TO CONQUER THEIR
FEARS, THEY MUST
MASTER THEIR SENSES ...

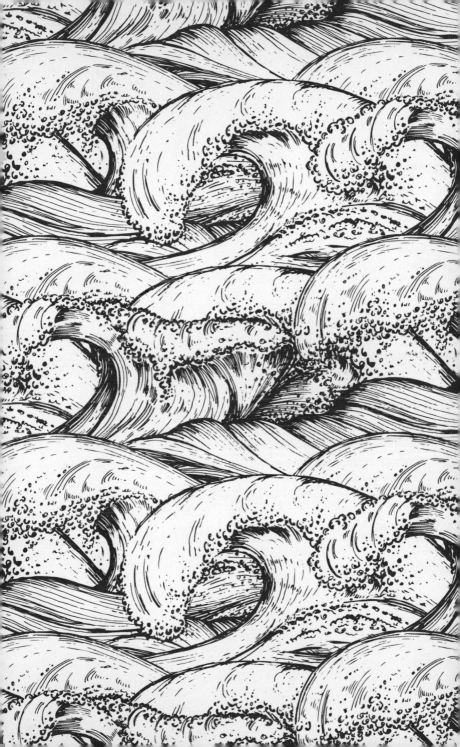

SCHOOL OF ALYXA

SECRETS & SHADOWS

R. L. FERGUSON

Willow
Tree

A CIP catalogue record for this book is
available from the British Library

This edition published by Willow Tree Books, 2019
Willow Tree Books, Tide Mill Way, Woodbridge, Suffolk, IP12 1AP

0 2 4 6 8 9 7 5 3 1

Series created by Working Partners Limited
Copyright © Working Partners 2019
All rights reserved.
Cover illustration by Dominic Harman © Willow Tree Books 2019
Typography © Willow Tree Books 2019
Endpaper art © Nadezhda Molkentin/shutterstock.com 2019

Willow Tree Books and associated logos are trademarks and/or
registered trademarks of Imagine That Group Ltd

ISBN: 978-1-78958-185-0
Printed and bound in Great Britain
by Bell and Bain Ltd, Glasgow

www.willowtreebooks.net

SPECIAL THANKS TO
GRAHAM EDWARDS

CHAPTER ONE

Finn couldn't decide which was worse – the relentless thumping of the party music or the sterile quiet of the hospital room. The soft beeping of the heart monitor only seemed to intensify the silence. But at least the beeping meant his brother was alive.

He checked his phone – 2.30 a.m. The last time he'd been up this late was New Year's Eve. They'd stayed up eating junk and playing board games, just Finn, John and their mum. John had been loud and funny, and he hadn't had an attack for months. All that seemed a long time ago now.

Finn's eyes were gritty and raw from too much crying and too little sleep. He closed them, but immediately his head filled up with memories of the evening. The party had seemed like such a good idea – the year over, summer ahead. And Amelie's house was amazing. The speakers pumping out music, the doors across the terrace opening on to the outdoor heated pool. Friends laughing and having fun. And no one had made him feel weird for being the youngest kid there by at least a year.

And then it had happened.

John, fine until that moment, falling to his knees on the kitchen floor, pounding the cabinets with his fists, the tendons of his neck like cords under his skin. People thought he was joking, but when his knuckles started to bleed the laughter had stopped. The screech of the speakers had risen to a deafening pitch before they'd blown, shattering the windows all around like a bomb going off. Everyone had ducked for cover, but Finn was transfixed on his brother. The way John had simply keeled over, stiff and staring blankly, would stay with Finn for a long time. He'd screamed for someone to call an ambulance, cradling John's sweating head in his lap.

After that was a blur. The spinning lights, the party breaking up, the smooth efficiency of the paramedics as they worked around his brother in the back of the emergency vehicle.

"Should we call your parents?" one of the nurses

had asked as they wheeled John into A & E.

Finn had looked at her blankly for a moment before answering, "It's just my mum. I tried her but she always turns off her phone when she's working."

"Would you like us to try for you?"

Finn had nodded and given her the number. He hadn't even known which restaurant she was working at, even though she'd have written it on the pad by the front door, like she always did.

He watched the jagged line of John's heartbeat flicking across the monitor. Only the top half of John's face was visible – the respirator strapped over his brother's mouth obscured his jaw. But it didn't hide the gash over John's eye, or the purple bruise on his cheek.

Finn touched the bandage on the side of his own left hand, where he must have cut it on broken glass. The way the windows had just burst inwards made no sense at all, but he couldn't think about that now. They were still waiting for the results of the CT scan. Until then, John's neck brace would have to stay on to protect his spine, and who knew what damage he might have done to his brain? All for the sake of a stupid party.

He was desperate for his mum to arrive. He needed her arms around him, needed her voice telling him everything was going to be all right. But he was dreading seeing her too. Dreading having to explain. They'd both known she would never have let them go, and so they hadn't told her.

The door opened and Finn rose expectantly, jolting the chair back and making its feet screech on the floor. Instead of his mother, a tall, well-built man with greying hair and sharp cheekbones entered the room. His suit was slate grey, his shirt collar open. Some sort of consultant, Finn guessed.

The man flicked his eyes over John, then studied the charts clipped to the end of his bed. Finn picked at the bandage on his finger, wondering how long he was going to be ignored.

"You're the brother?" said the consultant without turning.

Finn nodded. "Yes."

"Very good. I need to ask you some questions about what happened tonight. Is that all right with you?"

Finn shuffled his feet. "Sure." This guy didn't have much of a bedside manner.

The man leafed through the charts, then pressed his fingers against John's wrist to take his pulse. That was odd, given that Finn could clearly see his brother's heartbeat jittering across the monitor.

"This has happened to your brother before, yes?" said the consultant, releasing John's arm and letting it drop a little roughly on to the bed.

"Not like this," Finn answered, though he wondered what exactly this man knew, and how.

He thought back to the day John had broken the banister. At the time he'd just thought it was a fit of excitement brought on by his football team scoring the winner in extra time. But what about the following week, when John had started crying in the middle of a thunderstorm? Or when they were doing roadworks outside the house, and Finn had found his brother rolling around in agony on the bathroom floor? Mum had taken him to the doctors, and they'd run tests, but nothing had come back. And then months had passed without any further episodes. Finn guessed they all hoped the problem had gone away.

It hadn't. Two weeks before the party at Amelie's, he and his brother had been side by side on a new ride called Adrenalin Junkie, and Finn had thought John was screaming with the same excitement as himself. Only as he looked across, pulling four Gs, had he seen that John was actually in pain, slamming his head into the seat restraint again and again, eyes bulging and lips peeled back to reveal his gritted teeth.

Finn had seen someone having a fit before – Janie, one of the girls in his class, had epilepsy. This was completely different – this was real, conscious terror. "It felt like my brain was on fire," John had said afterwards, recovering on a bench. "You can't tell Mum. It'll just make her worried."

And for some reason, at that moment, Finn had promised to keep the secret. He could have kicked himself now.

"So this is the most extreme event to date?" asked the consultant.

"Yes."

The man leant close to John's head and then did something very strange indeed. He sniffed.

"Were the police called to the incident?"

John's heartbeat danced across the screen. The man in the suit remained utterly motionless, and in the reflection of the monitor his severe face was without expression.

"I didn't call them. Someone else might have, I guess. There was a lot of damage."

"How many witnesses?"

Finn shrugged. *Witnesses?* It wasn't a crime scene. "There were lots of people at the party. At least forty."

Putting the charts down, the consultant took a step forward and stood over Finn. For the first time, the man looked directly at him, and Finn realised he wasn't a consultant at all. His eyes had no warmth or kindness. They looked almost hungry. "What about you? Have you ever experienced symptoms similar to your brother's?"

Startled, Finn retreated until the backs of his legs rubbed up against the chair.

"What does this have to do with me? It's my brother who –"

"I asked you a question. Have you experienced similar issues?"

Finn had had enough. He squared his shoulders, even though the man was at least a head taller. "Sorry, who did you say you were again?" he asked.

The man smiled coldly through pale, thin lips. Finn stood his ground.

The door swung open. Finn had never felt more relieved to see his mother. She rushed in, heels clicking, sleek dress dishevelled. Tears stained the make-up around her eyes. Finn pushed past the stranger. "Mum!"

"I came straight from the tasting," she said, barely registering the man. "It went on so late. I thought … then I saw your messages." Her eyes fell on John. "Oh, my poor boy!"

She hurried to the bed and clasped John's bruised hands. "Finn – what happened?"

"We were at a party." Unlike earlier, the truth came out in one easy rush. "The music was so loud … I don't know … John had another attack." She flinched a little. "I wish we hadn't gone."

The man who wasn't a consultant closed the door

with a click. Folding his hands in front of him, he said, "Hello, Harriet."

Finn stared at him, dumbstruck, as the temperature in the room seemed to take a dive. *He knows her*. Oddly, his mother didn't even turn and look.

"Your son's injuries are superficial, this time," the man continued. "Harriet, we've been warning you that something like this would happen."

He took a step towards her. Finn saw the muscles tighten in his mother's jaw and moved to stand in the man's way. Why was he speaking to her like that?

"Who are you?" he said.

A groan rose from the bed and they all looked at John. Fumbling the respirator aside, Finn's brother regarded them through bleary eyes.

"Did someone die?" he croaked.

"Oh, John!" Still ignoring the strange man, their mum stroked John's messy hair, her tears rolling down her cheeks and on to his.

"Harriet," said the man, insistently. "I need to speak with you."

"Can't you see she's upset?" said Finn.

He wanted to say more, but his mother released John's hands, stood up, and touched Finn's shoulder. "It's all right," she said.

Plucking a tissue from her bag, she dabbed the tears

from her face. She paused, then wiped away most of the make-up. Her face looked strangely empty without it.

"Stay with your brother," she told Finn. "I'll be back in a minute." Then she turned her back on them both and followed the man out of the room.

Resisting the urge to go after them, Finn forced himself to sit back down in the chair. John raised himself on to his elbows, his movements made awkward by the neck brace.

"What happened?" John asked.

"Don't you remember?" Finn replied.

John frowned. "Not how I got here."

Finn regarded the bruise on his brother's cheek. "How's your head?"

"Epic," John replied. "But not in a good way."

"Do you remember anything?"

"Loud music. Flashing lights." He smiled. "A cute girl with blonde hair."

"Is that all?"

John's brow wrinkled. "I just remember having fun."

Finn could hear the muffled voices of his mum and the strange man coming from the corridor outside. They were arguing.

Crossing to the window beside the door, he lifted one corner of the blind with his finger. Through the gap he could see his mother waving her arms, not pleading, but sort of angry. Finn couldn't make out her words. He would have gone out, but the man didn't seem to be threatening her in any way. He was listening, motionless, with his arms folded across his chest. He spoke in short statements, his face impassive, and gave a couple of tiny shakes of his head. Eventually, Finn's mother's shoulders sagged and she fell silent. The man said a few more words, and she stared at him for a long time, then her body relaxed and she nodded, just once.

A shuffling sound came from the bed and Finn turned in time to see his brother sitting up. Before Finn could get to him, John had peeled back the straps of the neck brace and pulled it off.

"You should keep that on," said Finn, but John had already tossed the brace out of reach behind the heart monitor.

Their mother came back into the room, this time without the man.

"Mum, tell him," said Finn. "He can't just –"

"Shh, Finn. We don't have much time."

"Time?" said Finn. "Time for what? What do you mean?"

"I can't explain it all now."

There was something about her manner that made his skin go cold. The dullness in her voice, the pale clarity of her face.

"Mum?" said John.

She planted her hands against the sides of her head. The pose reminded Finn of John when he was having one of his attacks. Then her arms fell loose at her sides.

"I want to explain," she said. "I really do. But they won't wait. You just have to trust me."

Finn glanced at his brother, but all John had for him was another shrug. "Trust you about what? Mum, who was that guy?

"You have to go with him," she said. "Both of you."

Finn opened his mouth, but the words remained locked in his throat. He wanted his mother to look at him, but her eyes were fixed on the floor.

"I tried to protect you," she went on. "For years I've tried. Now I can't, not any more." Taking a deep breath, she finally looked at Finn. "There's a school. It will take you both, but you have to go tonight. It's the best thing for you, believe me, it really is. They know what you need. They'll look after you."

"Mum?" said John, rubbing his neck. "You're not making any sense. Are you okay?"

Finn continued to stare at her. "What school? We go to St Luke's."

Their mother shook her head. "I'm sorry, Finn."

"You're not making any sense!" said Finn, hating

the wheedling sound of his own voice.

His mum looked more than sad. She looked defeated. She inclined her head towards the corridor.

"That man's name is Geraint Kildair. He works for the school. That's why he's here. He's come to take you."

Take us?

"Do we get to pack?" said John. He sounded tired and confused.

She shook her head. "I'm sorry, I know this is a shock ..."

"A *shock?*" Finn exclaimed. The room was spinning and he felt sick. "Are you *kidding?*"

"I wish I could explain, I really do."

She crossed from the doorway to the bed and kissed John's cheek. Then she turned to Finn. He backed away. Nothing she was saying made any sense, but she was crazy if she thought he was just going to walk out of here with a weirdo.

"What is this school anyway?" asked John.

"Alyxa," said their mother in a whisper. "It's called Alyxa."

Finn continued retreating until he bumped into the edge of the open door. The hinges swung sideways and he stumbled, nearly falling. The walls of the room seemed to be closing in on him.

His mother reached for him. Her fingers brushed

the back of his hand and suddenly Finn had to run. Spinning on his heels, he bolted from the room.

"Finn!" she shouted after him. "Come back!"

He raced into the corridor and straight into Kildair. The man grunted and made a grab for him, but Finn ducked and ran on. He didn't know where he was running to. Just away. Out of here. He passed a drinks machine and what seemed like a hundred signs pointing to hospital departments with unpronounceable names. Then in the distance he saw a set of double doors and a sign that read: EXIT THIS WAY.

Reaching the doors, Finn crashed through them, dodged a nurse pushing an empty wheelchair, then vaulted over an unoccupied stretcher. He skidded around another corner and found himself in a wide lobby facing four sets of lift doors.

Gasping for breath, feeling dizzy, he hurried along the line of doors, stabbing each button in turn. *This isn't happening. This isn't right.* A sign on the wall told him he was on the third floor. According to the illuminated displays, one of the lifts was in the basement and the other three were on their way down from the upper levels.

"Come on!" he shouted, thumping the nearest button.

The grey-haired man swept around the corner.

He walked with menace and ease, and Finn thought of a leopard pacing towards its prey. His face wore an expression of strained impatience.

"Finn," said Kildair. "There is nothing to be gained from running away."

A set of lift doors hissed open. Finn hurled himself through and hit the button for the ground floor. He bent double, panting hard. His head was spinning and his breath felt like sandpaper in his throat. The seconds went by with agonising slowness before the doors began to close. Finn expected a foot to block them, but it didn't. The lift bumped into downward motion. There was one other person inside – a girl. Silver piercings crowded her ears and Finn saw more silver on the lapel of her denim jacket – a badge in the shape of a five-pointed star. She blew a pink bubble of gum and leaned casually back against the mirrored wall.

In his pocket, Finn's phone began to vibrate once, twice, three times. He ignored it.

"Aren't you going to get that?" said the girl. She blew another bubble, popped it, and went back to chewing again.

Wondering how she'd heard it, Finn plucked the silent phone from his pocket. It was his mum. He declined the call.

The girl smiled. She looked a few years older than

Finn – seventeen or so – but she was only a little taller than him. Her eyes were rimmed with black eyeliner and her dark hair was short and spiky.

"Let me guess. You're Finn, aren't you? The brother."

The brother. Her words echoed those of Kildair – even the slightly dismissive way she said it.

"What? How do you ...?"

She reached inside her jacket and drew out a short stick, like a black relay baton. Only relay batons didn't have silver switches at one end.

"What's that?" said Finn, backing into the corner of the lift.

"Sorry about this, kiddo," replied the girl.

She thumbed the switch and the end of the baton flashed red. The light punched its way into Finn's head, pressing his giddiness aside and replacing it with dazzling lines of fire.

CHAPTER TWO

Finn woke up suddenly. He couldn't see. Something soft was brushing his eyelashes – he tried to claw his hands up to his face, but his arms wouldn't move. A pounding noise assaulted his ears.

Thudda-thudda-thudda.

"Wait a second," said a voice. "Stop struggling."

Someone fumbled behind his head, then peeled away a strip of black cloth that had been covering his eyes. Finn blinked into darkness filled with blurry spots of light. When the view tilted slightly, his stomach lurched in sympathy.

As his vision finally came into focus, he realised he was looking through a window across a dark landscape dotted with city lights. The sky above it was black, but to his right and a little behind it faded to deep blue and the faint beginnings of a yellow dawn.

Thudda-thudda-thudda.

Finn looked up and around. He was sitting in the rear cabin of a helicopter. Curved walls met a low ceiling above his head, and on a nearby panel an electronic display flashed what looked like a moving satellite map. The whole cabin was filled with the judder of the rotor blades and the seat beneath him was vibrating. Thin cords strapped his wrists to the arms of the seat, and his ankles were tied to its frame. When he strained against the bindings, the cords bit painfully into his flesh.

John sat to his left, either asleep or unconscious, with his chin lolling on his chest. Unlike Finn, John's arms and legs were free.

Sitting opposite them in a pair of rear-facing seats were the thin man from the hospital and a sandy-haired boy who looked about seventeen. Kildair was gazing out of the window, but the boy's eyes were fixed firmly on Finn. His nostrils flared.

Trying to quell his rising panic, Finn pulled again at the cords.

"Chill," said the boy. "There's nothing to be afraid of."

"I'm not afraid," Finn snapped back. John stirred beside him.

"Really? You smell terrified."

"Let me loose!" As Finn struggled to free himself, his vision blurred again.

"We had to tie you up for your protection. You'll be free in a minute. You just have to wait for the overload to wear off."

Feeling helpless, Finn tensed his arms and legs and rocked in his seat. He wanted to shout, but something had locked up his throat.

"Bro, take it easy," said John, blinking his eyes open and yawning. "It's going to be okay."

The sound of his brother's voice calmed Finn. He relaxed his limbs.

"What did you mean – 'overload'?" he asked the blond boy.

"Sensory overload," said Kildair, turning his attention to Finn. "It's what Adriana used to subdue you." He held up his hand with his fingers splayed wide. "How many fingers am I holding up?"

"I don't care," Finn replied. "Just let me go!"

"Do you understand what I am saying to you?"

"Do you? I'm not your prisoner. I've done nothing wrong!"

"Mmm, you seem recovered to me." Kildair

straightened in his seat. "Now, I'm going to trust you not to do anything rash. When you're 12,000 feet up in the air, rashness is not advisable. Agreed?"

Finn glared, and gave the smallest of nods.

Kildair took one of the pens from his pocket and pressed the button at the end. Instead of a nib, a small blade shot out. With a few deft flicks, the man leaned across and cut through Finn's restraints.

Massaging his wrists and ankles, Finn peered ahead through the cabin and into the cockpit. It looked like a metal cave filled with blinking lights. Sitting in the co-pilot's seat was a boy perhaps a year or two older than John. The pilot was the gum-chewing girl from the lift – Adriana, presumably.

"So where are we?" Finn demanded.

"Our present location is unimportant," replied Kildair with a casual flick of his hand. "The only thing that matters is where we are going."

"And that's Alyxa, right?" said John.

"Indeed," the man replied.

Finn snorted. "Since when do schools have to kidnap their pupils?"

Kildair compressed his lips into the same thin smile Finn had grown to hate in the hospital. "It will all become clear soon. Until then, why don't you settle back and enjoy the ride?"

Suddenly remembering his phone, Finn drove his hand into his pocket, only to find it empty.

"Your phone is safe," said Kildair. "And so are you."

John elbowed Finn in the ribs. "We're here now, so we might as well go along with it. Anyway, check out that view!"

Finn turned away from his brother. Maybe John was happy to get swept along with all this, but Finn couldn't shake off the knowledge that their mother had just agreed to send them both away.

Dotted lines of light curved across the landscape, roads connecting the larger glowing patches that were towns and cities. The faint yellow band that hugged the horizon was more or less behind them now – that meant they were heading west.

Finn made some swift calculations. They couldn't have left the hospital much before three in the morning, and the sun rose early in the summer, so they could only have been flying for a couple of hours. In which case, they were still over the mainland.

He studied the display panel, but the satellite image was zoomed in too close to be of any help, so instead he peered out of the window again. There was a large city far to the north and beyond that was a vast expanse of deep blue that could only be the sea. Ahead, the countryside was relatively dark, with few roads and fewer lights. No big cities.

Kildair appraised Finn with a thoughtful gaze, then his stiff shoulders relaxed a little. "Do you have some questions for me?"

"Are you kidding?" said Finn.

Kildair's smile was as thin as ever, but was that a wrinkle of actual humour around his eyes? "Well, let me at least introduce myself properly. My name is Geraint Kildair – as your mother has probably told you – and I am the Dean of Alyxa."

Finn wasn't sure what that meant. *Is that like a headmaster?* "How do you know my mother?"

"We went to school together."

"Alyxa?" asked John.

The Dean nodded.

"And what's so great about this school?" said Finn.

"It is Alyxa's mission to nurture students with special ... needs," Kildair replied. "We usually accept pupils at the age of eleven. However, you two boys were allowed to slip through our net."

John seemed to accept this readily enough, but the Dean's explanation just left Finn more confused. He didn't have any special needs? He was top of his class at St Luke's in at least three subjects. This was about John. It had to be.

"Are you an Alyxa student?" Finn asked the boy

sitting opposite.

The boy pulled open his jacket and tapped a badge pinned to his shirt – a five-pointed star, just like the one Finn had seen on Adriana's jacket in the lift. By now, the yellow light had soaked further into the sky, and the whole world was growing bright.

Sunlight stabbed across the land, its low beams striking the eastern slopes of the mountains and firing long shadows far ahead into the west – like arrows, pointing the way. A coastline appeared and suddenly they were crossing a narrow channel of water, above an island with a castle, and then they were speeding out across the open ocean.

The sun continued to rise, painting the crests of the waves, and the hulls of the boats in a tiny fishing fleet. Below the helicopter there was water, and only water, until far ahead Finn saw a tiny speck of land come into view.

"Is that where we're going?" said John.

"Yes, it is," the Dean replied.

The waves came closer – the helicopter was descending. The speck swelled to become a squat island with a steep-sided mountain in the middle. White waves crashed against sheer cliffs to the north and lapped a dark sandy shore to the south. Lake water glistened halfway up the mountain, but the rest of the island was little more than a rolling carpet of barren moorland.

"I don't see a school," remarked John.

"This is AX-17 requesting permission to land," said Adriana, speaking into a microphone jutting from her helmet. She cocked her head, clearly listening to some response from the ground.

A tingle went down Finn's spine. *What kind of school teaches kids to fly helicopters?*

Adriana plucked the gum from her mouth and pressed it against the edge of the flight console. "Thank you, Control. AX-17 out."

"Manual landing, Adriana, if you please," said Kildair. "You know I don't like autopilots."

"Yes, sir," came Adriana's reply.

The helicopter swooped in low over the cliffs, scattering a flock of gulls. Ahead, all Finn could see was scrubby grass and the steep mountain slope.

Then the ground shimmered.

One by one, buildings began to appear in the landscape – a low barn, a line of huts, something that looked like an observatory. The outline of each building wavered briefly, as if Finn were seeing it through a veil of water, before suddenly snapping into solidity.

"That's impossible," Finn breathed.

"That's cool," said John.

The buildings were arranged in a broken ring around an empty patch of land the size of several sports fields. Now the air over the entire patch began to shudder. A vast shape began to materialise – it seemed almost to rise up like a whale breaching the surface of the sea. A single tremendous building, solid as a fortress, sleek and shining in the brilliant rays of the newly risen sun. Finn squinted into the reflections dazzling off its silver skin.

Looking down at the building from above, it was easy to make out its overall shape.

A five-pointed star.

The nose of the helicopter dipped and the *thudda-thudda-thudda* of the rotors dropped in pitch. Finn watched a line of slender trees sway in the sudden down-draught.

The co-pilot peered towards the building, then called back over his shoulder, "I see they've got a welcome party ready for you."

To Finn's eyes the building was just a mass of reflections – he couldn't see any party.

"I hope that includes breakfast," said Adriana.

The sandy-haired boy sniffed the air. "It does," he grinned. "Sausages, unless I'm mistaken."

As the helicopter approached the building, Finn grabbed John's wrist, wondering if his brother's heart was beating as fast as his own.

Who were these people? And what kind of school was Alyxa?

CHAPTER THREE

The helicopter hovered above the centre of the star-shaped building. Five silver petals folded back, revealing a recess in the roof. Finn was bounced in his seat as the chopper dropped sharply towards a bright blue landing pad surrounded by blinking lights, and he bounced again as it touched down.

With the blades still spinning to a halt, the sandy-haired boy pulled open the cabin door, admitting a blast of cool wind. Finn licked his lips, tasting salt. The boy went outside, followed by the Dean.

"After you, kid," said John, nudging Finn in the ribs.

Adriana and the co-pilot were flicking switches and

pulling off their helmets. Taking a deep breath, Finn hopped down from the helicopter.

The surface of the pentagonal landing pad was slightly spongy. Circular glass panels ringed the perimeter, set into the deck like transparent paving stones. Silver walls rose on each of the landing pad's five sides; in the centre of each wall was an arched doorway.

As John joined Finn on the pad, the doors slid open and five people emerged: three men and two women. Each trailed a long grey gown split down the middle, and as the wind whipped through the two halves they twined into lashing ribbons. The gowns were fixed at the collar by some kind of bronze clasp.

Finn watched as Adriana jumped down from the cockpit. "Stand up straight," she said to Finn. "Don't want to upset the Wardens on your first day."

The five figures gathered beneath the slowing blades of the helicopter, and they looked like they were from another age entirely. Kildair nodded to each of them in turn, but Finn noticed that he didn't look any of them in the eye, and the only word the Dean of Alyxa spoke was a terse, "Morning." After that, he marched briskly towards the nearest door with the sandy-haired boy following in his wake.

"So," said one of the robed men, "you are the brothers."

Finn looked at John, who just shrugged.

"I'm Finn," he said. "And this is John. Who are you? If you don't mind me asking."

The man touched a forefinger to the tip of his white goatee. He had a big belly and bright eyes that seemed to drill all the way into Finn's skull. The clasp securing his robe was embossed with the shape of a bird – some kind of hawk, Finn thought.

"My name is Professor Panjaran," the man said. "I am the Warden of Sight. I and my colleagues are here to greet you, as we greet every new student of Alyxa. We do this out of tradition, of course – Alyxa has a long history of tradition, as you will discover – but we do it also out of respect. Tradition attends the past, do you see, but only by attending to the present moment can we hope to attend the future."

The man's voice was soft and hypnotic, his words strangely slippery. Finn wondered if there was anyone here who would give him a straight answer to a simple request:

Just tell me what Alyxa actually is!

Professor Panjaran's shining eyes narrowed to slits. Never mind his skull – Finn felt like his entire soul was suddenly open to scrutiny.

"A winding path lies ahead for you," said Professor Panjaran. "On that path your feet may stumble. Be wary.

My eyes are upon you."

Was that a threat?

A second man came forward. He was as skinny as Panjaran was round, with a sharp chin and a smooth, bald head. His clasp, Finn noted, carried the shape of a coiled snake.

"Pietr Turminski," the man said. He shook first Finn's hand, then John's, each time flashing a toothy smile. "Don't take too much notice of old Panj here. He does waffle on."

"So you're a Warden too?" said John.

"I am the Warden of the Taste Clann. Which just goes to show I have taste! Ha, just my little joke! Now, tell me, do you know why you are here?"

"They think we've got special needs," said Finn slowly.

Turminski gave a mock frown. "Special needs, yes! But special gifts as well. And special people need a special place. A *safe* place. That is what Alyxa is: a safe place for students with abilities like yours."

Finn preferred Turminski's line of conversation to Panjaran's, but he was still confused. "What abilities?"

"Every student at Alyxa has unusually heightened senses," Turminski replied. "*Exceptionally* heightened."

"Senses?" said John. "You mean sight, hearing, all that?"

"Sight, hearing, smell, taste, touch." Turminski ticked off the list on his fingers, and beamed at them both. The other Wardens looked on in silence.

"Senses," Finn repeated. "That makes ... well, sense."

"Ha! You see, you make a joke too!" laughed Turminski.

Finn was thinking about the sandy-haired boy – how he'd claimed to be able to smell sausages from high up in the air. Then there was the way Adriana had heard his silent phone ...

Finn glanced at her now. She and her co-pilot were stripping off their flightsuits and stowing them in a hatch on the side of the helicopter. She caught Finn's eye and tapped her finger against her ear. The boy beside her grinned.

"Okay," said Finn. "I think I get it. But ... you said this was a safe place. Only, getting kidnapped doesn't exactly make me feel safe. And anyway, I haven't got any super-senses."

"Not yet," said Turminski. "They will emerge. You are siblings, no?"

"No," agreed John. "I mean, yes."

"Well then."

"Does that make a difference?" said John.

"All the difference in the world," Turminski replied.

Despite his own caution, Finn was pleased to hear the enthusiasm in his brother's voice. Only hours ago, John had been lying in a hospital bed. Now he was standing on a remote island with the ocean breeze wafting his hair, being told he was special.

Not just him, Finn thought. *Me, too.*

"John," said the third man in the group of Wardens. He was by far the biggest of the bunch, not rotund like Professor Panjaran, but solid – a huge square slab of a man with a thick blond beard and hands that looked as large as a baseball catcher's mitts. "You are John."

"That's me," said John, straightening his shoulders.

"I am Magnus Gustavsson," said the big man.

"And you're the Warden of ...?" asked Finn.

"I am Touch," Gustavsson replied. He adjusted his robe clasp, which bore the outline of a monkey. His fingers were like sausages, yet they moved with a strange precision.

"You're talking like you know me," said John.

"I do." Gustavsson brandished a wad of papers. "Tests. Very many of them. Of your brain."

"My brain?" John's eyes widened.

"Yes. The troubles you experience – we can help you."

"Really? How awesome is that?" said John. He elbowed Finn. "Right, bro?"

"Awesome." Finn was more concerned with how long they'd have to stay here being inspected by these five robed strangers. "Uh, when can we speak to our mother?"

Gustavsson glanced at Turminski, who looked in turn at the short woman standing to his left. She wore a badge with a dog emblem. Tipping back her head, she stared at Finn through thick spectacles perched on a long, beaklike nose. Finn guessed this one was the Warden of Smell. Which meant the other woman – the tall athletic one whose eyes hadn't opened the whole time they'd been here – was the Warden of Hearing. Her badge displayed the spread wings of a bat.

"Communication with the outside world is closely monitored at Alyxa," said the beak-nosed woman in a high-pitched voice. "For students, I'm afraid it's strictly forbidden."

"Forbidden?" said Finn. "I thought this was a school, not a prison."

"What Warden Blake says is indeed correct," said Professor Panjaran smoothly. "However, I urge you to dwell not upon the rules we make, but upon your own personal perceptions. Alyxa exists for your sake, and it will be whatever you choose to make it. Open yourselves to the possibilities we offer, and great rewards will be yours."

"But you can't just shut people away," said Finn. "What about human rights and ...?"

Professor Panjaran stabbed his forefinger firmly at the sky. "Save your questions. Today is a day for settling in. You, Finn, will join the Nurture Group." He beckoned to Adriana's co-pilot. "Ben - you will escort Finn to where he needs to be. John - you will go with Warden Gustavsson."

Before Finn knew what was happening, the Warden of Touch had moved between him and John with a speed that belied his tremendous size. At the same time, Ben appeared at Finn's side and gently took his arm.

"Wait!" cried Finn, shaking off Ben's hand. He pushed past Gustavsson and stood beside John. "You're not splitting us up!"

Professor Panjaran's face creased into a frown, and Finn heard a sharp intake of breath from the beak-nosed woman, Warden Blake. Then John was grabbing Finn's shoulders.

"Hey, bro," John said. "Take it easy. Everything's going to be okay."

"Like it was at the party?" Finn leaned in close and whispered, "Don't tell me your head doesn't hurt still, because I know it does."

"Alyxa cares deeply about the health of its students," said the tall woman. Even through her closed eyelids she seemed to be looking straight at Finn. He wondered how she'd heard him, then remembered Adriana. "The enrolment procedure includes a full medical check-up. Neither of you has anything to worry about."

Finn felt his fists clench. He forced himself to relax. Wind gusted past his face, bringing with it the scent of seaweed. Behind him, the helicopter's engine ticked quietly for a moment, then fell silent.

"Are you sure you're okay with this?" Finn said to John.

"Sure. I'll go with the big guy," his brother replied, grinning at Warden Gustavsson. "It's cool."

"And you can come with me," Ben said to Finn. "Are you okay with that?"

Sighing, Finn shook the boy's hand. "I guess so. I mean, yes, of course."

After a final glance at John, he followed Ben across the landing pad. As they passed the Warden with the closed eyes, Adriana trotted up to the woman and kissed her cheek.

"Hi, Mum," she said.

"You did well today, Adriana," said the woman, caressing her daughter's cheek without opening her eyes. Wind the clock back thirty years, spike up her hair, and the Warden could have been Adriana's twin. They turned and walked away together.

Ben led Finn not to one of the big arched doorways, but to a smaller door tucked into the angle between two of the five perimeter walls. Steps took them down into a long curving corridor illuminated from above by cool blue squares of light. The floor was tiled and their footsteps echoed.

"I know this all feels weird," said Ben to Finn, "but you'll get the hang of it. I was the same on my first day."

"Really?" Finn's eyes strayed to the logo on Ben's star-shaped badge: a coiled snake with three parallel lines beneath it. "What do the badges mean?"

"Okay, here's how it works. The snake means I'm a Taste student. The three bars mean I'm Level Three. Well, I was. See this?" Ben tapped a silver badge in his jacket's other lapel. One end was moulded into the shape of a pentagon. "That means I'm a prefect."

Finn nodded absently as Ben prattled on about his duties, which largely seemed to involve looking out for the welfare of the students. He was more fascinated by the lines of decoration on the smooth metallic walls. The markings showed cloaked people in various strange poses – were some of them doing yoga? – and they reminded Finn of Egyptian hieroglyphics.

"Everything works in fives here, in case you hadn't noticed," Ben went on. "Five houses – which we call Clanns – five Wardens, five animal mascots. Because

43

of the five senses, obviously. Although now we've got Dr Raj as well, but he's different. He's the one who keeps the White Wall powered up."

"The White Wall?" said Finn, but Ben had darted into a side passage. Finn followed, his nostrils flaring at the unmistakeable smell of ...

"Sausages!" said Ben, ushering Finn through another set of doors and into a canteen. No silver here – the walls and floor of the huge, round room were splattered with rainbow colours. It was like walking into the aftermath of a paintball battle. The whole place echoed with chattering voices and the clatter of cutlery.

In the middle of the canteen, standing behind a circular counter, a stout woman was serving sandwiches to a small cluster of kids. An overhead system of conveyor belts and suspended buckets delivered fresh orders down through a hole in the ceiling.

"Are you hungry?" said Ben with a grin. "I'm starving." He took two wrapped sandwiches from the woman, whose skin was even darker than his.

Finn's stomach gurgled. "Sausages," he said, opening the wrapper. "That's what the boy in the helicopter said breakfast would be. But we were so high up." He took a huge bite. There was one thing he could say for Alyxa – the food was awesome! "Was it some kind of trick?"

44

"You never know with Jermaine," said Ben, chomping on his own sandwich. "He's a Level Three too, so it could have been for real."

"Let me guess," said Finn, "these levels go up to five as well?"

"You're getting the idea. Not that the Wardens would know what to do if a Fiver came along. They get excited enough with the occasional Fourbie. Come on."

Heading towards the doors on the opposite side of the canteen, they had to circle a table where four students were sitting, two boys and two girls. One of the boys – a kid about Finn's age with a broad face and pale, sleepy eyes – stuck out his foot as they went past. Finn dodged it easily enough, but the attempt to trip him up was obvious.

"Who's your new friend, Benjamin?" said the boy. His voice drawled in an American accent.

"Good morning, Xander," Ben replied. "This is Finn."

Xander flicked crumbs of bread off the silver surface of his monkey badge. Touch student, Level Two.

"What's his Clann?" said Xander.

"That's to be decided," said Ben. "I'm taking him to Nurture Group."

Xander's three companions snickered.

"That's enough, Xander," said Ben, ushering Finn

away.

"Enjoy Numbskulls," Xander called after them.

Finn traipsed after Ben. Typical. Maybe Alyxa wasn't so different from the outside world after all.

Leaving the canteen, they entered yet another corridor. In complete contrast to everything Finn had seen so far, this passage looked ancient. Rugged stone walls supported a low ceiling strung with dangling lanterns. Finn had to duck occasionally so as not to bump his head. Then came a section lined with dark wooden panels, followed by more stone. The whole place looked like a hotchpotch of ancient and modern combined.

Fat cables ran from one section to the next, fixed to the walls with big metal staples and branching off to feed a variety of large monitors. Each screen displayed a table of information that reminded Finn of the departure gate screens at an airport. Mixed in with streams of numbers were the now-familiar symbols for the five Clanns of Alyxa: hawk, bat, monkey, snake and dog.

"It's the timetable," said Ben before Finn could ask. "It's not as complicated as it looks." He grinned. "Well, actually it is. We've got different classes, different ages of students, different abilities. Everyone's always on the move and the lesson plans are always changing. I tell you, the weather here is unpredictable, but it's nothing compared to the Alyxa timetable! Ah, here we are."

Ben stopped at a door that might have been taken from a medieval castle. A wooden plaque clung to the stone wall, carved with a curved, segmented shape that Finn at first took to be a seashell. He looked closer, and realised it was a chrysalis.

Ben pressed his thumb to a round metal plate in the corner of the plaque. The door clunked and swung open.

"You'll be able to do that once your prints have been scanned," Ben said. "Go on in. Take a look around."

The room was small with blank grey walls. There was a small square window, but most of the light came from the ceiling, which emitted a flat, white glow across its whole surface. A white-framed bed spanned one wall. A narrow wardrobe nestled behind the door. A thin wall sectioned off the far corner to make a little en-suite bathroom. That was all. It wasn't the castle dungeon Finn had been expecting, but it did feel a little like a prison cell.

"Very homely," he said.

Ben laughed. "It's supposed to be like this. Sort of a neutral space for students who need to recover."

"Recover?"

"From sense loss. It happens. Or confusion. The plain surroundings help you relax and find your way again. That's the idea, anyway."

After the rainbow of colours in the canteen, and the constantly changing corridors, the grey walls were actually kind of a relief. But relax? Everything that had happened to him in the last twenty-four hours was swilling around inside his head. His brain felt ready to explode. He eyed the bed and realised he'd hardly slept. Yet his day at Alyxa was only just beginning.

Ben opened the wardrobe to reveal a rack of grey jumpsuits.

"They're your size," he said. "Come on – let's meet the others."

Others?

An adjoining door took them into another room, bigger than Finn's dorm but just as grey and featureless. Here, two girls wearing identical grey uniforms sat in small white chairs.

"This is the common room," Ben said. "Lucy, this is Finn."

Lucy was an Asian girl, of maybe Indian heritage. She had the same light brown skin as Saanvi from his class at school, with long black hair tied in a glossy ponytail. *My* old *school*, he reminded himself with a sudden pang.

"Hi, Finn," Lucy said. "Welcome to the Numbskulls. Zoe – this is the part where you scowl."

The other girl, a freckled redhead, just stared at the

opposite wall. At least, Finn assumed that was what she was staring at – the dark goggles she wore hid her eyes almost completely.

"She likes you!" Lucy exclaimed, offering Finn the palm of her hand. He obliged her with a high five.

"She does?" he said.

"Sure. If she didn't, she'd have burnt you to a crisp with her microwave laser vision."

Finn gaped at Zoe's tinted goggles.

"Just kidding!" said Lucy. "It's not like the movies here. Life at Alyxa is really extraordinarily dull."

"Really?" said Finn. "Or are you still kidding?"

"That's for me to know and you to find out."

Finn liked Lucy already. After the robed Wardens and the school that appeared out of nowhere, she seemed pretty normal. He took in the rest of the room, such as it was. He counted six doors in total.

"What's through there?" he asked, pointing at the nearest door.

"That's my room," said Ben. "If you need anything, just knock."

"Your room?" said Finn, surprised. "You're in the Numb ... Nurture Group too?"

"Didn't I say? I lost my powers a while back."

"How?" said Finn.

"I overtrained. You should watch out for that. Work

49

hard and you'll do well at Alyxa, but try not to end up like me." Ben slapped Finn's shoulder. "There you go, day one, and you're already getting some top tips."

"It's time to get ready," said Zoe, still facing the wall. Her lips were the only part of her body that moved.

"She speaks!" cried Lucy.

"Thanks for the time check, Zoe," said Ben.

"Ready for what?" said Finn.

"Assembly," said Ben. "Get changed into your uniform. When you hear the bell, it's time to go."

"Chop-chop," said Lucy. She flapped her hands at Finn, then leapt out of her chair and vanished through another of the doors. Zoe sat motionless for a moment, then plodded into her own room.

Finn returned to his little dorm and flopped down on the bed. He stared up at the glowing ceiling, suppressing a yawn and remembering how tiny the island had looked when he'd first seen it appear in the wide ocean. He imagined himself small like the island – no, smaller, a scrap of driftwood floating alone in a hostile sea. The thought made his stomach churn.

He jumped off the bed and ventured into the en-suite. Running cold water into the sink, he splashed his face. As he dried himself on a grey towel, a bell jingled in the corridor outside. The combination of splash and sound seemed to drive his tiredness away.

He snatched a uniform from the wardrobe. No sooner had he shrugged off his T-shirt and jeans than someone knocked on the door.

"Assembly time!" came Lucy's muffled voice. "You've got thirty seconds."

"I'm coming," said Finn, hastily pulling on the grey jumpsuit. The silver star on the lapel was blank: no animal emblem, no stripes.

From top of the class to the bottom in less than a day, he thought. *All thanks to you, John!*

There were boots in the wardrobe too, along with underwear and pyjamas. Everything in his size ... and everything the same dull tone. He wondered what sort of fancy room and clothing they'd given to his brother.

Was it really true that John had strange sensory powers? It was an exciting thought. Maybe that explained his attacks. The sensitivity to noise. As for Finn – well, all this had to be a big mistake.

"Time's up!" Lucy called.

"Coming," said Finn.

He ran his fingers over the smooth metal of his badge. *Was there an animal hiding under there, just waiting to appear?*

CHAPTER FOUR

Finn squeezed into a small lift with his new companions. Ben thumbed the controls, and Zoe, her eyes unreadable behind her dark goggles, stood motionless with her hands plunged deep in the pockets of her jumpsuit.

Finn wondered why Lucy and Zoe were in Nurture Group. *Had they worked too hard and lost their powers like Ben, or was it something else? Would it be rude to ask?*

Three floors down, they stepped out of the lift into a wide passage filled with kids all heading the same way. Finn let the flood carry him along, making sure he didn't lose sight of Ben. After a few steps, Lucy grabbed his hand.

"Can't have you getting lost on your first day," she said.

The passage delivered them into a huge, five-sided hall. Wooden seats rose on each side, turned inwards to face a central stage. Coloured banners hung over each of the five sections, displaying the different Clann emblems. High, high above, a ring of circular skylights fired bright sunbeams down from a pentagonal ceiling.

We're underneath the landing pad, thought Finn.

Lucy steered him to a small seating area set a little apart from the five main blocks. Zoe joined them. Ben gave Finn a small salute, then joined Adriana on the stage – she was sitting next to the Dean along with Jermaine and two other older students. The benefits of being a prefect, Finn supposed. The five Wardens were there too, seated in a ring of high-backed chairs around a platform in the middle of the stage. Curled up on the floor beside the beak-nosed woman was an overweight bloodhound, and was that really a snake wrapped around Pietr Turminski's neck?

He looked up and around, feeling a little dizzy. The auditorium was nearly full now, and buzzing with countless murmured conversations. Hearing a familiar laugh, Finn spotted John. He was chatting and joking in the middle of a gang of kids in the Touch zone and, to

Finn's astonishment, he had a small black monkey on his shoulder. It was playing with his hair, as if rooting for ticks.

Finn half-stood from the Nurture Group bench. He wanted to call out to his brother, but John was too far away, and the noise in the chamber was too loud.

Lucy tugged at Finn's jumpsuit.

"Sit down," she said. "Here we go."

The noise ebbed as the last few students took their seats, and stopped completely when Professor Panjaran took the platform.

"Welcome, students," he announced, turning slowly as he spoke. "Welcome, all. This assembly is late, due to the Dean's delayed return, so let us turn our minds immediately to the biggest event of the calendar – this year's annual Hunt."

Whoops and cheers rang around the chamber. Finn nudged Lucy.

"What's the Hunt?" he said.

Lucy flashed her teeth. "You know sports day?"

"Of course."

"The Hunt is like that, only way more exciting."

"I remind you that all team lists must be submitted before one o'clock tomorrow afternoon," Professor Panjaran continued. "Let me also remind you that the Hunt is not an excuse for frivolity. It is a serious competitive event. Irresponsible behaviour leads to accidents – as recent events have shown."

Several heads turned towards Zoe. Her body tensed and Finn saw a blush rise from her neck into her freckled cheeks.

"Moving on," said Professor Panjaran. "I am pleased to announce that one of our leading students has achieved her next Torath."

"What's a Torath?" Finn whispered to Lucy, but she just shushed him.

"I ask Adriana Arnott to please step forward," said Panjaran.

Finn watched as Adriana joined Panjaran on the platform. He half expected her to blow a pink bubble in the Warden's face, but on this occasion she'd abandoned the gum. In silence, she handed her old badge to the Warden and pinned the new one he gave her to her lapel.

"Torath means growth," whispered Lucy. "This one takes her up to Level Three. She's Hearing, in case you hadn't guessed. Their symbol's a bat, but Adriana thinks she's the queen bee."

As if to prove her extraordinary hearing abilities, Adriana targeted Lucy with a withering glare.

"My final announcement," said Professor Panjaran as Adriana returned to her seat, "concerns the arrival of two new students."

Heads turned again, this time towards John. He smiled, and the monkey climbed on top of his head and offered a jaunty salute. Laughter rang out. Then attention turned to Finn. Some students regarded him with wide eyes, while others cocked their heads at odd angles. Several sniffed.

"I trust you will all join me in welcoming John Williams and his brother Finlay," Panjaran said. "Tend to their needs today, for in the future you may need them to tend to yours."

Everyone clapped and at the height of the applause, a piercing screech signalled the descent of a large bird of prey from somewhere near the ceiling. Spreading wide red wings, it swooped low over the platform, leaving a trail of white splatters behind it. Shaking his head, Professor Panjaran removed a spotted handkerchief from his pocket and started to mop up the hawk droppings.

The bird returned to its perch, the fourth creature Finn had seen in the hall this morning. "Where's the bat?" he asked Lucy. "There must be one around here somewhere."

"It only comes out at night, stupid," Lucy replied.

The clapping dissolved into laughter, and the assembly broke up.

Not sure where to go next, Finn started forcing his way through the crowd towards John, hoping to catch his brother before the Touch students whisked him away. He was halfway there when Ben intercepted him.

"Not so fast," Ben said. "It's time for your medical."

* * *

Outside, the morning sunlight was dazzling. The silver walls of the star-shaped Alyxa building seemed to concentrate the heat, like a lens. Yet the sea breeze was cool on Finn's face and hands.

"Is it far?" he said as Ben led him along a path running beside the wall.

"Nowhere is very far on the island," Ben replied. "Although that doesn't mean you can't get lost."

"What's that?" Finn pointed towards a ring of huge stones jutting from the scrubby grass a few hundred metres away. They looked like giant teeth. They also looked like a perfect freerunning course. Finn suspected that really would be against the rules.

"That's the Small Ring," said Ben. "It's one of the old Druid sites."

"Druids?"

"Yeah. This place has a lot of history. A lot of myths and legends too."

"It looks old."

Ben shrugged. "The Dean says it's first century, but

I'll bet nobody really knows."

If that's the Small Ring, Finn thought, *what does the Large Ring look like?*

At the end of the path, the silver wall turned back on itself at a sharp angle. Finn realised they'd reached the southernmost point of the enormous star-shaped building. Angular windows reflected the sunlight, too high above their heads for Finn to see inside. Not for the first time, he wondered how all this was paid for. He was pretty sure his mum didn't have money for tuition.

Some of the wall panels were cracked and twisted. Metal scaffolding held them in place. Below the scaffolding was a revolving door.

"What happened here?" asked Finn.

"There was a big storm last month," said Ben. "Terrifying, actually. Force nine gales, lightning strikes, the whole thing. They're getting it fixed."

Finn eyed the door. "And what's through there?"

"The infirmary. You can get to it from inside, but I thought you'd like the fresh air. So this is where I leave you."

"Wait," said Finn as Ben turned to go. "How do I find my way back?"

"Nurture Group is in this arm of the star. If you get lost, tap on one of the wall screens and you'll be able to access a map." Ben grinned. "If all else fails: follow your senses!"

After Ben left, Finn spent a brief moment feeling very small, and very alone. Then he summoned his strength and went through the revolving door into a long, triangular lobby dominated by a spiral staircase and an enormous potted palm tree. There was a small reception desk, but there was nobody behind it. Finn dithered for a moment, then a young woman descended the stairs with a clipboard pressed to her blouse. She wore a crisp white uniform with an embroidered snake's-head badge. Her blonde hair was tied in a tight bun.

"Finlay Williams?" she said, glancing at the clipboard.

"Uh, yes, that's me," Finn replied.

"I'm Dr Forrester. You're right on time."

She turned smartly on her heels and ascended the stairs again. Finn followed. The palm tree's fronded leaves draped over the handrail, and he let his hand brush over them as he climbed.

At the top was another triangular room, two sides of which were mostly glass – the windows he'd seen from outside. The view was spectacular: sunlit grass rolling down towards a broken cliff edge, with craggy rocks rising beyond, then the sea and a vast blue cloudless sky. A black-headed seagull hovered in an updraught, barely moving its wings.

"This way," said Dr Forrester, leading him into an area filled with white cabinets, smooth worktops and strange steel gadgets. A couple of technicians worked quietly with test tubes and glowing tablets. "Try to remain quiet."

They reached a small cubicle, where Dr Forrester told Finn to sit before turning her attention back to the clipboard.

"I see you're one of the Taste people," Finn said to break the silence.

She granted him a brief smile. "That's one way of putting it. I am a graduate of Alyxa and, yes, as a student I was in Taste Clann."

The smile revealed creases around her eyes, and Finn guessed that she was probably about the same age as ...

"My mother came here," he said. "I think she was in Taste Clann too?"

"What makes you think that?"

"Well, her job. She used to be a sommelier, you know, sort of a wine waitress. Now she writes restaurant reviews and everything."

Dr Forrester nodded. "Harriet was very talented, in her own way."

Finn clutched the edge of his chair. "You knew her?"

"She was two years above me. My own powers of

taste are very different from hers, of course – that's why I stayed on to do this job."

Finn tried to imagine his mother here at Alyxa, walking its corridors, attending assemblies, sitting in the canteen. Perhaps she'd even eaten sausage sandwiches with Dr Forrester.

"My talents lie in the field of emotional well-being," Dr Forrester continued. "Wine and food are one thing – quite straightforward to be honest – but my powers allow me to taste happiness, sadness, anger, frustration; the entire spectrum of human feelings."

Finn ignored the barb at his mother. "So taste comes in lots of different, well, flavours?"

"That's one way of putting it."

"And your flavour makes you sort of a mind-doctor?" said Finn. "Like a psychiatrist?"

"Oh, I'm a lot more than that. I can also taste airborne pathogens. Viruses. Certain types of disease. My powers are holistic, Finlay. Do you know what that means?"

Finn was pleased that he did. "It means you do a bit of everything."

"I prefer to think of it as caring for the whole patient. Now, shall we begin with a basic eye test?"

She picked up a remote control and pressed a button. The cubicle went dark and a panel lit up on the far wall. On it were rows of letters, numbers and animal symbols, gradually decreasing in size. Finn read them aloud, although he struggled with the really tiny row of symbols at the bottom.

"I guess I won't be making it into Sight Clann," he said when the lights came up again.

"Everyone has trouble with that last line," said Dr Forrester.

"You're wasting your time," said Finn. "There's nothing special about me."

"I doubt that," Dr Forrester replied. "Now, let's assess your hearing."

***

Finn watched glumly as Dr Forrester sealed the cotton pad in a plastic envelope. He ran his tongue around the inside of his cheek, which still felt a bit weird from where she'd taken the swab.

"It will take a few days to process the DNA data," said Dr Forrester.

"But nothing showed up in your tests, did it?"

The doctor ran her finger over her lips and gave Finn a long, appraising stare. "Everyone's different. Some people develop their powers at quite a young age. For some it takes a little longer. Sometimes it comes all in a rush, just when you least expect it."

Despite her words, Finn could tell she had her doubts.

"The Dean said your students normally start here at eleven. I'm thirteen, and still no powers. Are there any others who haven't shown their powers after two years?"

"Be patient," said Dr Forrester. "You can't rush nature."

Finn was going to protest, but kept it to himself. How long was he supposed to be patient? *I can't put my life on hold just because these people think I might be special.*

There was a knock at the cubicle door and a man poked his head inside. He was short, with a smooth, round face and a little pair of spectacles perched on the end of his nose. His green jacket clashed horribly with his yellow trousers. The bright red turban didn't help.

"Am I too early?" the man said. "Too late? Just right?"

"Just right, Dr Raj," said Dr Forrester. "I've finished with Mr Williams."

Dr Raj clapped his hands. "Then this is the perfect time for me to do my thing! Care to join me, Finlay? Or do you prefer 'Finn'?"

"Uh, Finn is good," said Finn, eager to get out of the

infirmary.

"Excellent! Walk this way."

Dr Raj's office adjoined the clinic. Finn counted no less then twelve computer monitors mounted on the big desk in the middle. A pot of pens and pencils looked hopelessly out of place. A wide window looked into a large room that was as black as the infirmary was white. In the gloom, screens flashed, lights blinked, and in the far corner sparks sizzled around a piece of apparatus that looked as if it was made mostly of bedsprings.

A mobile phone buzzed on Dr Raj's desk. He swiped the screen to reject the call and beamed at Finn.

"Never mind what they want," he said. "How are you?"

Finn eyed the phone, remembering what Warden Blake had said about outside communication being forbidden for students. Was that really true? Even if it was, there had to be a way around it.

"I'm fine, thanks."

He scanned Dr Raj's jacket, looking for a badge. When he saw none, he said, "So what's your power?"

Dr Raj pantomimed a shifty glance at the door. Beckoning Finn closer, he placed his finger to his lips and whispered, "Don't tell a soul, but I haven't got one."

"Oh, um, really?" said Finn. "I mean, I won't say anything if ..."

Dr Raj burst out laughing. "Oh, do forgive me, Finn. I'm just messing around. It's true I don't have a power, but it's no secret."

"So not everyone at Alyxa has super-senses?" Finn relaxed a little – maybe he wasn't the only odd one.

"Most people do, but not me, alas. My wife was the talented one, and our daughter takes after her. She's here at Alyxa, by the way."

"Your wife?"

"My daughter. You might meet her if you ..." Dr Raj slapped his forehead theatrically. "Wait! You're attending Nurture Group – of course you've met her!"

Finn suddenly saw something he recognised in the little man's dark skin, broad grin and mischievous eyes. "Your daughter's Lucy."

"Indeed she is! Now, let's measure your brainwaves!"

Dr Raj's laboratory was filled with a soft thrumming sound. Somewhere unseen, something beeped intermittently. Finn picked his way across a dimly-lit floor covered with tangled cables and wondered if anybody had ever told Dr Raj about health and safety in the workplace.

When they reached the buzzing, sizzling contraption in the corner, Finn pulled up short.

"Is that thing dangerous?" he said.

"Not particularly," Dr Raj replied. "Don't worry. I

will sit you at a safe distance."

Ushering Finn into a nearby metal chair, he grabbed a tangle of wires with pads connected. The other ends of the wires disappeared into some sort of box that looked like a computer router.

"It won't hurt," said Dr Raj cheerfully as he attached the pads to Finn's temples.

"What *will* it do?" said Finn.

"Between you and me, it will do exactly what the Wardens of Alyxa don't want it to do. They want to know what powers a student has. What I want to know is why they are different. Where exactly in the brain does this phenomenon occur?"

"Why don't they want you to find that out?" said Finn.

Behind him, the machine let out a long, rasping fart, then began to chug like a steam locomotive. A spark leapt from the router box, but Dr Raj didn't look concerned.

"Because they're not interested in scientific explanations. The Wardens ask questions like *who?* and *how?* but as a scientist I want to know *why?* As soon as you understand why something happens, you immediately unlock its potential. You can switch it on and off, like a machine. It will be predictable. Take sense-enhancement, for example. If you can find a thing, you can change a thing. Make it bigger, more powerful. Give it a megaboost. Now, while you're sitting still ..." He wheeled himself over on a chair, holding a small tablet. "I need your palm for the biometric scanners."

Finn obliged, laying his right hand on the screen.

"Very good," said Dr Raj, tossing it aside. "Ah-hah! You're cooked!"

The machine sputtered into silence and Dr Raj removed the pads, leaving Finn to massage his temples. His ears felt hot and tender.

"I don't know about enhancing things," Finn said, thinking about John's terrible attacks. "Whatever it is my brother's got, it needs dialling down, not up."

"Yes, I have read John's file. Inhibition is possible, in theory. I've been working on a device." He quickly crossed to the end of a workbench, and proudly whipped a sheet off an object that looked like a hollow golden disco ball. "I haven't given it a name yet, but it taps into the various sensory lobes and augments or reduces the signals received in the brain.

"Like a booster helmet," said Finn.

"Exactly!" said Dr Raj. "I might use that, if you don't mind?"

Finn laughed.

Dr Raj replaced the cover. "The difficulties your brother is experiencing are common," he said seriously.

"The staff here at Alyxa will teach him the necessary control."

Finn prised himself out of the chair. "You haven't seen what he gets like. The last attack ... it was really bad. Maybe you could try your device on him, just a little bit ..."

Dr Raj backed away with his hands raised. "Your concern does you credit. But it's far too dangerous. Inhibiting something means boxing it in. Do you really want me to box in your brother's brain? What if I make the box too small? The human mind is a fragile thing, you know. Fragile and squishy."

Finn shuddered. "You'd never get him to wear one of those things anyway. It would mess up his hair."

On the way back to Dr Raj's office, they passed a steel carry case filled with short black batons. Finn snatched one up and ran his finger over the silver switch at the end.

"Adriana used one of these on me in the hospital," he said. "Another one of your gadgets?"

Dr Raj removed his spectacles and wiped them with the end of his tie. Without them he looked vulnerable and, Finn thought, rather shamefaced. "I don't like it when they take Overloaders off the island," he said. "But Mr Kildair insisted it was a security situation."

Finn dropped the baton back in its case, and tried

to shake off the memory of being zapped in the lift. "Security for who?"

Back in the office, Dr Raj summoned his toothy smile again. "Alyxa is a good place, Finn. The best place, actually, for you and your brother. Now, before you go, will you promise me one thing?"

Finn didn't like the way the cold, heavy Overloader had felt in his hand. But it was hard not to like Dr Raj. "Of course," he replied. Dr Raj's phone was still on the desk. Finn only wanted to borrow it for a moment, just to let his mum know he was okay.

"Keep an eye on Lucy," said the doctor. "She's a bit of a live wire, and I'd hate for her to get into any trouble."

"Sure," said Finn. He turned, swiping a mug full of pens off the desk. They scattered across the floor. "Oh, I'm so sorry!" he said, stooping to pick them up.

"Never mind!" exclaimed Dr Raj, bustling over to help.

Finn stood up quickly with a handful of pens, grabbed the phone from the desk and dropped it into his pocket. He knew it was wrong, but then so was kidnapping. Anyway, he only wanted to use it once, then he'd give it back.

Once they'd replaced the mug and its contents, Dr Raj directed him down a set of stairs, which took Finn outside. Before setting off down the path he turned to face the sea. Somewhere beyond the horizon was his home, his life. It might as well have been on the moon.

He trudged back along the path until he came to a bulky air-conditioning unit jutting from the wall of the building. It looked quite dilapidated, and Finn wondered if it too was a victim of the recent storm. Ducking behind it, he pulled out the phone and dialled his mother's number. For a moment he was convinced she wasn't going to answer. Then he heard a voice so warm and familiar that his legs turned to rubber.

"Hello?"

"Mum!" Finn cried. "It's me!"

"Finn? What are you ... you're not supposed to call me. You're not supposed to call anyone."

"You've got to get me out of here."

"Just calm down and ..."

"I don't want to calm down! I want to come home. I don't belong here. This is all a huge mistake."

"You do belong. Alyxa is the best place for you. If I didn't believe that, I wouldn't have ..."

"It might be the best place for John, but not for me."

"No. You both need to be there. You're both special."

Finn couldn't believe his ears. Was that really what she thought? He stared up at the shining silver wall, then out at the distant ring of standing stones. He wiped stinging tears from his eyes.

"Why didn't you tell me about this place?" he said.

There was a long pause at the other end, then an equally long sigh. "I think I just hoped it wouldn't come to this. I wanted to believe that you and John would never have to go to Alyxa. I was kidding myself."

"Come and get me, Mum," said Finn. "Please, I want to get off this island."

"Finn, darling ..." He heard tears in her voice. He hated himself for doing it, but he knew she was close to breaking.

"Mum, if you don't, I'll find my own way. I'll –" A shadow blotted out the sun as a hand snatched the phone from his grip.

"Hey!"

Finn looked up into the glowering face of Kildair.

"I decide who leaves this island," said the Dean of Alyxa. "And I decide who stays. Now, would you care to explain exactly what you are doing with this phone?"

CHAPTER FIVE

"I just wanted to talk to my mum," said Finn.

"Where did you get this phone?" demanded Kildair. With the sun behind him, the Dean was made of shadow. He'd ended the call, Finn noticed; he hadn't even had a chance to say goodbye to her.

"I borrowed it," Finn said.

The Dean's eyes locked on to his coldly. "I knew you were trouble. So did Professor Panjaran - the moment he set eyes on you he saw a shadow in your future."

"He didn't say anything about shadows to me," Finn replied. His cheeks felt hot. "He just went on about some path or other."

Kildair raised a finger. "Do not challenge me, Finn.

Go back to your room and wait."

"Wait for what?" said Finn.

The grey-haired man shifted his balance and the sun flashed out from behind his head. Finn squinted his eyes against the glare.

"I think you mean 'Yes, Dean.'"

Finn glared at the ground. "Yes, Dean."

His face burning, Finn stalked back along the path until he found the door that he and Ben had used to exit the building. He yanked it open, marched inside and slammed it shut behind him. Day one and he was already facing detention. Or whatever sanctions they had here at Alyxa. Whatever. The sooner he was out of here the better.

He set off down the corridor and lost his sense of direction almost immediately. It wasn't that everywhere looked the same – every passage just looked so different. He gave up trying to navigate and just walked, passing rapidly from a wide corridor with slick metal walls to a dark twisting tunnel of stone. After several false turns, he eventually found his way back to his door.

He pressed his palm to the chrysalis sign, wondering if the palm print taken by Dr Raj had worked its way into the Alyxa security system. To his relief the door clicked open immediately, admitting him into his room – the closest thing he had to a sanctuary in this madhouse.

The grey room wasn't empty. Finn stopped dead. Zoe was standing in front of his wardrobe and rifling through the uniforms hanging there.

"Hey!" he said. "What do you think you're doing?"

She threw him a guilty look. Her tinted goggles were up on her forehead, and for the first time Finn saw her eyes. There was something odd about them, but he got no more than a glimpse before she yanked the goggles down again.

"Mind your own business!" She slammed the wardrobe door shut. Light from the little window glanced off the lenses of her goggles.

"This is my business," said Finn.

He noticed that Zoe was wearing a hawk badge. *Had it been there before?* He couldn't remember. She stalked out of his dorm and past the chair where Lucy was sitting, heading for her own room. Finn followed.

"Come back," he said. "I want to know what you were doing in my ..."

Zoe slammed her door in his face. Finn was about to hammer on it when Lucy called to him.

"Give her some space," she said.

"Why should I?" said Finn.

"She's having a hard time."

"I'm not exactly having a great day myself."

"Seriously," Lucy said, "just come and sit down."

Finn considered telling her to mind her own business as well. Then he reminded himself that Zoe was the one he was mad at. He slumped down in the opposite chair and glowered at the wall.

"Zoe lost her sister recently," said Lucy.

Finn's breath caught in his throat. "You mean she ... died?"

"Two weeks ago."

"Oh ... oh, that's terrible. I didn't know." He glanced at Zoe's door, trying to imagine how awful she must feel. "What happened?"

"Her name was Kylie," Lucy said. "She fell off the South Cliff."

That had to be the same cliff Finn had seen through the infirmary window. He remembered the waves crashing against the distant rocks. The sea had seemed a very long way down.

"In the storm?"

Lucy shook her head. "No, after that. Some people thought the storm might have weakened the cliffs, but ..." Lucy tailed off, looking at Zoe's closed door.

"Is this the accident Professor Panjaran was talking about in assembly?" said Finn.

"Nobody really thinks it was an accident," said Lucy quietly. "She took off her shoes first – they found them up there." Lucy paused. "She jumped."

Finn stifled a groan. Why had he lashed out at Zoe? If only he'd known something was wrong.

"She'd been going through a bad patch," Lucy went on. "She was in Smell Clann. They'd recently made her a prefect and she was, you know, really flying high. Then she split up with her boyfriend, and her grades started slipping. One thing led to another and she ended up here in Nurture Group." She nodded towards Finn's door. "That was her dorm."

A shiver ran down Finn's spine.

They've given me the room of a dead girl.

He thought about the broken cliff edge, and the long fall to the sharp rocks far below. He tried to imagine how Zoe must be feeling, and it wasn't hard, because he knew if John had done anything like that ...

He couldn't think of anything worse.

And he couldn't help his mind turning to John's attacks. *Had Kylie suffered from something similar?* he wondered. Maybe problems like that were commonplace at the school.

They'd told him it was a place of safety, that John would be fine. Finn wasn't sure Zoe's sister would have agreed with that.

***

At lunchtime, Finn and Lucy headed for the canteen together. Halfway there, Finn was pleased to discover he remembered the way. Maybe he wasn't going to need Ben's maps after all.

The canteen was crowded and noisy. Noon light poured down through slots in the ceiling, turning the paint-splatter decoration into a kaleidoscope of colour. Even the tables looked like paint palettes.

A red-faced woman and a man with an enormous moustache busied themselves behind the circular counter, snatching fresh ingredients off the ever-moving vertical conveyor belts, griddling food, filling plates and handing them over to the waiting students.

Following Lucy's lead, Finn took a tray from a stack near the door and joined the queue.

"I saw your dad this morning," he said as they inched forward. "After Dr Forrester had finished with me."

"Did he put that contraption on your head?" said Lucy.

"He wired me up to something!" said Finn. They laughed together, then Finn said, "He mentioned your mum. That she had a power, but not him?"

Lucy's smile vanished. "Oh, she had this really unique talent."

"What was it?"

"The ability to forget all about her family. Next question?"

"Uh, no, I'm done," said Finn hurriedly.

The line of kids shuffled forward. Before they could move with it, a tall boy wearing white shorts and a sports vest rushed out of nowhere and squeezed into the gap.

"Hey, watch it!" said Finn, then belatedly recognised his brother. "John – trust you to jump the queue."

"Hey, bro! How's it going?"

Finn couldn't help but grin. Seeing John made the incident with the Dean and the mobile phone seem unimportant.

"I'm all right," he said. "I'm fine."

"Me too!"

The line reached the counter and Lucy circled around to the section where the man was serving. Finn and John waited in front of a line of square metal tubs filled with hot food.

"I had a medical this morning," said Finn.

"Yeah? They got me doing gym. Did they find anything interesting?"

"Not really." Finn hesitated. "Not about me, anyway. But someone did tell me – his name's Dr Raj – he said that your attacks are, well, they're actually pretty common. He said they should be able to do something about them."

He tensed himself, waiting for John to object to the word "attacks". Instead, his brother regarded him with solemn eyes.

"Really?" John said. "That would be awesome."

Finn relaxed. "Yeah, it would. So how are things going in Touch Clann?"

"Oh, everyone's cool. Some of the kids there can do amazing things. There's this girl called Sara. She's got ten times as many ridges on her fingers as the rest of us. She can climb walls like a lizard. Extra friction, or something. It's incredible. And this boy called Wayne, he can put his hand in boiling water without getting, you know, cooked."

One of the women behind the counter tapped her serving spoon on Finn's tray.

"Have you two decided what you want?" she said brightly.

"Eggs and hash browns," said John at once. "Pile them up, please."

"I'll have the same," said Finn. "Only not quite as much."

Carrying their loaded trays, they caught up with Lucy at the cutlery dispenser. She'd picked up a dish of something that looked like grey oatmeal.

"Where are you sitting?" said John. He kept glancing at a table near the outer perimeter of the circular canteen. Four kids were beckoning frantically at him.

"It's all right," said Finn. "Go and sit with your friends. I'll be fine."

"Okay. Catch you later."

Clearly relieved, John made his way to the table, where he was greeted by a chorus of chatter. *How does he do it?* Finn thought. *He's been here for a morning, and already he's Mr Popular.*

Looking around for Lucy, Finn spotted Zoe sitting on her own nearby. He wondered if she always ate alone now that her sister was gone.

He took a step in her direction, then another. It wouldn't be hard to say sorry, but what if she started kicking off again? The last thing he wanted was to make a scene on his first day.

So he followed Lucy to a round table splashed with red and yellow streaks, and started tucking in.

"This food is way better than at my last school," said Finn. He plunged a hash brown into a runny egg yolk, added a generous splash of ketchup and crammed it into his mouth.

"The chefs are all Alyxa graduates," Lucy replied, stirring her dish of sludge.

"So what are you eating? It looks ... nice. *Ish*."

She laughed. "It's soy. My taste buds are all messed

up – sort of hypersensitive. That's why I'm in Nurture Group. I'm only supposed to eat stuff that doesn't taste like anything. They throw vitamins in so I can pretend it's a balanced diet. Want a try?"

Finn scooped up a dollop on the end of his knife and tasted it. His first thought was "cardboard" but even cardboard tasted of something. This stuff just made his tongue feel numb.

"Yuck!" he said, grabbing his glass and gulping down a mouthful of water. "That's disgusting."

"Hey," said a familiar drawling voice, "if you're going to stay, I suppose I should welcome you to Alyxa."

Finn turned to see the grinning face and sleepy eyes of Xander. "Thanks," he said warily. "You're not going to try and trip me up again, are you?"

"No way," said Xander. "I was only kidding. Shake on it."

He held out his hand. Finn glanced at Lucy, who shrugged.

"All right," Finn said, taking Xander's hand. "I suppose I ... yow!"

Sharp pain stabbed his fingers, like he'd grabbed a cactus. Finn yanked his hand away and pressed it to his mouth.

Still grinning, Xander raised his own hand and wiggled his fingers. Bright sparks danced between them. *What is that?* thought Finn. *It can't be electricity – that's impossible.*

"Shocking, right?" laughed Xander.

"Get lost!" said Finn.

"Get a life!" Xander turned his back and began walking away.

Finn wasn't sure why he did it, but he flicked the grey sludge off the end of his knife and it splatted on to the back of Xander's neck.

The entire canteen fell silent.

Xander turned slowly round. His face was red. Finn could almost see the line of his gaze sweeping the room like an angry lighthouse beam. Xander's eyes settled on Finn.

"You'll pay for that."

Xander began to advance, but suddenly John was there, standing between them.

"It's our first day," he said. "Don't ruin it."

Xander looked John up and down, and for a moment Finn thought he was going to swing a fist, but someone hissed, "Kildair!"

Then the Dean was there, gliding towards them, his eyes glittering in his gaunt face. Wherever he went, students fell back with fearful expressions. It was like watching a shark cut through a terrified ocean.

"What's happening here?" he asked.

"Nothing, sir," said Xander.

Kildair ran his index finger through the ketchup on Finn's plate. *What's he doing?* The watching students pulled back a little. The Dean smeared a line of red sauce first on John's cheek, then on Xander's. Reloading his finger, he approached Finn. For some reason, Finn found he couldn't move, as the Dean marked him in the same way across the forehead. He had no idea what it meant, but it was unnerving.

"Clean yourselves up," said Kildair, then he walked silently away.

Xander grabbed a napkin and wiped his face, then slouched off. Finn handed a napkin to John. "You didn't have to do that," he said. "I could've handled it."

"I know you could," said John.

"That was *almost* exciting," said Lucy. She handed Finn another napkin. "You've missed a bit, by the way."

CHAPTER SIX

"It's time for PE," said Lucy, scanning a large monitor on the canteen wall. "Come on."

Finn gave up trying to interpret the constantly-shifting graphic display and trudged after her, still massaging the hand that Xander had zapped. It felt as if he'd plunged it into a clump of stinging nettles.

"How far is it to the gym?" he said as Lucy led the way through a labyrinth of black tiled corridors.

"That's not where we're going," she answered. "You're in Alyxa, don't forget. Everything is different here."

"They don't do parkour, by any chance?"

"What, like freerunning? Is that your thing?"

"Yeah. I just thought that, you know, with all the stones and rocks on the island ..."

Lucy seemed to consider this. "Maybe they should build it into the Hunt. Trouble is, all the Touch students would be too good at it. There's a kid called Eloise who can run the hundred metres in under ten seconds."

"No way!" Finn thought about it for a moment. "Hang on, there must be loads of Alyxa kids who can do things that are ... well, superhuman. Isn't it cheating?"

"Why? They're not taking drugs – it's a natural gift they're born with."

"Yeah, but if other people don't know ..."

"Relax," said Lucy. "Alyxa has a strict code for graduates. Most just slip back into normal life. Sure, they have interesting jobs – your mum's a sommelier, you said – but anything that draws attention is frowned upon."

"Forbidden?" said Finn.

"Let's just say, discouraged," said Lucy.

Finn wondered what she meant. It wasn't a stretch to imagine the Dean showing up on a doorstep in the middle of the night with words of "discouragement" for an Alyxa graduate who'd overstepped the mark.

The corridor took them to a rectangular yard roughly the size of a tennis court. The floor was covered in sand and the roof was open to the sky. Basketball hoops hung on posts at either end, but what caught Finn's eye was a wooden rack filled with long silver poles, each nearly as tall as he was.

Six other students were there already, wearing shorts and vests just like those John had paraded in the canteen. They all looked about his age. He saw badges from all five Alyxa Clanns, though none had more than two bars below their animal emblem.

Standing before them, dressed in a long black cloak, was Magnus Gustavsson, the burly Touch Warden. When he spotted Finn and Lucy, he beckoned them over with one of his plate-sized hands.

"You come to me late," Gustavsson said as they joined the semicircle of students. "But you are new, Finn, so I forgive you." He eyed Lucy sternly. "You, Miss Raj, should know better." He scratched the shelf of chin hidden beneath his thick blond beard. "Now, where was I?"

A mousey-looking girl with a hawk badge on her vest raised her hand. "You were telling us about animal instincts, sir."

"Thank you, Karensa. Animals and humans. Hmm, well, humans are animals, you might say. But the world we have built has changed us." He spread his arms to indicate the surrounding courtyard. "We live in clean, square places. We think clean, square thoughts. The

86

more we do this, the more we lose our instincts. Our animal selves. Our ability to *feel*." He paused. "We lose our senses."

Karensa glanced at Finn and Lucy's grey jumpsuits. Finn wanted to tell her he wasn't like the rest of Nurture Group – he hadn't lost his powers.

Because I never had any in the first place.

"So we fall back on what we know," Gustavsson continued. "We use whatever sense is strongest, according to our needs. Alyxa will help you build on those strengths." Another pause. "It will also help you find strengths that you have forgotten."

The Touch Warden clapped his massive hands together, and the sound echoed through the courtyard.

"I need volunteer!" Gustavsson boomed in his clipped English.

Everyone moved except Finn, not towards the Warden but away from him in a series of small, shuffling steps. Despite the urge to follow them, Finn held his ground and looked Gustavsson in the eye.

"Our new recruit," said Gustavsson, curling one fat finger in Finn's direction. "Come with me."

Finn followed the big man to the wooden rack. Gustavsson plucked a pole from its slot and tossed it through the air as if it weighed no more than a matchstick. Finn caught it clumsily.

The pole was a bit like a long broomstick, and about as heavy. Its silver surface felt odd – smooth and cold like metal, yet grainy like wood. One end was capped with a slotted red sleeve. The other end ran into a red leather pouch just large enough to contain his fist. Halfway along its length, the pole threaded through a similar pouch. Hand-protectors?

Gustavsson seized a second pole from the rack.

"These are *gefelsticks*," he said. "The materials are modern, but the Druid settlers used such weapons to defend their island. Hold a gefelstick, and you hold the past."

Wedging the pole under his arm, Gustavsson plucked a strip of black cloth from his pocket and tied it around his head so that it covered his eyes. Then he took the gefelstick in his hands and held it vertically before his face.

"Now," he said. "Hit me."

Finn glanced at Lucy, who gave him an enthusiastic nod.

Inserting his right hand into the leather cowl at the end of his gefelstick, Finn gripped the middle of the stick with his left. After a couple of practice swings, he made a cautious jab towards Gustavsson's slab-like midsection. Despite the blindfold, the Warden deflected the blow easily, and returned instantly to his resting

88

position.

"Strike harder," Gustavsson said.

"But you can't see me."

"Do as I say."

Spreading his feet wider in the sand, Finn jabbed again, this time leaning his body weight into the blow. Again Gustavsson knocked his gefelstick aside with ease. The two weapons made a sharp cracking noise as they connected, sending vibrations through Finn's hands.

"Strike as if you mean it," said the Warden.

Finn breathed deeply and tried once more, only to be thwarted for a third time. *How is he doing that? Can he see through the blindfold?*

"There is no focus in what you do," said Gustavsson. "Unlike your brother this morning. He struck with a purpose."

Finn could feel the eyes of the other students boring into his back. And even though Gustavsson's eyes were hidden beneath the blindfold, he could feel the big man's gaze upon him too. Except it wasn't his gaze. It was something else.

"To fight well, you need a strong heart," Gustavsson said.

Finn tightened his grip on the gefelstick, squeezing his fingers hard against the thin film of sweat that had gathered beneath them. He wondered why he had to fight at all.

"Do you have a strong heart, Finlay Williams? A heart as strong as your brother's?"

Finn's mounting frustration suddenly snapped. With a yell, he leapt forward. This time, instead of jabbing with the gefelstick, he swung it like a sword, bunching the muscles in his arms and aiming the weapon squarely at Magnus Gustavsson's head. Air whistled faintly through the slots in the gefelstick's red cap.

Gustavsson ducked, bending his knees while keeping his back straight. Finn's gefelstick sliced the air above the Touch Warden's head, missing him by a hand's width. The momentum spun Finn round, throwing him off balance. He staggered and nearly fell. Behind him, the watching students laughed and for the second time that day he felt shame burning his face.

"Better," said Gustavsson, peeling off the blindfold. "Far to go, but better. Now the roles reverse."

Finn's dismay grew as the Warden set his pole aside and tied the black cloth around his head instead. Finn's eyelashes brushed the coarse fabric, reminding him instantly of the moment he'd woken in the helicopter. What was it with Alyxa and blindfolds?

"I can't see a thing," Finn said.

"That's the idea," a boy called from behind him.

Hands shaking a little, Finn held the gefelstick up in front of his face, just as he'd seen Gustavsson do.

"What do I ...?" he began, then something hard prodded the left side of his chest. He jerked the gefelstick towards it, but the weapon met only empty air.

"Your heart is there." Gustavsson's voice floated in the darkness. "Use it."

Finn waited, listening hard. Maybe if he could follow the sound of the Warden's footsteps in the sand ...

Gustavsson's gefelstick hit his right shoulder. This time it hurt. Again he tried to parry the blow late.

The next blow hit his thigh, hard enough to make him cry out. A girl – Karensa maybe – chuckled.

This is hopeless.

Trying to anticipate the next attack, Finn waved his gefelstick left and right, left and right. Each time he met no resistance, heard nothing but the thin hiss of the air through the slots in the end of the weapon. He whirled around – maybe Gustavsson was behind him. But there was nobody there either. Panting hard, disorientated, he turned a slow circle, brandishing the gefelstick, waiting for the next blow to come out of the blackness.

"Calm yourself," came Gustavsson's voice. The big man was somewhere to his left. Finn turned towards the sound. "Empty your mind and fill up your heart. Open your senses to the world. If you cannot see, then hear. If you cannot hear, then touch. Taste the threat. Smell your enemy. Take it all in."

Finn closed his eyes behind the blindfold. It made no difference to his vision, but it did seem to help his focus. He listened hard. *Was that soft crunch the sound of the Warden's boots in the sand? Did that subtle breeze mark the movement of Gustavsson's gefelstick through the air?* Robbed of his sight, he tried to will his other senses into life.

With a painful whack, Gustavsson's weapon slammed into his elbow. Crying out, Finn dropped his gefelstick and clapped his hand against the pain erupting through his arm.

"Enough!" roared Gustavsson.

Finn snatched the blindfold off his face, blinking into the sudden flood of light. Through the glare, he saw disappointment flicker on the Warden's bearded face.

"Pick up your weapon," Gustavsson said, holding Finn's gaze briefly before turning to the other students. "Break into pairs. Duelling practice. Begin!"

Rubbing his aching arm, Finn joined Lucy in a corner of the courtyard.

"I suppose you're good at this," he said as he planted his hands back into the gefelstick's guards.

"Not really," Lucy replied with a sunny grin.

They began trading gentle blows. The crack of their gefelsticks joined the chorus of impacts resounding through the courtyard. Finn soon realised that his partner was holding back.

"You don't have to go easy on me," he said.

"I'm not," Lucy replied. "You're good."

"I wish."

Lucy closed her eyes, but continued to fight as they settled into a rhythm of clashing sticks. "It's early days." *Knock*. "Duelling practice is a great way to focus on your power." *Knock. Knock.*

"You're just showing off."

"Try it too," she said.

Finn closed his eyes, swinging his stick smoothly. *Knock. Knock. Knock.*

"Ouch!" Her pole caught his forearm and he opened his eyes.

"Sorry!" she said. "If you do it regularly, you'll soon –"

"I don't want any stupid power. I just want my old life back."

Finn rubbed his arm, taking a moment to watch the rest of the students. Gefelsticks flashed silver in the sunlight, cutting back and forth. Sometimes they moved in silence; sometimes he heard the whoosh and whistle as they slashed the air. Each time a pair of poles made contact, a sharp popping sound rang out. It was like listening to a chorus of whipcracks, like watching a dance.

Practice continued for twenty minutes. By the end of the session, it wasn't just Finn's hands that were sweating. His armpits prickled and his brow was dripping. His body felt bruised all over.

In contrast, Lucy looked as fresh as when she'd started.

"Don't worry," she said as they dropped their gefelsticks back in the rack. "You'll get the hang of it."

He was following her out of the courtyard when Gustavsson's massive hand landed on his shoulder.

"She is right," the Touch Warden said. "You will learn to do this and more. But first you must learn to let go."

Finn regarded the big man. "Let go of what?" he said.

"Many things," Gustavsson replied. "Pride. Self-consciousness. Embarrassment. Perhaps anger."

"What have I got to be angry about?"

Gustavsson's shoulders heaved in an almighty shrug. "Only you can know this. I cannot see into your thoughts."

***

Back in his dorm, Finn changed his sweat-soaked jumpsuit for a fresh one. He was about to close the wardrobe when he caught sight of his reflection in the rectangular mirror hanging on the inside of the door. A red weal striped his left cheek – the remnant of one of Lucy's blows. He'd probably have a black eye tomorrow. That would really give them something to laugh about in the canteen.

The frame of the mirror was coming loose. He pushed it back into place and examined his knuckles. They were red too, from where they'd rubbed against the inside of the leather hand guards. His reflection regarded him with a silent frown. Not for the first time he wondered what on earth he was doing here. Sure, his brother seemed to be thriving, but that's because this place was an answer to his problems. For Finn, it was just the problem. When he said to his mum that he'd find his own way back, he'd been trying to push her, but now, as he stared at himself, battered and angry, he began to think of it more seriously. *Could he get away, if he wanted to? How far was the mainland? They'd try to stop him, and get him back, but what if he managed to get to a police station?* He found himself grinning a little at the fantasy. *What if he contacted the press?*

A harsh splintering sound made Finn jump, and a crack appeared that split the mirror completely from one side to the other. *I must have jammed the frame back too tightly*. He lifted the mirror off its hook. The two pieces of glass grated against each other, but the frame stayed rigid and kept the whole thing intact. He was about to put it back in place when he spotted something scratched into the surface of the grey wardrobe door: the unmistakeable pattern of the Alyxa star.

Finn put the mirror carefully on the floor. He ran his finger over the graffiti, wondering who'd carved it there. Then he paused. It was a star all right, but it wasn't the star of Alyxa.

The star on the wardrobe door didn't have five points, but six.

Icy fingers brushed Finn's spine. *Was there a draught coming from somewhere? No. The window was closed.*

He wasn't sure why the symbol was freaking him out. He'd seen far worse scratched into the toilet cubicle doors at his old school. But there was something brutal and crazed about the deep gouges. *What had made them - a knife?*

Someone knocked on the outer door of his room, startling him out of his reverie. Hurriedly he hung the broken mirror back in place, closed the wardrobe and opened the door.

John stood in the stone corridor, still in his sports kit. Beside him was Adriana. The Touch Clann monkey squatted on John's shoulder, watching Finn with beady black eyes.

"Woah! What happened to your face?" said John, his smile dropping. "If Xander ..."

"No," said Finn. "I just had a tough intro to the gefelstick with Gustavsson."

"You don't say," said John. "He's cool, isn't he?"

"Erm ... that's one way of putting it," said Finn. He wished he felt more pleased to see his brother. "Everything okay?"

"Everything is excellent," John replied, with a sideways smile at Adriana. "I stopped by to tell you there's a dorm party tonight."

A party? Tempting as it was to shut himself away for the rest of the day, Finn thought it might be fun to mix with the rest of the Alyxa students. Maybe if he got to know a few people ...

"The trouble is, I've got to look after Pogo," John went on. The little monkey chirruped and curled its long tail affectionately around John's neck. "So I was wondering."

"Wondering what?" said Finn, his heart sinking.

"If you'd look after her," said John.

Beside him, Adriana breathed on her new stripe and polished her badge with the sleeve of her black jacket.

"Is that allowed?" said Finn. "I mean, I'm not even

in your Clann."

"You don't have to tell anyone," Adriana said without looking up. "We won't."

"Come on, bro," said John. "It's only for a couple of hours. I've got to go to this thing – it's part of my initiation."

Pogo chirruped again, then extended one tiny paw towards the red mark on Finn's cheek. He recoiled, prompting laughter from John.

"She likes you!" said John. "So you'll do it?"

Finn raised a reluctant arm. Pogo leapt on to it, scurried up to his shoulder and settled herself against his neck.

"Awesome!" said John, putting his arm around Adriana and striding away down the corridor. "Catch you later!"

Finn closed the door slowly and glared at the blank, grey wall of his Nurture Group dorm. His brother had turned him into a babysitter.

Coiling her tail loosely around his neck, Pogo began purring like a cat.

"I hope you haven't got any bad habits," said Finn. "And you'd better do as you're told."

Pogo's enormous eyes shone like a pair of black polished mirrors, each containing a perfect reflection of Finn's angry scowl.

CHAPTER SEVEN

It was hard to stay angry at John for long. Actually, Finn liked the idea of his brother going through some kind of initiation ceremony.

"So how does it feel to have your face on a badge?" he asked Pogo. "I suppose you think you're some kind of celebrity."

The Touch Clann monkey chattered through her little yellow teeth.

A knock sounded on the door to the common room.

"Finn?" It was Lucy's voice, slightly muffled. "Is someone in there with you?"

"No," Finn answered, mentally willing Pogo to keep quiet.

"Oh. Anyway, I've got food."

Finn opened the door a crack and peered out. Lucy was there with a cardboard box in each hand. A delicious smell reached his nostrils: sweet and sour sauce, if he wasn't mistaken.

"It's takeaway night," said Lucy.

"They deliver to the island?" said Finn, amazed.

"No, silly! The canteen just lets you bring stuff back to your room. Do you like Chinese?"

"I do," said Finn. "Thanks."

He reached through the narrow gap and took one of the boxes. The cardboard was hot and slightly sticky. Steam puffed from beneath the lid.

Lucy loitered in the doorway.

"What are you doing in there?" she said.

"Just chilling," Finn replied, feeling bad that he couldn't invite her in. At least, he couldn't with the monkey around. "That okay with you?"

"Sure. Everybody needs some me-time." She hesitated a little longer. When Finn didn't invite her in, she raised her own takeaway box in a half-hearted salute. "See you later then."

"See you."

After closing his door, Finn sat on the bed with his back against the wall. No sooner had he opened the box than Pogo was there beside him, pawing expectantly at the cardboard.

"So *now* you want to make friends," he said.

***

Finn levered himself off the bed and saw at once that he was back in his old bedroom. His desk, his shelf of books, his bathrobe hanging on the back of the door. Dark outside. Relief flooded through him, overwhelming the confusion. Just a dream. All of it! And he felt stupid for ever believing any of it. A school magically hidden on an island! Ha! He circled the room, touching everything, the smile growing on his face.

He wandered out on to the landing. Dark inside too. John's door was open, his room empty. *What time was it?*

Finn descended the stairs, so happy it felt like his feet were floating above the treads. He heard classical music coming from the kitchen.

"Mum?" His voice was thin and reedy in his ears.

"Finn!" His mother's voice was all tangled up in the music. She sounded anxious, and he felt a twinge of fear. "I can't see you. Where are you?"

"I'm here," he said. "Turn on the lights." He leapt down the last few steps. "Mum?"

Finn crossed the hall. He couldn't remember

where the light switch was. The music wobbled as if the orchestra was playing underwater.

"Don't come in," his mother called.

Ignoring her, fear mounting, he entered the kitchen. The floor was wrong. Grey and cracked. His toe caught in a deep crevice and he nearly tripped. As his eyes adjusted to the gloom, he saw that the table was gone, and he was walking over a broken jigsaw of ancient flagstones. Stone columns loomed on either side, rising towards a shadowy vaulted ceiling. Round a hidden corner, candlelight flickered.

Finn stumbled on, breathing in cold, damp air.

"Mum – where are you?"

He rounded a column and there she was, dressed for one of her restaurant openings. But her face was gaunt and her eyes were hollow. She didn't look right. Not right at all.

Finn's stomach climbed into his throat. Cold as the surrounding air was, he could feel the perspiration clinging to his neck.

"You shouldn't have come here," said his mother.

"What's wrong?" he replied. "I'm home, aren't I?"

Her sunken eyes grew suddenly wide. Reflections flashed inside them – something moving behind him.

He heard its breath, or its thoughts. The rumbling sound was the thunder of its heartbeat. He felt its pulse as it lunged towards him, heard the boom as it knocked the air aside. He turned to meet it, not knowing what it was and not wanting to know.

**

Finn woke gasping for breath, his hands gripping the duvet he'd been sprawled across. Grey walls stared back at him, dull beneath the flat light of the glowing ceiling. The air in the dorm was hot and stifling.

He sat up, heart hammering, inadvertently planting his hand in the sticky remains of his takeaway. He pushed it off the bed in disgust.

Kneeling on the bed, he opened the small window, using the hand that wasn't dripping with sweet and sour sauce. The flood of fresh air was cold and welcome. Outside, a crescent moon hung low in the clear night sky.

Finn went to the sink and washed off the mess. He splashed his face with cold water, driving away the last remnants of the nightmare.

Something chattered. He spun around, his pulse racing all over again. There was Pogo sitting on top of the wardrobe. The black fur on her body lay flat, but her blonde mane was sticking out in an angry-looking ruff. As he met her eyes, she lashed her tail and bared her teeth.

"Hey, calm down," he said to the monkey. "It's not my fault my brother left us in the lurch." He checked his watch: it was nearly half past midnight.

Pogo chattered again, then stood upright. Flexing her long legs, she leapt from the wardrobe on to the bed and trampolined up on to the open window ledge.

"No, no, no ..." said Finn, hands splayed as he reached for her. "Don't you dare, you little ..."

Pogo hopped out into the night and Finn gaped at the open window. *Oh, great!*

Gathering his senses, he jumped on to the bed and peered outside. He saw moonlit grass and the dark shadows cast by distant buildings. No sign of the monkey.

For a moment he considered just shutting the window and going back to bed. But he couldn't do that to his brother. He hadn't *wanted* to look after the monkey, but he'd given his word he would.

Getting through the window was a tight squeeze. Perched on the outer sill, Finn appraised the distance to the ground. The drop was enough to break an ankle if he landed badly.

The wall to his right was smooth and sheer. To his left, however, the silver cladding bulged around some kind of ventilation duct. He threw himself towards it, letting his thigh muscles absorb the impact as his feet struck the curved metal surface. Rolling sideways around the duct, he planted his hands on the cold metal and pushed off, propelling himself away from the building. The instant his heels hit soft grass he let his body fold and roll.

Springing to his feet, he looked up at the window and wondered how he was going to get back in again.

Never mind that. I've got a monkey to find.

He set off along a narrow path leading away from the main building.

"Pogo!" he hissed, not daring to shout.

Something chirruped in the distance and he hurried on.

The path took Finn between a cluster of sheds and past a small stone cottage before bringing him to a sloping field covered in gorse and heather. Heading downhill, Finn was rewarded by the sight of a tiny animal springing over a far-off rocky outcrop.

"Pogo!" he called.

Finn began to run. The moon lit up the island landscape well enough. As the downward slope steepened, he picked up another path. Tiny pawprints peppered the sand-covered trail, which led him through a small copse. The breeze made the trees move, and then suddenly the night air itself seemed to be moving. Finn ducked as a stream of black shapes poured past his head, and for a few seconds his head was filled with a series of strange whistles that were almost too high to hear.

He spun around and watched as the black things soared up past the moon, revealing themselves for what they really were. Bats.

Finn continued to slip and slide down the sandy path for what seemed an age, until he arrived at a wide beach. Waves lapped the shore, the dancing edge of a moonlit sea so flat it looked like a mirror.

The monkey was nowhere in sight. All Finn could hear was the wash of the waves on the sand. No more pawprints. The trail had gone cold.

Wandering down to the water's edge, Finn gazed out across the empty ocean. He couldn't believe how calm it was. It was tempting just to throw off his jumpsuit and dive in. He was a decent swimmer. If he knew the right way to go, he might even reach the island or the mainland. *Or I might just freeze and drown ...*

He started walking along the beach, parallel to the shoreline. Ahead, a high cliff jutted out to sea like the prow of some vast, craggy ship. Its upper edge was broken, and jagged scars ran down its face to a pile of rocks half-sunk in the water. Was this the same cliff he'd seen from the infirmary?

The same cliff that Zoe's sister, Kylie, had jumped

from?

Finn turned away, and immediately saw a line of little pawprints running through the damp sand. Following them, he eventually reached the place where the cliffs cut across the end of the beach.

Here, the sand gave way to piles of shingle and scattered boulders slick with seaweed and covered with clinging mussels. There were rock pools everywhere, and Finn deduced that this whole area must be below water at high tide.

A cave mouth gaped in the base of the cliff, directly ahead of where Finn was standing.

Squatting on a rock near the entrance to the cave was Pogo.

"Come here!" Finn called, gesturing wildly.

The monkey remained.

Finn began clambering toward the cave on all fours, skirting the rock pools and jumping from one boulder to the next. Once, when his hand slipped into a pool of water, a crab skittered away beneath his fingers. The stench of seaweed was incredibly strong.

"I'll bet you think this is funny," he said to Pogo when he reached the mouth of the cave.

The monkey immediately jumped down from the boulder and started pawing at the shingle that surrounded it. Crouching beside her, Finn saw something shiny sticking up from between the tiny glistening stones. He pulled it free and held it up in the moonlight. It was a silver pin with a pentagon at one end.

A prefect's badge.

Lucy said they made Kylie a prefect not long before she ...

Finn gazed up the enormous wall of crumbling rock. The sea clawed at the shingle with a low rasping sound. So this was the place.

Pogo let out a sudden screech and bolted away over the boulders. Finn made a grab for her, but he was too late and the darkness beneath the cliffs swallowed her up.

He was about to go after the monkey when a sudden movement caught his attention. Turning, he looked back down the beach.

A tall figure was making its way across the sand – a man, Finn thought, although his face was mostly hidden by the hood of his long cloak. He carried a flaming torch, which stained the night air with red light. The sea breeze turned the cloak into a tail of twisting shadows. Beneath his boots, the shingle shrieked like shattered glass.

The stranger – whoever it was – was walking straight towards Finn.

CHAPTER EIGHT

Finn ducked down behind the boulder.

"I know you're there," said the figure.

Finn recognised the voice at once, and slumped further into the shingle at the sound of it. He thought about making a run for it, then decided it was pointless. He'd been found. He had to face whatever came next.

Slipping the badge into his pocket, he got to his feet and said, as casually as he could manage, "Evening!"

Kildair stood with his feet planted either side of a narrow rock pool. The sea breeze whipped the split ends of his cloak around his head. The moonlight sculpted the bones of his cheeks and turned his eye sockets to hollows.

"It is past one o'clock in the morning," said the Dean.

"I lost track of time," Finn replied.

"Boys like you always do." Kildair was perfectly still in his whipping clothes. The flame from his torch danced. "Do you know what I do to students who break the rules?"

Finn wasn't sure what to say, so he simply mumbled, "What rule have I broken?"

The breeze dropped and the Dean's cloak fell still.

"Tell me, what are you doing on the South Beach in the middle of the night?"

He took a step forward. Gulping, Finn took a step back. The easiest thing would be to come clean and tell the Dean about Pogo. But if he did that, he'd have to explain why he'd been babysitting the monkey in the first place. Which would get John into trouble.

"It's a nice night," Finn said, swallowing his fear. "I felt like a walk."

The Dean's face contorted with sudden fury. "A *walk*?"

As if shaken by his voice, a shower of stones rattled down the sheer drop towards the cave entrance. They were followed by a trio of big boulders. Two of the boulders embedded themselves deep in the shingle; the third struck a half-buried rock and smashed into pieces, right where he'd been standing a few seconds before. Finn really hoped Pogo hadn't hung around.

"There are places on the island that are free of danger," said the Dean when the echoes of the impacts had died away. "This beach is not one of them." He drew back his cloak to reveal a stubby black cylinder hanging from his belt. When he saw the Overloader, Finn flinched.

Waves crashed against the shore, louder than they had been earlier. Finn realised the tide was coming in, and for the first time understood how easy it would be to get cut off here.

"It's all right," he said. "I'll just go straight back to my dorm."

"Oh, you'll go back," said the Dean. "But you won't be seeing your dorm again for some time."

The Dean turned his back on Finn and started making his way towards the path that led back to Alyxa.

***

As the Dean led him to a plain-looking door near the end of one of the building's five pointed arms, tucking the torch into a sconce on the outside wall, Finn's mind was on the Overloader. Surely Kildair wouldn't use it on him? The Dean pressed his palm against a glowing red panel, which immediately turned green. The door clicked open. Finn followed the Dean into a round lobby with rough stone walls. Water dripping from cracks in the domed ceiling landed in shallow puddles on the floor.

A wheezing lift took them down several floors before releasing them into a long stone corridor. Pipes covered in green lichen trailed along the walls. Some kind of ancient basement, Finn supposed, a part of Alyxa lying deep underground. The thought made him uneasy.

"Where are you taking me?" he said.

Kildair remained silent. He used another palm-scanner to unlock a steel door. Pressing his hand into the small of Finn's back, he pushed him through the opening.

"Wait!" Finn called, spinning round. "What sort of ...?"

The door slammed shut. Finn ran to it, but there was no handle on the inside, only another scanner on the wall beside it. He flattened his hand against the screen. Nothing happened. He tried to force his fingers into the crack around the door's edge, but it was hopeless. He thumped the door once, twice, three times, all to no avail. He was trapped.

I was trapped the minute I got to the island, he thought

in despair.

Wiping sweat from his shaking palms, Finn took in his surroundings.

The little room was as gloomy as the tunnel outside felt clean and modern. The walls were dank stone, there was no window, no furniture, and the only light came from a single bare bulb hanging from the ceiling. The air was damp and tasted sour. He lowered himself to the stone floor and sat with his back to the wall. He wiped his nose on his sleeve and gritted his teeth. He wasn't going to give them the satisfaction of seeing him lose it.

Despite the fear bubbling through his veins, and the hardness of the floor, Finn dozed for a while. When he jerked awake his backside was numb. He shifted his weight and checked his watch: quarter past two. *How long is this going to last?*

He stood and massaged the backs of his legs. Then he ran on the spot for a moment. This at least warmed him up a bit. His footfalls were loud in the empty room, but it was odd that they didn't echo. There was something strange about the air in here. It wasn't just dry – it felt ... dead.

Experimentally, Finn kicked his heel against the floor. It made a short, dull thud. He rapped his knuckles on the wall. The sound was exactly the same. Weird.

He cocked his head and listened. *Was something humming?*

He walked slowly around the perimeter of the room, turning his head this way and that, trying to locate the strange sound. But he couldn't. First it seemed to be coming from his left, then from his right. Now it was behind him, now in front. *I'll bet there's a hidden camera*, thought Finn. *He just wants to watch me crack.*

Finn pressed one ear to the wall. Maybe the humming was coming from an adjacent cell. Maybe somebody else was ...

The door clicked open. Finn jumped away from the wall, feeling oddly guilty. The Dean strode in.

"What do you think you are doing?" he said.

"I'm trying to work out why you've put me in a prison cell," Finn replied.

To his surprise, Kildair laughed. But there was no humour in his expression.

"This is not a cell," the Dean said. "This is a meditation chamber."

"Meditation?" said Finn.

"An important part of the Alyxa curriculum." The Dean's eyes narrowed. "As you may yet come to learn."

"I don't think there's anything you can teach me," said Finn. "You might as well just send me home."

The Dean crossed to the far wall and stroked his

hand against it. "This is Alyxa," he said. "You don't need home any more." The skin of his palm rasped across the stone. "Tell me what you were doing on the beach."

"I did. I went for a walk."

The Dean suddenly lunged, and gripped Finn hard around the lower jaw. Finn tried to protest, but he couldn't get out more than a muffled cry as the Dean pulled Finn's face towards his own. Then the Overloader appeared in the Dean's other hand, pressed close to Finn's temple.

"Tell me!" roared Kildair.

Finn stopped fighting at once. He felt the Dean's eyes drinking in his fear. If he could have explained about Pogo in that instance, he would have, but the Dean shoved him hard. Finn landed on the floor, and pressed himself back into a corner.

"You can't do that!" he said. "It's assault!"

Kildair took a deep breath, and stowed the Overloader. The rage seemed to have left his body. Finn was breathing hard. He massaged his jaw.

"You know that your mother was a student here," the Dean said. His tone betrayed no hint of the violence that had just occurred.

"What does that have to do with anything?" said Finn.

"Perhaps nothing," replied the Dean. "Perhaps

everything." His mouth curved into a sickle-thin smile. "You didn't know about her connection with Alyxa, did you?"

"So what if I didn't?"

"In fact, you don't know very much about your mother at all." The Dean stopped. Finn felt boxed in. "Or your father."

Finn glared. "Leave my dad out of this!"

"Have I touched a sensitive spot?"

"If you know so much about me, you'll know he's dead."

"My condolences."

"Go to hell." Finn spat out the words and got to his feet. He didn't favour his chances against Kildair in a fight, but if he tried anything like that again, Finn knew he'd go out with fists flying.

"Do you remember him?"

"I was two."

"So you don't. Just like you don't remember why you went to the beach."

The humming sound returned to fill the silence that followed. It was very loud now – almost loud enough to drown out Finn's thoughts. He shook his head, trying to drive it away.

Pushing past his interrogator, Finn ran to the door and slammed his hand against the scanner. No response.

He did it again, then again. He thumped the door then whirled round.

"Interesting how your walk led you straight to the cliffs where Kylie Redmayne took her life."

"What's that got to do with anything?" said Finn.

"You've been spending time with her sister, Zoe," Kildair said. "What has she told you about Kylie?"

"Nothing," said Finn. Why was the Dean so interested in Kylie all of a sudden?

"I doubt that."

Finn slammed the door with his palm. "You can't keep me here."

"I can keep you here as long as I like," said the Dean. "Be in no doubt of that. On this island, my authority is absolute. I'll ask you again: what did Zoe Redmayne tell you?"

The humming was so loud that Finn could hardly think, let alone answer the Dean's question. It varied in pitch as it throbbed in his ears, sounding like some low, mournful song. *Were there words in there? Was that actually a voice?*

The Dean's gaze intensified. "Finlay?"

Finn grimaced. "There's someone else down here. I can hear them. Who is it?"

"Tell me what you hear," said the Dean.

"You can't hear it?" said Finn. He clapped his hands

to his ears, but the sound intensified. The Dean gripped his wrists, and pulled them away, and then the sound was gone. Kildair pushed his face close to Finn's.

"There is nobody else down here, Mr Williams. Trust me when I say that you are entirely alone."

CHAPTER NINE

At breakfast, Finn again saw Zoe sitting on her own. He picked an empty table opposite hers and sat down. Zoe's dark goggles made it impossible to tell if she'd seen him, so he just nodded in her direction and started eating.

Actually, he didn't mind being alone. With Pogo still on the loose, he needed time to work out what he was going to tell John. Assuming he could get his brain to work the right way. Even after the Dean had let him go, and once he'd found his way back to his dorm, sleep had eluded him. He'd tossed and turned in his bed, trying to work out what it was the Dean had really wanted from him.

He said he was going to punish me, he thought. *But that was more like an interrogation.*

He was just thinking how weird it was that Pogo had led him straight to the prefect's badge on the beach when a tray clattered down next to his. On it was a plate piled high with scrambled eggs and beans. Finn looked up to see his brother grinning down.

"Mind if I join you?" said John, throwing himself into the next chair. Adriana sat beside him with her own breakfast – a dish of fruit and cheese.

"Be my guest," said Finn, yawning.

"Late night?" said John.

"You have no idea."

"Only, I was wondering –" John lowered his voice "– what happened with Pogo?"

Finn's breath caught in his throat. "I'm really sorry," was all he managed to say.

John gave him a friendly nudge. "You must have worn her out – she's fast asleep in the Touch common room."

It took Finn a moment to compute what his brother was saying. When he realised he was off the hook, he gave a silent sigh of relief. "I'm glad she's safe," he said.

"Unlike you," came a voice from the table behind him.

Finn looked round and there was Xander, hanging

over the back of a chair with a sly grin on his face.

"What's that supposed to mean?" he said.

"Don't you know?" said Xander. "It's all over the school."

"What's all over the school?"

"Finn trying to do a 'Kylie' off the South Cliff! The Dean talked him down!"

On the opposite table, Zoe dropped her spoon with a clatter. Her neck flushed red. John was looking puzzled.

"Shut your mouth, Xander," said Adriana without looking at him.

Xander made a face, but went back to his breakfast, much to Finn's relief. He swallowed more oatmeal and sneaked another glance at Zoe, who was still ignoring him.

"Finn?" said John. "What's he talking about? You okay?"

"You were at the cliffs?" said Adriana, frowning.

"Yeah," said Finn. "I just took a walk and ended up down there." He managed a grin. "Kildair was *not* happy."

"You're crazy," said Adriana, with a hint of respect. "It's really dangerous, Finn."

"I can't see what the fuss is about."

In his peripheral vision, he saw Zoe take her tray to

the drop-off area and walk out.

"Well, don't get yourself killed before the Hunt," said John, lifting a forkful of egg to his mouth.

"Oh, sure." Finn tried to remember what Professor Panjaran had said about the Hunt at yesterday's assembly.

"Adriana's almost finished putting her team together, haven't you, Ady?" said John.

She nodded. "Nobody lower than a Level Two."

"So what exactly is the Hunt?" said Finn.

"It's what it sounds like," said Adriana. "You hunt down members of the opposing teams. And try not to get hunted down yourself."

"Don't worry," said Xander. "They don't expect Numbskulls to take part."

Finn shrugged. "Doesn't bother me. I stopped playing hide-and-seek when I was six."

"Hide-and-seek, right," said Xander, moving off with his tray. "The Hunt is hardcore, rookie. People get hurt."

"Are you going to finish that oatmeal?" said John. "I'm still kind of hungry."

Glancing down, Finn realised he'd been stirring his half-eaten breakfast around and around in its bowl. He dropped the spoon with a sigh.

"Can I talk to you for a minute?" he said.

"Sure, go ahead," said John.

Finn flicked his gaze towards Adriana. "Uh, just you and me?"

"Oh, right. Is that okay with you, Ady?"

She smiled. "Sure."

Picking up his glass of water, John weaved his way through the maze of tables. Finn followed.

"What's up?" said John once they'd reached a private spot. A fan with multicoloured blades turned slowly above his head, making a soft whirring sound.

"Pogo escaped last night," said Finn. "I had to go after her. She must have made her way back to you on her own, but the thing is ..." He hesitated.

"What's the thing?"

Finn took a deep breath. "That's how I ended up at the South Cliff. It's the place where ... there was this girl, and she ..."

"Kylie?" said John. "The girl who jumped?"

"Yes," said Finn.

"Adriana told me. It happened not long before we came. It really cut Ady up – they were friends. Must have been horrible."

"Right. Only, the Dean turned up while I was down there and he was ... I don't know. He was really shifty. I think ... I think he might have been mixed up in it somehow."

John shook his head. "Finn – he's the *Dean*. Kylie was pretty messed up, you know. Something to do with a boy, I think. It was just a really bad thing that happened."

John's argument was reasonable. That didn't mean Finn had to agree. "Maybe. Only, later on, the Dean kept asking me about Kylie."

"He's bound to be concerned."

"I know, but ..." A massive yawn caught Finn unawares.

"You're tired," said John, clapping his shoulder. "I feel guilty, making you look after Pogo."

Finn sighed. "You're totally not welcome."

John grinned and raised his glass to his lips, then stopped. "Hey, bro. I've got to show you this!"

"Show me what?"

Frowning with concentration, John balanced the drink on his outstretched palm. He ran his other hand through his hair, then lowered it towards the glass.

"Ready?" he said.

"Ready for what?"

John touched the tip of his index finger against the side of the glass. Ice crystals formed instantly on the inside, shooting through the water like little blue bolts of lightning, crackling softly as they spread. The crystals continued to branch out, forming a delicate spider's web

124

that grew until it filled the entire glass. Then all the gaps between the crystals turned white.

Upending the glass, John held it over Finn's hand and tapped the bottom. A cylindrical lump of ice fell out. Finn caught it, laughing at its cold, slippery weight.

"Warden Gustavsson taught me that," said John. "He says I have massive potential."

Finn blinked in disbelief. This was only day two at Alyxa, and his brother was already working miracles.

Unlike me, he thought glumly. *I'm just getting deeper and deeper into trouble.*

***

When the assembly bell rang, Finn joined the tide of students converging on the large central hall. He made it a few steps before someone shoved him against the wall.

"Hey!" He turned angrily around, fully expecting to see Xander's grinning face.

It was Zoe. "What's your problem?" she said. Another jab, this one hard enough to hurt.

Students continued to hurry past. Most ignored Finn and Zoe, but a few gave them curious looks. Finn shrugged his shoulders at them: *What can you do?*

"I suppose you think it's funny," said Zoe, lowering

her voice.

"What's funny?" said Finn.

"You humming that tune," said Zoe.

Finn rubbed the spot on his chest where she'd jabbed him. "I really don't know what you're talking about."

Zoe hummed a few notes of a lilting melody. "Recognise that?" she said.

Before Finn could reply, an older boy pushed roughly between them both, barking at them to get out of the way. When he'd gone, Finn ushered Zoe into a quiet alcove.

"What is that tune?" he said, running the little melody through his head. It sounded oddly familiar. Had he really been humming it?

"It's our song," said Zoe. Her lower lip pouted and trembled a little. "Mum made up this special song to sing to my sister and me at bedtime. That was it."

"Hum it again," said Finn. She did, and after just six notes he had it. "Last night! That's what I heard last night, in the meditation chamber!"

"The Dean put you in one of the meds?" said Zoe.

Finn nodded. "To start with it was all quiet, but then I started hearing this humming. It didn't sound like anything at first. Towards the end, it sounded like music. It was that tune. I know it was."

With a trembling hand, Zoe pulled the goggles down and let them hang from their strap around her neck. For the first time, Finn got a good look at her eyes. Like his, her irises were blue, but they were completely overwhelmed by her enormous pupils.

"They don't react as quickly as normal people's," said Zoe, clearly aware that he was staring. "They let in everything. Sometimes it really hurts."

Even as Finn stared at the fixed black discs of her pupils, tears pooled in Zoe's eyes and trickled down her cheeks. He told her to wait for a second, then rushed back into the canteen for a paper napkin and handed it to her. She wiped her face. By now the corridor was empty except for a last few straggles of students.

"You'd better not be making this up," she said.

Finn shook his head.

"I thought I heard a voice, right at the end. But look – it might have been someone else singing."

"I told you, my mum made it up," Zoe replied with a sniffle. After a pause, she added conspiratorially, "They never found her body, you know – Kylie."

Finn wasn't sure what to say. What she was saying? If Zoe was grieving, maybe she was grasping at straws.

"You think she's ... that she might be alive?"

After a hesitation, Zoe's face closed down. "No," she said quietly. "They searched everywhere. We all did.

The Wardens, the Level Fours. We found her shoes at the top of the South Cliff."

Finn thought of the cave beneath the cliffs. The prefect badge. *Could she somehow have got inside?* He dismissed it. That didn't make sense. She couldn't have climbed down barefoot without ripping her feet to shreds. There was a much easier explanation for the badge. Kylie had jumped, and it had torn free when her body was bashed against ...

He didn't want to think about it.

And anyway, the med chambers were a long, long way from the cave.

"Did you hear anything else?" asked Zoe.

Finn remembered how the underground tunnel had felt sort of haunted. Probably not a great idea to start talking to Zoe about ghosts, though. "Only that the music made me feel ... sad," he said.

"Kylie was sad," said Zoe. Her pupils had at last shrunk to pinpoints and she was breathing in short, hard gulps. "It was all because of Alyxa. When she came here, Callum had to stay on the mainland. He was her boyfriend. She tried to make it work but in the end they split up – that long-distance relationship thing, you know? She hated being here after that. She used to say her powers were a curse."

Finn thought about his mother, how far away she

seemed. How isolated this little island really was. "I can understand that," he said. "It must have been awful when she ..."

"It was," said Zoe. Her breathing had slowed again. "It still is. I just have all these questions. That's why I sneaked into her room – I mean, your room. I'm sorry about that."

"It's all right."

"It's not, but ... it's just that I keep looking for reasons. Clues. I need to know what really happened that night."

For the first time since meeting Zoe, Finn felt like he was talking to a real girl and not a brick wall. He wondered if he should hug her or something. Instead he just said, "I'm really sorry."

Zoe wiped the tears away with the screwed up remains of the paper napkin. "Kylie had this journal, only now it's disappeared. We always used to tell each other everything, but I can't stop thinking there must be something in the journal that she *didn't* tell me. I have no idea where it is – I've looked everywhere."

A thought flowered in Finn's head. "Did you look in my wardrobe?" he said.

"No. Why?"

"The mirror broke," said Finn. "I took it off and there was something behind it. Sort of like graffiti."

"What sort of graffiti?"

"A star," said Finn. "A six-pointed star."

All the colour drained from Zoe's face. "You've got to show me," she said. "Right now."

Finn looked along the deserted corridor.

"What about assembly?" he said.

"Assembly can wait."

***

Finn carefully lifted the cracked mirror off the door and put it down on the floor. Zoe peered at the symbol scratched into the grey panel.

"Oh, Kylie," she said, her voice wavering.

"Does it mean something?" he said.

"It's this stupid old story," said Zoe. "It's what they tell the new kids to scare them."

"I'm the new kid," said Finn. "Nobody's told me."

Zoe glanced again at the hexagram on the door. A shiver ran through her shoulders.

"Back in the old days – I mean *really* old – there was this cult," she said. "That's what the story says, anyway. Sort of like a secret society. They performed all these rituals that were supposed to summon up the sixth sense."

"The sixth sense?" said Finn. "I thought there were

only five."

"There are. Like I said, it's just a story. The sixth sense is some baloney about body-hopping. It's like bad sci-fi. I remember the first time I heard it. This prefect told me to watch out for the ghost that roams the halls of Alyxa after dark."

"Whose ghost?" said Finn, thinking again about haunted cellars.

"The ghost of the Sixth Warden," Zoe replied. She hugged herself. "He was called Morvan. I thought Kylie was just having boy trouble. I never imagined she was mixed up in anything like this."

"Is it that bad?"

Someone knocked at the door to Finn's room. Zoe had just enough time to snap the goggles back over her eyes before the door swung open and Lucy poked her head around it.

"There you are," she said. "Ben sent me to find you. Assembly's about to begin." She eyed Zoe. "I didn't think I'd find the two of you together."

"We'll be there in a minute," said Finn.

Lucy's gaze settled on the hexagram. Her eyes grew wide and her mouth dropped open. "Who drew that?" she said. "What's going on?"

"None of your business," said Zoe, moving swiftly between Lucy and the wardrobe. "You didn't see anything."

"But I ..."

"Seriously, you need to leave," said Zoe. "Now."

Lucy's hand tightened on the edge of the door and her shoulders stiffened. For a moment Finn was convinced she was going to argue. Maybe even sound some kind of alarm. Then her shoulders relaxed again. "Suit yourselves. I'll just tell Ben you've eloped." With a toss of her head Lucy stalked away, leaving the door swinging.

Zoe turned back to Finn. "Can you cover that thing up, please?"

After he replaced the cracked mirror, Finn drew out the silver badge and handed it to Zoe.

"It's a prefect's badge, isn't it?" he said as she examined it. He told her where he'd found it.

Zoe fingered the badge for a moment before pressing it back into his hand. "I suppose it could be Kylie's."

"That's not the only thing," Finn said. "The Dean was down on the beach too."

"The *Dean?*" Zoe shook her head, clearly bemused. "What was he doing there?"

"At first I thought he might be following me," said Finn, "but I'm not sure. I think he was going to the cave."

"Cave?" said Zoe, sounding thoroughly confused

now. "What cave?"

"In the cliff. I think it only appears at low tide. I think ..."

"Wait." She held up her hand. "Slow down. What exactly happened with the Dean?"

Finn considered telling Zoe the whole story from the beginning – the phone call he'd made to his mum, the Dean's threatening behaviour, taking him to the cell, the questions he'd asked about Finn's father. But the more he thought about it, the more his memory stuck on just one thing.

"He wanted to know about Kylie," he said slowly. "In the end, it was all he wanted to talk about."

Zoe didn't move. "What exactly did he say?"

"It was more what he *didn't* say." He paused, trying to remember the Dean's exact words. "He wanted to know if you'd told me anything."

They gazed at each other.

"Are you thinking the same as me?" said Zoe.

"He's in on it, somehow," said Finn, nodding.

Zoe crossed to Finn's bed and stared out through the little window with her fists clenched at her sides. "I knew she couldn't have killed herself, no matter how bad things got. I knew it!"

Finn's pulse was pounding in his temples. He closed his own fist around the prefect's badge and felt the cold metal jab into his skin. "Do you think the Dean ...?"

Zoe whirled round. "I'm not sure. But he *knows* something."

"Maybe we should go back to the cell," said Finn.

Zoe shook her head. "That's not where she is. The cell's just a meditation chamber, remember? It amplifies your senses, lets you tune into stuff that could be miles away. Which means *Kylie* could be miles away."

Finn joined her at the window. Outside, the clouds were thick in the sky. "Or she could be closer than we think." He hadn't wanted to jump to conclusions, but Zoe's excitement was contagious. "The cave on the beach," he said. "I bet it was inaccessible during the search. That's where we need to start."

***

Finn had never felt more conspicuous than when he and Zoe crept into assembly. Professor Panjaran had already taken the platform. As they made their way towards the Nurture Group bench, he looked up from his tablet and tracked them with his gaze. On the seats behind him, the Wardens were frowning. Even the bloodhound sitting next to the Smell Warden managed to look unimpressed.

Worst of all, the eyes of the Dean followed Finn all

the way to his seat.

"So you decided to come," muttered Lucy as they settled in on the bench beside her.

"Better late than never," Finn replied.

He gazed up at the skylights. The light filtering down was thin and grey. Finn wondered if it was raining outside. A winged shadow was circling around up there – the Sight Clann's hawk.

Professor Panjaran started saying something or other about the Hunt. Finn found it hard to tune in. He kept thinking about the six-pointed star, and Kylie's song, and the mysterious cave beneath the South Cliff. If only there was a way to get down there without being followed.

"... South Cliff," said Panjaran from the stage. Finn's ears pricked up. "As you know, the recent storm has made that entire region unstable." He aimed his gaze at Finn. "Adventuring on the beach is strictly forbidden, whether by day or by night."

Finn heard snickers, and to his horror realised that once again everyone was looking at him. Xander had obviously been right: news of his exploits last night were all around the school.

"This year's Hunt is therefore confined to the north and west of the island," Professor Panjaran went on. "There will be monitors at all striking-off points to make sure the rules are obeyed." He swiped his finger across the tablet. "You have the rest of the morning to finalise your teams. After that, team captains must report to their supervisors at one o'clock this afternoon. As soon as the Quarries have gone to ground, the Hunt will begin!"

Cheers echoed around the enormous chamber and students started rising from their seats. Finn kept his head low, not wanting to catch the Dean's eye.

"I heard that Nurture Group isn't allowed to take part in the Hunt," he said to Zoe. "Is that true?"

It was Lucy who answered. "It's not against the rules," she said. "It's just that nobody wants a Numbskull on their squad. Why? Thinking of trying out your parkour skills on the course?"

"It crossed my mind," said Finn.

Zoe huddled close, clearly interested. "But who would want us?"

"Which is exactly the point I just made," said Lucy, looking away from Zoe. Finn hoped she wasn't cross about the hexagram business. But then she shouldn't have barged into his dorm like that.

"Then let's form our own team," said Finn.

"It's not that easy," said Zoe. "You need five people, one from each Clann."

"What about your brother?" said Lucy suddenly.

"What?" said Finn.

"John. He's Touch and I'm Taste. Maybe Ben would be up for it too. That gets us most of the way there. John would make a great Hunter, don't you think?" Lucy's eyes shone as she spoke his name.

"And me," said Zoe. "I'm Sight, not that my eyes are up to much."

Finn had to agree that his brother would be a great asset. And a good ally in case anything went wrong. "Okay," he said. "I'll ask him. But what about me?"

"You can be our Quarry," said Lucy. "That's the person who has to hide."

This was getting more interesting by the second. "You mean somewhere like in, I don't know, say, a cave?" said Finn.

Lucy shrugged. "That's kind of obvious. But whatever. You'll get a head start, so there should be time to pick somewhere really good."

"Time to search around?" Finn glanced at Zoe and raised his eyebrows. She nodded imperceptibly. "Time to really investigate your surroundings?"

"It's not an exploration," said Lucy, rolling her eyes. "It's a Hunt. And don't get too excited. You probably won't last very long."

CHAPTER TEN

Finn managed to intercept John on his way out of the assembly hall with a bunch of his new Touch Clann friends.

"Got a minute?" said Finn, pulling John aside.

"Make it quick," his brother replied. "I've got to get to the language block."

"That's right," said Adriana, trotting up to join them. "Can't be late for these things." She grinned at Finn.

"Okay," said Finn, glancing at her. "Here it is. We want you on our team for the Hunt."

Adriana suppressed another smile. John looked puzzled, but said nothing.

"Will you do it?" said Finn.

John shook his head. "Sorry, bro, I can't."

Can't? Finn thought. *Or won't?*

"I looked after Pogo for you, didn't I?" he said through clenched teeth.

"I know, bro, but I already agreed to be on Adriana's team."

Adriana tugged at John's shoulder. "Come on," she said. "We really should go."

At that moment, Lucy and Zoe turned up with Ben in tow.

"There you are," said Lucy to Finn. "Any luck?"

Finn shook his head. "It's still just the four of us."

"You're not seriously planning to do this, are you?" said Adriana.

"Why shouldn't we?" said Finn.

Adriana looked at Ben. "Can you talk some sense into them?"

Ben shrugged. "It's been done before, I think. Not that I'm saying it's a good idea."

"But why shouldn't we take part?" said Finn, trying to set aside his growing frustration. "Haven't we got as much right as anyone else?"

"Of course you do," said Adriana. "But it's not that. The idea of the Hunt is that you have to use your sense powers. That's the whole point of the competition. If you're in Nurture Group you're just ..." she waggled her hand uncertainly.

"Numbskulls," said Lucy gloomily.

Adriana laughed. "You said it, not me."

"Maybe there are other skills that count," said Finn.

Adriana shook her head. "It's a knockout contest. Winner takes all. Even if you do manage to pull a team together, you probably won't make it past the first elimination." She linked her arm with John's. "Come on, we really have got to go."

She steered Finn's brother down the nearest corridor. John had time to throw an apologetic glance over his shoulder, then he was gone.

"She was no help," said Finn.

"Like I said," Lucy remarked. "She thinks she's queen bee. Comes from being the daughter of a Warden."

"Adriana's all right," said Zoe. "She stood by Kylie when things got bad."

"And she's right about us not having much chance of winning the Hunt," added Ben. "Sorry, but it's true. Look – if you really want to go through with this, I'm in. But I don't see how you're going to make up a full team."

"Me neither," said Finn. "We'll just have to find a way."

***

Walking into the history room was like entering a museum. Everywhere Finn looked he saw a different display case crammed full of ancient pottery, stone tools, grimy jewels and stuffed animals. Bookcases bulged with huge, dusty encyclopedias and the walls were covered in maps and timelines. Dominating one corner was a huge statue of an armour-clad woman riding a horse. Everything smelt of mildew.

In the middle of the room, three lines of desks faced a large silver table that looked to Finn like a prop from a science fiction film. Now *that* was different. Lights blinked at its corners, little antennae rotated and tilting screens displayed unfathomable charts. Finn liked the way Alyxa mixed things up, as if someone had taken an assortment of ancient artefacts and futuristic machines and put them through a blender.

Finn chose a desk near the back, with Lucy on one side and Ben on the other. Alyxa's complicated timetable had sent Zoe to a maths lesson instead. He counted twelve other students, none of whom paid them any particular attention. In fact, most of them had their heads down, and one boy looked ready to doze off.

"What is this, the sleep lab?" he said to Lucy.

"It's the Hunt," she replied. After the awkwardness in front of the hexagram in his dorm, Finn was relieved that she seemed back to her normal self. "Everyone's trying to conserve their powers for this afternoon."

Suddenly realising he didn't have anything to write with – much less an exercise book to write in – Finn lifted his desk lid. The desk was empty.

"I don't suppose you have a spare pen," he said.

"Oh, we don't write anything down at Alyxa," said Lucy.

"What?"

"You won't need exercise books here. You just have to remember what the teachers tell you."

"So what's the catch?" he said. "I suppose the exams are mega-hard?"

Lucy beamed. "No catch. And no exams. It's all about tradition – that's a big thing at Alyxa, in case you hadn't noticed already. Beaky says that learning is all about telling stories."

"Stories?"

"Yes. In the old day, everything was passed down by word of mouth. Facts, fiction, everything. Beaky calls it the oral tradition. It was only later they started writing things down."

No books? No exams? Finn thought about the huge bag he'd had to lug around at his old school. And the endless hours of studying he'd had to do for exams. Maybe Alyxa wasn't so bad after all.

"Who's Beaky?" he said.

"The Smell Warden, Marissa Blake," said Ben. "Shh – here she comes."

Finn immediately recognised the woman who walked in as one of the Wardens he'd encountered on the landing pad. She was short and wore a tweedy skirt and jacket with a sprig of heather in the lapel. Half-concealed behind the purple flowers was a badge with a dog's-head emblem. Behind her plodded the bloodhound. Unlike the sharp-featured animal on the badge, it had saggy jowls and a sad expression.

Planting her hands on the high-tech table, the Warden scanned the rows of desks. Her head was tilted slightly back, presenting Finn with a startling view of her nostrils, which were truly enormous. A girl seated in the front row looked up, but the rest of the class hardly seemed to register her presence.

With a grunt, the bloodhound flopped down beside her and appeared to go to sleep.

"What are you staring at, Finlay Williams?" Beaky said, settling her gaze on him. Finn squirmed in his seat.

"Nothing, Miss," he answered, trying not to stare at her long, chiselled nose. "Just paying attention."

"Good. The more you can learn at Alyxa, the less of a hindrance you will be."

Lowering her face almost to the surface of the table, Beaky peered through her spectacles at one of the glowing screens. However good her sense of smell might be, Finn guessed the Warden's eyesight wasn't up to much.

Beaky swiped the screen twice, then prodded it with an outstretched finger. A hatch opened in the table top and a stalk emerged with a large, round lens on the end. Light flared, and suddenly a hologram of a man's head was floating in the middle of the room. The man looked chubby, and had a curly beard that went all the way under his chin without ever coming near the rest of his face.

"This is Nero," said Beaky, her high voice cutting through the dusty air. "He was Emperor of Rome from AD 54 to 68. He's famous for all sorts of things, like arranging the murder of his mother, and playing a fiddle while Rome burnt around him. He also waged wars, including one that sent people running for the hills."

The girl at the front jabbed her hand in the air. "Are you talking about the Druids?"

"Indeed I am," said Beaky. "Very good, Chandice. Nero's general, Gaius Suetonius Paulinus, sent his troops to the nearby island to crush the Druids who'd fled in an attempt to escape Roman rule. 'Why?' you might ask. If any of you were listening."

A boy raised his head, then his hand. "Why, miss?"

Beaky's thin eyebrows shot into her hairline. "Why,

indeed. The answer lies in what the Druids represented."

"They were sort of like magicians," said Chandice.

Finn chuckled, unable to stop himself.

"Is something funny, Finn?" said Beaky. "Perhaps you'd like to share it with us."

Finn's skin prickled as the other students stared at him.

"It's just that, well, we studied the Druids at my old school," he said. "They weren't magicians. They were more like, you know, religious leaders."

Beaky nodded. "Religious leaders, yes. Also doctors and law-keepers. The Celtic authorities, if you like. But ordinary people at the time probably *did* think of them as magicians, simply because that was the way they saw the world."

Finn shrugged. "There's no such thing as magic."

"I didn't mean the Druids were actual magicians, you idiot," Chandice replied.

Beaky regarded them both for a moment, then rattled her fingers across another screen. Words appeared in the air, superimposed over the floating face of Nero:

A MYSTERIOUS OR SUPERNATURAL POWER.

"The dictionary definition of *magic*," said Beaky. "It may not mean what you think it means, Finn. But it does mean something."

She swiped her hand and the words vanished. Chandice made a point of catching Finn's eye, then looking huffily away.

"Rome's armies were impressive," continued Beaky, "but conquering a country isn't simply about enforcing your might. It's about persuading the natives of that country that you can make their lives better. Often, the Romans were successful because they *did* offer something the natives could appreciate. Technology, roads, an impressive pantheon of gods. They would work with the chieftains and the native leaders. It was a takeover, but a bloodless one. However, that didn't work with the Druids. They weren't interested in bowing down, and their people held their leaders in such trust that they fought the Romans tooth and nail."

"So Nero decided to wipe out the Druids?" said Finn.

Beaky tapped the screen and the hologram of Nero changed to a three-dimensional map of the coast, an island clearly visible in the top left corner. As Finn watched, cartoon boats sailed from the island out into the open sea.

"The Druids put their trust in their gods and journeyed west," said Beaky. "Eventually they reached this island. They carved words on a stone in the East Cove, presumably not long after they landed. Who can tell me what it says?"

More text appeared in the air, a whole paragraph this time. Finn scanned the first few words:

VENIMUS, VIDIMUS, AUDIVIMUS ...

Finn hesitated, then put his hand up again.

"It starts off, 'We came, we saw, we listened,'" he said. "Or 'we heard'. I guess it's the same thing."

"Hearing is not the same as listening," said Beaky. "But your knowledge of Latin is impressive."

Finn glanced at Chandice, expecting the girl to blank him again. Instead, she pursed her lips around a smile and waggled her head: *Not bad, new kid.*

"Can you read the rest of it?" Beaky said.

Finn frowned. He'd always been interested in the Romans, and he'd studied a Latin module for a couple of terms, but this was a lot trickier than the simple passages he'd worked on before.

"It says something about how they were running away," he said. "Then 'over the sea' ... something ... and 'the island became our home'."

"Very good," said Beaky. She fiddled with the desk controls and the hologram changed again, this time to a slowly spinning ring of upright stones. Finn recognised it at once. "There are more carvings on the stones in the Small Circle. If you read each carving in turn, they tell the story of how the Druids devoted their

147

lives to the study of their new island home. The more they investigated, the more they found, and the more attuned they became to their natural surroundings."

Beaky stepped out from behind the futuristic table to stand beneath the revolving hologram. The bloodhound lifted its head, peered into the light, then lowered it and closed its eyes again. The Warden raised her arms, allowing her outstretched fingers to brush through the glowing boulders.

"The Druids searched here for inspiration, and they found it," she said. "When they searched here for truth, they found that too. They searched with all their senses, and as they did so their senses became sharper than ever before." She paused. "And that is how they first unlocked their powers."

Finn gazed at the floating stone circle, wondering if the meditation chamber worked in the same way. Despite what Zoe had said, maybe there was more to be discovered in that dank stone cell.

He put up his hand again.

"Was that when they discovered the sixth sense?" he asked.

Several of the other students looked round, suddenly paying attention. Some chuckled uncomfortably. Beaky raised her hands.

"You are here to learn real history," she said sternly.

"Not joke about legends."

The hexagram scratched into Finn's wardrobe door was no fairy tale. "Aren't most legends based on truth, though?" he said.

That brought a few sucked-in breaths from the other students. Beaky shot him a glare. "Don't get clever with me," she said.

Finn shrugged. "So the sixth sense isn't real?"

Beaky pursed her lips and spoke with weary patience as if she was addressing a toddler. "The Druids always saw themselves as one with nature. That was the purpose of their efforts. Some of them thought it possible to go further, to explore a spiritual realm where they merged with nature and with each other. They sought to uncouple their consciousness from their bodies, to let their minds roam unencumbered by flesh."

"Body-hopping!" said Finn, remembering what Lucy called it.

At the adjacent desk, Lucy shook her head in mock despair.

"That's a particularly crude way of putting it," said Beaky.

"One of the standing stones has got a six-pointed star carved in it," said a small boy of about eleven. He blushed. "At least that's what I heard."

By now, everyone in the history room was sitting

up straight and alert.

"This school has been here since the Dark Ages," said Beaky. "The Druids might have been more attuned to the physical world than many of their contemporaries, but they were people of their time, too. Superstitions grow like weeds from ignorance, and like weeds they are hard to eradicate."

"So the sixth sense is just superstition?" said Finn.

All the class groaned, and Lucy just shook her head. "The sixth sense is about as real as that statue of Morvan in the woods," Chandice went on.

"As in the Sixth Warden, Morvan?" said Finn.

Now everyone went quiet. Beaky laid both hands on her desk, with a sigh that suggested she was close to losing her patience. "I don't know where you've heard this nonsense, young man," she said. "Morvan was not a Warden. He was just a madman, a demagogue spurned by the Druidic community for his nonsense ideas."

"But there's a statue of him?" said Finn.

Chandice looked over, rolling her eyes. "It's just this old rock that's been shaped by the weather. It doesn't even look like a man."

"It's just a bedtime story," said Ben.

"Nightmare story, more like," said Rufus. "Someone told me that Morvan had this ritual where he sliced open ..."

Beaky flapped her hands in an agitated fashion. "That's quite enough," she said.

There were no more interruptions as the Warden moved her focus to Druid traditions and customs. Charts and diagrams came and went on the holographic display, but all Finn could think about was six-pointed stars. There was nothing funny about the one that Kylie had carved behind her mirror. Every scar in the wood looked deranged and violent.

Beaky ended the lesson with the suggestion that they all spend the rest of the time prior to the Hunt in meditation. "Even if it doesn't prepare you for the ordeal," she said, "at least it will rid your minds of far-fetched stories."

As they filed out of the history room, Finn ignored the wary glances he got from the other students. He was thinking about what Beaky had said. *Minds unencumbered by flesh and roaming consciousness.*

Sort of like a … ghost. Was that what he'd heard – the spirit of a dead girl?

Out in the corridor, Lucy tugged his sleeve.

"Nice going," she said. "You made yourself look like a total freak in there."

"That's what I get for taking an interest in things," said Finn.

"It's what you get when you take an interest in

something imaginary, like the Easter bunny," said Lucy. "I'm going back to Numbskulls Central. You coming?"

Finn was about to say yes, then changed his mind. "If we're supposed to meditate, I thought I might try one of the meditation chambers."

Lucy wrinkled her nose. "There's no point. We haven't got a team, remember?"

"So what are we supposed to do when everyone else is off having fun?"

"I'm going to see my dad for a while," said Lucy. "He likes to lecture me at least once a week."

Finn looked at Ben. "I'm going to the courtyard," said the older boy. "If you like, we can duel. I know some cool moves I'd be happy to teach you."

Finn shook his head. "Thanks, but I really do want to meditate."

Ben shrugged. "Suit yourself. Can't hurt."

When he reached the dark, clammy passages of the meditation level, Finn saw that there were about a dozen chambers lining both sides of the corridor. Each had a print scanner outside the door with a red or green glowing light above. A girl went past him, opened a door with her palm and disappeared inside. The light changed from green to red.

"What am I even looking for?" Finn muttered to himself.

He went to the nearest vacant chamber and let himself in. Like the cell the Dean had interrogated him in, the walls were ancient stone, like a medieval dungeon. He wondered how long these chambers had been here. It wasn't hard to imagine the early Druids using them.

Finn looked around the bare room, then closed his eyes and tried to focus on his hearing. It took a few moments to shake the six-pointed stars from his thoughts, but soon, all he could hear was his own breathing.

No humming. No singing.

He tried sitting cross-legged on the floor, like a yogi, but that just made him feel stupid. He hadn't bothered with all this the night the Dean had brought him here. The voice had just come to him.

I heard something all right, he thought with a tremor. *But what was it? A voice from beyond the grave?*

Shutting his eyes once more, he brought his breathing down to a slow, steady rhythm. Finn imagined that his breath was a wave, and he was surfing on it.

As he opened his mind to this idea, Finn felt his muscles relaxing and his heart rate slowing. His breath washed in and out of his lungs, just like the sea splashing on the shore. He could almost hear the sea, in fact, almost feel the water washing over him.

And there, at the edge of his consciousness, the lilting music began.

He tried not to panic, not to follow the music, but to let it come. He was afraid that if he strained to hear, it would disappear. And as he gave himself to the distant sounds, he felt another sensation. First on the tips of his fingers, then across his skin. *Water ...*

... cold and wet, holding him until he floated, drifting, surrounded by a moving ocean, a constantly shifting tide. It held him, cradled him, but there was nothing else at all.

Someone knocked on the door. "How long are you going to be in there?" said a voice.

The spell was broken and Finn was back in the cell, surrounded by stone walls. He wasn't at all sure what had just happened. Slightly unsteady on his feet, he went to the door and opened it. It was Chandice.

"Oh, it's you!" she said. "You've been in there nearly two hours, you know."

Finn frowned. *Two hours?* It had felt like less than ten minutes! "Sorry," he mumbled.

Chandice shook her head. "Yeah, well - do you mind?" and she shoved past him.

Gaining control of his shaky legs, Finn headed for the lifts.

CHAPTER ELEVEN

Finn spent most of the lunch break pushing clumps of rice and chunks of chicken around his plate, wondering if he should tell the others about his vision. Or whatever it was. Had he heard Kylie's song again, or had he just wanted to hear it? Maybe his mind had just summoned it up because he was thinking about it too hard. Whatever the case, he couldn't feel anything but negative about that watery, bodiless sensation. If somehow he'd tuned into Kylie, what could it mean except that she was floating at the bottom of the sea somewhere.

Or in a flooded cave.

Not that it mattered, because his chances of

reaching a cave were zero.

Zoe nibbled around the edges of a sandwich. Lucy stared dismally at yet another dish of unappetising grey slop. When the bell rang and the canteen emptied, they stayed put.

"Cheer up, team," said Lucy. "At least we get the afternoon off."

"We're not a team," said Finn. "That's the whole problem. We've only got four people."

"Make that five," said a familiar voice.

Finn looked around to see Xander hovering by the door. He held a paper napkin, which he kept folding and unfolding.

"I thought you were on Adriana's team?" Finn said.

Xander's fingers continued to work the napkin. "I was, until your brother wheedled his way in."

"Why would you lower yourself to hunt with the Numbskulls?" said Lucy.

Another shrug. "I want to be in the Hunt. It's you or nothing. Take it or leave it."

Finn stood up with a smile on his face. "You really mean it? And you won't mess us about?"

"Nobody messes about on the Hunt," said Xander. He balled up the napkin and lobbed it across the deserted canteen. "Like Panjaran says, it's a serious business. So do you want me or not?"

"Are you kidding?" said Finn. "Of course we want you." He turned to Lucy and Zoe. "Numbskulls – we've got ourselves a team!"

Zoe pointed at the clock on the wall. "And we've also got ten minutes left to register."

They raced along the main corridor in the north-west arm of the star-shaped Alyxa building, with Lucy leading the way. The school was empty, and eerily silent. Awaiting them at the end of the arm was a wall marked with yellow and black diagonal stripes. Ben stood before a closed steel door, his prefect's badge prominently displayed on his grey jumpsuit. Finn craned his neck to peer through a glass panel in the door and saw a sea of heads spotlit in a dark hall.

"You're just in time," Ben said. "At least you can be spectators."

"No need," said Finn. He pointed to Xander. "Meet our fifth team member!"

Ben gaped at Xander, then his face creased into a smile. "Really?"

"Really," said Lucy. "Now are you going to let us in or not?"

Ben fiddled with his prefect's badge. "A team from the Nurture Group," he said. "Oh boy."

"Hey," said Xander. "We're not all Numbskulls!"

Ben turned a metal wheel. The door hissed open.

"Then what are we waiting for?" he said.

Finn followed Ben along a zigzag path made of tiles that glowed faintly green. Up ahead, the illumination came from dazzling spotlights; through their glare, Finn saw that the enormous hall came to a point, like the infirmary. They'd clearly reached the tip of the north-west arm.

At each turn of the path, a different group of five students stood on a low platform. Finn felt their eyes following him as he hurried with the others towards the big black desk at the end of the path.

They reached the desk just as Pietr Turminski – who was standing behind it – reached towards a tall, narrow computer screen.

"Warden Turminski," said Ben. "Don't shut it down. We want to register."

Turminski beamed, revealing all his teeth in one go. "Hurry, then."

One by one they gave their names. When Turminski realised that Xander was the only one who officially belonged to a Clann, his smile became a frown.

"Four out of five from Nurture Group? Two of you with previous Taste affiliation, and no representative of Smell at all?"

Gustavsson joined him, and regarded Finn and his ragtag team with bewilderment. "The odds are not in your favour. You will lose."

Thanks for the vote of confidence, thought Finn.

"Come on," Ben said. "The Dean's about to kick things off."

"Wait," said Turminski. He handed Ben five leather thongs, each strung with what looked like a small black stone. "Your team's *guthas*."

"What's a *gutha*?" said Finn.

"You'll find out," Ben replied.

Finn's stomach knotted as he gathered with his teammates on a vacant platform. A hush descended. The spotlights went out. Then, deep grinding sounds began to echo in the darkness. Finn rubbed his eyes. All he could see was the pale green glow of the zigzag path. Where was the Dean, and Professor Panjaran?

Something rang like a gong. Suddenly, a narrow line of light appeared directly overhead. Blinding white, it was swiftly joined by four others, two on each side, lower down on what Finn assumed were the walls of the hall. All five lines met at a point in the distance.

The grinding noise subsided, and a thin whine took over. The lines of light widened, gaped. Cool air gusted against Finn's face, bringing with it the taste of the sea and the scent of pine needles.

"The walls are opening up," he said, astonished.

"Sadly there's no prize for stating the obvious,"

said Xander.

Finn stared as the sides of the hall folded back. Sunlight poured in revealing gigantic robot arms, and hissing pistons worked smoothly together to peel away the walls. In less than a minute, they were standing not in a dimly-lit cavern, but on a triangular section of black floor pointing straight at the mountain in the middle of the island.

Ahead, a rolling meadow blended swiftly into a craggy mass of rock outcrops. Squinting into the glare of the sun, Finn watched a flock of seagulls wheel over the boulders before swooping towards a distant pine forest. Mountain slopes climbed beyond the trees.

"What do we ...?" he began to say, and then a platform rose up from behind the reception desk. On it were standing all five Wardens and Kildair. The wind flung the double ribbons of their cloaks around their shoulders.

"Teams," said the Dean, his voice booming out. If he was using a microphone, Finn couldn't see it. "The Hunt is on. As ancient tradition dictates, it falls upon me to remind you all of the rules."

"Yeah, yeah," said Xander. "Get on with it."

"Shut up, Xander," said Ben mildly.

"Each team has nominated one of its members to be the Quarry," the Dean went on. "The Quarries benefit from a thirty-minute head start. They must use those thirty minutes wisely by trekking out across the island in search of a hiding place."

"That's you," said Lucy, giving Finn a nudge. "Think you can do it?"

"I'll do my best," said Finn.

Half an hour. Would that be long enough to find the cave, search for clues about Kylie and find somewhere to hide?

It's going to have to be.

The Dean spread out his arms. "After thirty minutes, the teams will send out their remaining four members. These are the Hunters. They will use their combined powers to track down the Quarries of the opposing teams. Once discovered, the gutha of the Quarry will signal defeat. When their teammates receive the signal, they must give up and return to Hunt Base."

Ben handed around the thongs. Finn took his, running his fingers over the smooth polished surface of the stone.

"So how am I supposed to signal that I've been found?" he said. "There aren't any buttons."

"The gutha will do it for you," said Ben. "As soon as you send the signal, our guthas will whistle."

"And we'll know you've messed up," added Xander.

"What do you mean, 'The gutha will do it for you'?"

said Finn. "How does it know?"

"Oh man, can you get any dumber?" said Xander.

"Teams are eliminated until only two remain," the Dean was saying. "At this stage, the Hunt becomes a race to see which team of Hunters can locate the opposing Quarry first." He paused, then his voice deepened. "I must stress that the moment the Quarries leave Hunt Base, they are on their own. All communication with the rest of their team is strictly forbidden."

The difficulty of the challenge ahead was beginning to dawn on Finn. Twenty or more teams of Hunters, all with unbelievable sense powers, all searching for any Quarry they could find. *All searching for me.* The more he thought about it, the more his confidence was ebbing away. Maybe Gustavsson was right.

"So how do the Hunters actually catch you?" he asked Ben quietly. "Is it like tag – do they just have to touch you?"

"It's not as simple as that," said Ben.

"One of our students has asked a good question," said Susan Arnott, appearing on the platform beside the Dean. "Warden Gustavsson – kindly demonstrate the method by which the Quarries are tagged."

Finn shut his mouth with a snap, and wondered if he'd ever get used to the unnatural powers of the Hearing Warden.

What if she hears literally everything? he thought with a shiver.

Magnus Gustavsson opened a box at his feet and drew out a silver bow. The short, curved arms were connected by a tangle of thin wires and tiny pulleys. He adjusted something on the bow, then picked up a long black arrow with yellow feathers at one end and a silver ball at the other.

"Archery is ancient, noble sport," Gustavsson said. "It is sport for lords; sport for commoners. Archery is at heart of Alyxa tradition." He paused. "Archery is heart of the Hunt."

Planting his feet a shoulder's width apart, Warden Gustavsson straightened his back. He gripped the bow in his right hand and extended his right arm straight out in front of him. He nocked the arrow on the string, drew it back until his left hand was brushing his ear and tilted the bow up towards the sky.

Then he waited.

Finn held his breath.

A seagull flew overhead. Gustavsson adjusted his aim and released the arrow. The arrow flew fast, curving slightly as it sped skywards. It struck the seagull a glancing blow, and Finn watched in wonder as bright sparks flowered around the point of impact.

The seagull's wings collapsed and the bird began

to plummet towards the ground. Finn felt his shoulders tighten.

"Dr Raj has improved the technology," said Gustavsson as the seagull fell towards him. "We expect no repeat of last year's ... mishaps."

A few metres above the ground, the seagull's wings jerked open again. Flapping in a panic, it stopped itself from hitting the ground, then soared up into the sky once more, apparently unharmed. Finn allowed himself to relax a little.

"A direct hit will stun the Quarry," Gustavsson said with a small, satisfied smile. "The discharge from the arrow will also trigger the Quarry's gutha to signal defeat. It will cause no permanent damage, and it is almost painless."

Finn rubbed his chest, remembering what it had felt like when Adriana zapped him in the hospital lift. If those arrows delivered even half the jolt of an Overloader, he was determined to stay out of their way.

The Dean raised his hands once more.

"The time has come," he announced. "The Hunt is on. Quarries ... go to ground!"

Cheers rose up as one student from each team ran out across the meadow. Finn held Zoe's gaze for a moment.

"Do your job," she said.

"I will," he replied, knowing that she wasn't talking about the Hunt.

Setting off at a jog, he weaved his way through a cluster of platforms towards the edge of the grass. Just as Finn reached the last platform, John sprang down and started running beside him.

"Good luck," John said, clapping his brother on the back. Then he sprinted away into the distance.

"You're brave," Adriana called to Finn. "I'll give you that."

It took Finn just a few minutes to ascend the sloping meadow. By the time he reached the jumble of rocks on the far side, John and the rest of the Quarries had vanished. Beyond the trees, the mountain loomed.

He paused, fingering the smooth coldness of the gutha hanging around his neck. He felt suddenly very alone.

Aware that time was short, he went straight along the route he'd taken to the beach the night before, only to come upon a short steel post planted in the middle of the sandy path. As he circled it, a camera perched on top swivelled to face him and he stopped dead.

"Turn back, Quarry," said a disembodied voice. "Or you will be disqualified."

Great! So that's what Professor Panjaran meant by "monitors". This just got trickier.

Pasting a fake smile on his face and waving casually, Finn backed up until he was out of sight of the camera, then broke sideways across the scrubby grass. There must be a place he could sneak past the cameras. But moments later he came across another monitor post.

"This is your second warning," said the voice through a hidden speaker.

Cursing under his breath, Finn retraced his steps to the top of the meadow. Five minutes gone already and he was practically back where he started.

This isn't going well. He thought about just disobeying, but he guessed he wouldn't get very far before they brought him in. And then who knew what the Dean would do.

Maybe they'll turn those things off when the Hunt's over, he thought.

In which case, his priority right now was to go along with the game and find himself a hiding place. If he was lucky, he might get time to conduct his own personal hunt later on. *Find somewhere high up. One secret spot, that's all you need*.

A quick glance over his shoulder revealed the Alyxa building sprawling like a silver starfish. One arm of the star was splayed open. On the triangular black deck of Hunt Base, a crowd of students watched and waited.

Hunters.

Finn made for the trees, leaping easily from one boulder to the next. Back home, his favourite place for running had been the new garden on the main street, but he was starting to think that craggy rocks were better than concrete walls any day. His trainers gripped the rough stone, and his hands moved easily from one handhold to the next. The wind whipped past his face. He could almost convince himself this was fun.

He entered the forest and jogged for another ten minutes through the trees. Checking his watch, he confirmed that he'd now used up more than half of his thirty-minute advantage. He was sweating already – no doubt a good Hunter would smell that. Spotting a ridge to his left, he jogged to a clump of ancient oaks nestled deep amid the pines. The enormous trees were gnarled, and carried huge boughs thick with leaves. This could be a good spot?

But before Finn could investigate further, a boy who looked about John's age appeared from behind a holly bush and shoved past him.

"Find your own place," said the boy. "This one's mine."

Bending his knees, the boy sprang upwards. Finn watched in astonishment as the boy flew in complete defiance of gravity to a branch at least ten metres off the ground. Landing lightly in the crook where the branch met the trunk, the boy melted into a hollow in the rough bark and disappeared.

Finn ventured deeper into the forest, his footsteps crunching into the debris on the ground. The wind ticked in the canopy of oak leaves and pine needles, marking off the relentless passage of time. He listened hard, wondering if he might be able to pick out the melody of Kylie's song from the natural chatter. Reluctantly, he admitted to himself that the music just wasn't there.

Spotting a stream, he smiled, and struck out into the shallows. His feet were immediately soaked, but it would confuse any Smell Clann tracker.

After fifty metres or so, he squelched on to dry land again. He followed a contour, ducked under a fallen tree, then came to a halt. A gigantic stone lay in his path. It was as big as a bus, standing on end. Moss clung to its rounded form. Strands of lichen nestled in the spiral patterns etched into its surface.

Finn circled the stone. Behind it was a kind of shelter, also made of stone. The interior was dank and dark. Cracks ran through the walls, which were engraved with some kind of writing. Finn peered at the engraving, wondering if it was more Latin. But it was impossible to read, so weathered was the stone.

Another Druid place, he told himself, wondering if this was part of the Large Ring he supposed must exist somewhere on the island. He shivered. Not only was it cold here, it felt so *old*.

He checked his watch. Five minutes left.

Finn felt the first stirrings of panic fluttering in his stomach. He needed to find a hiding place, and fast.

As he backed out of the shelter, his fingertips scratched the edge of the wall. The stone felt strangely warm. Lichen lodged beneath his fingernails.

Beneath his feet, the ground began to throb.

Finn stumbled to his knees. He tried to stand, but the throbbing climbed his body and filled up his head. He staggered, clutching dizzily for the nearest tree trunk, but all the trees seemed to be flying away from him. His vision blurred, so that he could no longer tell if what he was seeing was real.

He blinked and the forest was gone.

More standing stones had appeared around him, each as immense as the first. Even bigger was the mountain, which was now covered in snow. Above it, the sky sang with electric colours and everything swam before his eyes, as if he were underwater.

And he was not alone. Five men sat in a huddle beneath the stones. They wore long brown robes, and blue tattoos covered their lined faces. The men spoke to each other in deep, guttural voices. Finn had no idea what language they were speaking. As he watched, one of the men held up a dead rabbit and peeled off its skin. The man pressed the shining carcass to his mouth and gnawed on its flesh.

Finn gagged. At the sound, the five men turned in his direction, but their eyes darted loosely. One raised a crude axe, another a dented sword. The third snatched a stone knife from his belt.

The man who had been eating the rabbit lowered his feast and snarled. His teeth and lips were bloody.

Finn staggered away with a cry. His foot caught in a tree root and he fell on to his back. The men gathered over him, their inked faces masks of curiosity as they looked down at him.

"No!" shouted Finn, raising his hands to ward them off. "Leave me alone!"

The dead rabbit swung above his face, dripping blood.

With a flash, Finn came to. He lurched, hit his head, then clambered woozily to his feet. He tottered forward, rubbing his head. He looked around.

One standing stone again, and the forest just the way it had been. No men, no weapons. No dead rabbit.

What happened to me?

Something snapped in the woods behind him. Finn whirled, nearly falling as a fresh wave of giddiness washed through him.

"Over here!" cried a voice from the trees. "I can taste him!"

Hunters!

Finn bolted. Legs pumping, he sprinted away from the standing stone towards a path running upslope through the forest. Crashing sounds followed him, getting louder.

"This way!" someone shouted.

A rock rose up before him, completely blocking the way. He leapt sideways, pushed off a broken stump and sprang right over the obstacle.

That should hold them up, he thought.

But he'd already seen a boy get halfway up a tree with just one leap. Who could say what his pursuers were capable of?

"I see him!" shouted a girl to his right.

Finn darted left, heading for a gully. His breath burned in his lungs. Forget going high. Maybe if he led them downhill ...

The air whistled. Something punched him between his shoulder blades. Bright pain skewered his back, and all his teeth seemed to sizzle. It wasn't as bad as the shock he'd got off Adriana at the hospital, but it was close.

So much for "almost painless", he thought, as stars shot across his vision.

CHAPTER TWELVE

F inn found the rest of his team waiting at Hunt Base. As he got closer, he saw the streaks of mud on their jumpsuits and the miserable looks on their faces. Otherwise the Base was deserted, which confirmed his fears.

"Great job, newbie," said Xander. "You were the first Quarry found."

Finn's hand went to the gutha on its leather thong. It didn't feel any different. He supposed it must have broadcast its signal during his brief period of unconsciousness.

"So what were you doing out there?" Xander went on. "Admiring the scenery?"

Finn wondered if there was a way to wipe the sarcastic smile off Xander's face. Recounting his peculiar experience at the standing stone might do it, he supposed. But he'd already decided to keep that to himself.

"I thought maybe you'd got lost," said Zoe. Could the others hear the hopeful tone in her voice? "Maybe found yourself somewhere you weren't supposed to be?"

"Nothing like that," Finn replied. "I had to stick to the course. I had no choice."

Her disappointment showed in the slump of her shoulders.

"Don't beat yourself up," said Ben, patting Finn's shoulder. "You did your best. Actually, just getting a team together at all was pretty amazing, under the circumstances."

"We knew this was a long shot," said Lucy. "At least we got to take part."

Xander pretended to stuff his fingers down his throat. "Yeah, yeah - it's not about winning, it's about taking part. So long, Numbskulls."

Lucy pulled a face at Xander's retreating back, then turned to Finn. "Well, that's all over for another year," she said. "Maybe we'll all be back in our Clanns by the time the next Hunt comes around."

"I don't even have a Clann," said Finn.

"Don't worry," said Ben. "You'll find your place here, sooner or later. Everyone does."

"So people keep telling me," Finn replied.

"I'm going back to the common room," said Lucy. "You coming?"

Finn looked around. The Dean and the Wardens were busy behind the control desk. Above it, the silver petals of the folded walls looked suddenly like the jaws of some monstrous ocean creature.

"I think I'll enjoy the fresh air a little longer," he said.

"Don't stay too long," said Ben as Lucy departed. "Nurture Group is there for a reason, you know. You should rest." He glanced at the desk, where Kildair was waving. "The Dean wants me. A prefect's work is never done. Are you sure you're okay, Finn?"

"I'm fine," said Finn. "You go. I'll see you later. And thanks."

"For what?"

"For taking a chance on the team."

Ben gave him a broad smile. "Any time."

When he was gone, Zoe spoke up. "So you didn't manage to get down there?"

Finn shook his head. "I didn't even come close."

Zoe made a show of looking around the empty base. "Then let's make the most of what we've got."

"What do you mean?"

"Isn't it obvious? All the kids are out on the Hunt, and the staff are all busy keeping an eye on them. The rest of the school is practically deserted."

Finn nodded. This was his opportunity to tell her about the meditation chamber. The problem was he couldn't think how to start. "Okay, I'm in," he said. "But listen - I already tried the med chamber ..."

Zoe put her finger to her lips, glancing over towards the Wardens, then came right up close to him, cupping her hands to his ear. "There's somewhere else I want to try," she said.

***

As they approached the polished wooden door to the Dean's office, Finn's heart was thumping.

"Are you sure about this?" he said. "If we get caught -"

"I don't care," she said. "They can expel me if they want. He knows something and I'm going to find out what it is."

It's not expulsion I'm worried about, thought Finn. If the Dean really had something to do with Kylie's disappearance, there was no saying what he might do to protect that secret. He pointed to the security panel on the wall. Unlike some of the others, it was a number code rather than a palm print. Part of him was relieved though – this crazy mission was over. Assuming it was a four-digit code, like an average PIN, that meant ...

"Ten thousand," he said mournfully. "That's how many combinations it's got. If it's a six-digit code, it's a million." He started turning away. "Maybe it's just as well. I mean, what do you think the Dean would do if he caught us in his private quarters?"

"Wait a minute," said Zoe. She bent close to the keypad and lifted her goggles away from her eyes.

"What are you doing?" said Finn.

"Concentrating. Shush."

Finn went out of the lobby and into the hallway to check that nobody was coming. When he returned, Zoe was just slipping her goggles back into place.

"Two, four, six, seven," she said, standing up straight.

"What?"

"Those are the numbers. Two, four, six, seven."

"But how did you ...?"

Zoe regarded him through her goggles. "There's a thin layer of dirt on the display," she said. "You probably can't see it, but I can. The numbers that get used the most are cleaner than all the rest."

Finn looked at her with renewed admiration.

"That's incredible!"

"But I don't know the order."

Finn made a quick calculation. "Okay. Four numbers can be arranged in ... twenty-four different ways."

Zoe smiled. "In my book, *that's* incredible," she said. "I was never much good at maths."

They punched out the possible sequences one after the other.

2, 4, 6, 7 ...

2, 4, 7, 6 ...

2, 6, 4, 7 ...

Then Finn tapped in *6, 7, 4, 2* and the door lock emitted a loud click.

"Bingo!" said a girl's voice behind him, and suddenly there was Lucy. Her eyes were bright above an excited grin. "Man, you two are going to get in a whole world of trouble!"

"You just can't keep your nose out of it, can you?" said Zoe.

Lucy held up her hands. "Don't attack me. I'm just here to make sure you don't do anything *really* stupid.

"This has got nothing to do with you," said Zoe.

Lucy's face grew serious. "Yes, it does. I saw that hexagram on the wardrobe door." She turned to Finn. "And I heard you asking all those questions about the sixth sense in Beaky's class. Why don't you just tell me what's going on?"

"Why?" said Zoe. "So you can scurry off and tell the Wardens?"

"I'd never do that," Lucy said defiantly. "I thought I was your friend."

Zoe's expression remained rigid for a moment, then her face collapsed. "You are," she said. "I'm sorry. I've been keeping this bottled up for so long. I just ... I just need to find out what happened to my sister."

Lucy nodded. "I knew this was about Kylie." She looked at Finn over Zoe's shoulder. "So - are you going to tell me what's going on?"

Finn looked at Zoe, who nodded. "It's a long story, but we think the Dean knows what really happened to her."

Lucy's eyes widened. "I thought she ... y'know ..."

"She didn't," said Zoe, with complete conviction. "I know it sounds hopeless, but we're looking for clues. Anything."

Lucy peered into the room, and for the first time since Finn met her, she looked unsure of herself. "Okay, then, let's do it."

The Dean's office was almost as sparsely furnished as the rooms in Nurture Group. In place of the plain grey decor, however, it had wooden panels on the walls and a rich cream carpet. The large desk was bare except for a leather pad and a small screen displaying a feed from the Alyxa timetable. A sleek cluster of steel spotlights hung from the ceiling. The air was stuffy.

Zoe crossed at once to the bookcase.

"They're all in alphabetical order," she said as she scanned the shelves.

"Trust the Dean to make his books obey the rules," said Lucy. "Listen, are you saying the Dean had something to do with Kylie's disappearance?"

Hearing Lucy, the arch cynic, say it like that made Finn doubt himself even more. *What are we really talking about here? Conspiracy? Murder?* The more he thought about it, the more he thought that the vision he'd had was a watery grave.

"Exactly," said Zoe.

Finn went across to a tall white filing cabinet. He expected the drawers to be locked, but the top one slid open easily. *I guess the doorpad is supposed to be all the security he needs.*

"Looks like all the student records," he said. "Personal files, everything. Paper copies. You'd think he'd keep it all on computer like other schools."

"Alyxa isn't like most schools," said Lucy. "Hey, where's my file? I want to see what they've got to say about me!"

She started leafing through the folders that were

hanging on a rail in the drawer. Finn's eyes dropped to the bottom drawer, which almost certainly contained a pair of files on two boys whose surnames began with the letter W.

Finlay Williams.

John Williams.

He was tempted to look, but stopped himself. The Dean could be back any minute and they were here for a reason.

Lucy pointed into the drawer. "There she is: Kylie Redmayne."

Finn pulled out the file, surprised by its weight.

"It's thicker than all the others," he said, letting it drop on the Dean's big wooden desk.

Between them, he and Zoe searched through the reams of paper inside the file. There were medical reports signed by Dr Forrester, charts of duelling scores recorded by Magnus Gustavsson, class attendance records, school photos charting her five years at the school, looking older in each, always smiling. Apart from the most recent. Maybe it was because Finn knew her story, but in the one dated three months before, Kylie looked ... empty. She seemed to be staring right through the camera with dead eyes. Finn could feel Zoe trembling against his shoulder and realised how hard this must be for her.

Towards the back of the file, Finn came across a sheaf of pages covered in neat, hand-written script.

"It's a sort of day-by-day account," said Zoe, scanning the writing. "It's ... it's like somebody was spying on her, tracking all her movements and writing them down."

Finn glanced over her shoulder, and read aloud: "*KR attended morning lessons but spent afternoon in library researching local tidal patterns.*" Then another. "*KR stayed in dorm claiming sickness but no evidence of ill health. Later appeared recovered but in a depressed state.* There are dates on them all."

Zoe flicked through from one page to the next, the frown across her forehead deepening. Finn could almost feel the intensity of her gaze through the dark lenses of her goggles, and realised she must be memorising each, reliving the final weeks of her sister's life. Her hands trembled.

But what did it mean? Sure, the Dean was watching Kylie for some reason. But from what Finn had seen, Kildair liked to keep a close eye on everyone. It didn't mean he killed Kylie.

Lucy, meanwhile, was searching the desk drawers.

"Prefect badges," she said, lifting up a handful of little shining spears. "There's loads of them."

"Not surprising," said Zoe, still focusing on the

folder. "The Dean decides who gets them. Alyxa isn't exactly a democracy."

As she read, Finn spotted a photo on the wall above the desk. In the picture, a tall man with slicked back hair stood on an expensive-looking yacht surrounded by a group of people. His arm was around a slim young woman in a striped swimsuit. The buildings that clung to the hillside in the background looked Greek, thought Finn.

He looked closer. There was something about the woman in the swimsuit.

Finn gasped.

"What's the matter?" said Lucy.

"That's my mother." He was barely able to get the words out.

Zoe stopped reading, put her sister's file on the desk, and came over to peer at the photo with Lucy.

"She looks about twenty," said Zoe.

"Wow, he was really out of his league," said Lucy.

"She wasn't his girlfriend!" snapped Finn. But was that true? His mother hadn't told him about Alyxa. What else might she have been hiding from him? Suddenly he didn't want to look at the picture any more. "Are we looking for clues about Kylie or not?"

Zoe waved her hand at the filing cabinet. "We've got clues," she said. "That weird spy's diary in the file. The badge you found on the beach. We know something's going on, and we know the Dean's behind it. I vote we tell the Wardens."

"Woah!" said Lucy, slamming the desk drawers. "Tell the Wardens? You just went from zero to sixty without even blinking."

"Lucy's right," said Finn. "None of it's really evidence. It's all – what do they call it? – *circumstantial*."

"All right," said Zoe. "Then let's just tell Arnott."

"Susan Arnott?" said Lucy. "Adriana's mother? Are you crazy?"

"Why her?" said Finn.

"Because she always listens," said Zoe.

"She's always listening, you mean," said Lucy. "Totally different thing."

"She kind of scares me," said Finn. "She's ... I don't know, very straight."

"That's the point," said Zoe. "I trust her. Adriana was Kylie's best friend."

Finn could feel his eyes being drawn back towards the photo of the Dean and his mother. He turned his back on it.

"I don't know," he repeated. "I just think telling anyone is risky." He checked his watch. "I also think our time is running out. We should get out of here."

Zoe let out a shriek of frustration. She ripped off her

goggles and flung them across the room. Finn ducked as they flew past his head, then stared at her in shock as she advanced towards him, her pale eyes wet with tears.

"Whose side are you on?" she shouted.

"Yours!" said Finn.

"Well, act like it!" said Zoe. Finn had never seen her so angry. "The Dean's done something with my sister," she went on. "I know he has!"

She was standing right in front of him now, her eyes locked on his. Slowly, he picked her goggles off the floor and held them out to her.

"I know I heard your song," he said gently. "And I'm sorry she's gone. But until we know what happened, we can't just go around accusing people -"

"You don't understand," Zoe said curtly, snatching the goggles. "You don't care. Neither of you care."

"That's not fair," he replied. "I just don't want you building your hopes up. But we do understand."

"How can you? You never lost anyone!"

Lucy's face turned red. "Oh, so you've seen my mother around lately, have you?"

Finn chose not to mention his dad, because he could see Lucy's words had already taken the wind from Zoe's sails.

"I'm sorry," she said. "That was unfair. I just can't ... not if there's any chance ... Finn, would you listen again? For the song, I mean? It's the only real proof we've got that I'm not going mad."

"Listen? What song?" said Lucy.

"I heard music," said Finn. "When I was down in the meditation chamber being grilled by the Dean."

"A song our mum used to sing," said Zoe. "And how could you have heard it, unless she's alive?"

Lucy looked perplexed as she processed the information. "You never mentioned that bit. Do you think that could be your power coming through? Hearing."

"I don't know," said Finn.

"Try, *please*," Zoe said. "Before we have to get out of here."

Finn took a deep breath. He had to tell her now. It wasn't fair to keep her hopes up any longer.

"I need to talk to you about something," he said.

Zoe flinched. "What?"

"When I was in the med chamber this morning ... I did feel ... something."

Zoe stared at him fiercely. "You heard Kylie?"

"Not exactly," he said. "It's hard to describe, which is why I didn't say. I don't know what it means."

Zoe came right up to him, close, and gripped both arms surprisingly hard. "Just tell me," she said.

Finn tried to hold her gaze, but couldn't bear the

desperation he saw there and looked away. "It felt like I was underwater," he said. "Like I was floating in the deep somewhere. It was sort of ... peaceful."

Zoe's gaze softened. "You mean dead," she said. "If that's what you mean, just say it. You think she's drowned, don't you?"

Finn looked to Lucy for support, but she only shrugged.

"I think so, yes," he murmured.

Zoe released his arms, staring distantly.

Something buzzed and warm air began to waft through a grate in the ceiling, bringing with it a faint aroma of heather. Lucy looked at Finn in alarm.

"It's all right," he said. "Just the air conditioning." A panicked thought flashed in his brain. The Dean might have set it to come on; he might be returning soon.

Zoe seemed to be coming to her senses, taking in the room dully. "We need to hide any traces we were here." She picked up Kylie's file again and went back to the cabinet. Finn felt awful for dashing her hopes, but relieved too that he didn't have to hide it any longer.

As Zoe was replacing the file, she suddenly froze and a hand shot to her mouth.

"Oh my God."

"What?" said Finn and Lucy at the same time.

Zoe turned to them, speechless, then back to

the drawer. Slowly she reached inside, and when she withdrew her hand again she was holding a book bound in bright green plastic. Finn was confused.

"It's my sister's journal," said Zoe. "Why has the Dean got my sister's journal?"

"Are you sure it's hers?" said Lucy.

"Of course I'm sure!" said Zoe. She opened the journal's green plastic cover, then half-closed it again. "Kylie caught me trying to peek at it once. She went nuts."

Finn gawped at the book, then at Lucy, and wondered if he looked as shocked as she did. He'd suspected the Dean of something all along, but this was real evidence. Kylie's property. Stolen.

A beep came from the desk. Finn saw that the little screen was no longer displaying the regular timetable. Instead, a red panel displayed the text:

THE HUNT IS OVER.

ALL STUDENTS MUST CONVENE IN ALYXA HALL FOR THE ANNOUNCEMENT OF THE WINNING TEAM.

"Time to go," said Finn.

Zoe was gripping her sister's journal with white-knuckled hands.

"We've got to put it back," said Finn quietly. He held out his hand.

Zoe retreated, clutching the book tighter than ever.

"No way."

"Finn's right," said Lucy, going back to the bookcase. "If the Dean …"

"I said no!"

Zoe rushed to the door and flung it open, then ran out into the corridor. Finn moved to follow her, but Lucy caught his arm.

"Let her go," she said.

"But what if she does something stupid?" said Finn.

Lucy made a show of looking around the Dean's office. "I think the horse has bolted on that one. Come on, we'd better hurry. You want to find out who won the Hunt, don't you?"

Finn checked the room over before they left. Apart from the diary, he was pretty sure it was as they'd found it. The air conditioning would hopefully clear out any trace of their presence from the air.

"What's the Dean's sense of smell like?" he asked Lucy.

"I think he's an all-rounder," she replied. "Level Two across the board."

Finn closed the door behind them, then gave the keypad a wipe with his sleeve. He felt like a criminal leaving the crime scene. Which wasn't all that far from the truth.

CHAPTER THIRTEEN

They reached the hall to find the announcement already made and the celebrations in full swing. Triumphant music echoed from hidden speakers, helium balloons bobbed on silver strings, and strands of multicoloured foil littered the floor, the occasional piece still floating down from the ceiling. The Sight Clann hawk was circling through the aerial clutter and Beaky's bloodhound was baying like a wolf at the moon.

A huge crowd of students had clustered around the victors. In the middle of the throng, four members of the winning team clung to each other, holding the fifth up on their shoulders.

It was John.

When he spotted Finn, he scrambled down and started pushing his way through the crowd. Finn forced his way in and met his brother in a crush of laughing boys and girls.

"Nice one!" Finn shouted over the tumult. Their hands met in a resounding high-five.

"Thanks, bro!" John shouted back. "It was a close one."

Adriana appeared and snaked one arm around John's waist.

"They had him cornered by the Hammerhead Lake," she said. "So he froze it."

"You did *what?*" said Finn.

"The whole thing," said Adriana. "Then he ran out on to the ice."

John grinned. "They followed me out and when I got to the other side, I, you know ..."

"What?" said Finn.

"Defrosted it," said John.

Adriana pointed to a group of dripping wet Hunters standing away from the crowd. Finn recognised Jermaine, whose sandy hair hung limp around his miserable face.

The music died away and Professor Panjaran stepped up on to the hall's central platform. He was about to speak when a strip of foil landed in his mouth.

He spat it out and everybody laughed.

"On behalf of the Wardens ..." Panjaran began.

Somewhere a balloon popped with a loud bang. Another cheer went up.

The Sight Warden tried again. "On behalf of the Wardens, I heartily congratulate the winning team. I am also most delighted to report that this year's Hunt concluded without major incident."

"It ended with a splash!" shouted a boy from the depths of the crowd. There was more laughter, and it took Professor Panjaran nearly a minute to calm everybody down.

"In the tradition of Alyxa," he said, "now that the Hunt is concluded, there will be no more lessons today."

Uproar. Adriana turned to John and planted a kiss on his cheek. Finn spied a momentary grimace on the face of her mother, Susan Arnott, who was turned in their direction from her place on the platform. Then hands grabbed for John and up he went again.

"Party in my dorm tonight!" John called down to Finn.

"Is that an invitation?" said Finn. "Or am I on monkey duty again?"

John was still grinning, but Finn caught a flash of discomfort on his brother's face, then he reached up and rubbed his temple. Finn called to ask if he was okay, but

191

it was too noisy and John looked fine again anyway. He watched as his brother bounced away on the shoulders of his triumphant teammates.

While the proceedings descended into chaos, Professor Panjaran mopped his brow and fiddled with his goatee. Magnus Gustavsson and Pietr Turminski clapped him on the back, grinning. But Finn wasn't interested in them.

Behind the group of Wardens, half in the shadows, the Dean stood with an expression like stone.

As Finn and Lucy followed the crowd to the canteen, he couldn't shake the look from his head. *Does he somehow know what we did?*

"They put Chef Kapoor in charge of the Hunt Buffet," Lucy said to Finn as she tried to pull him along with her. "There's samosas and yogurt dips and about a thousand different sorts of bhajis. Just for once, I'm going to forget the rules and eat some *real* food!"

Hungry though he was, Finn told her to have a good time and went in search of Zoe.

He found her in the Nurture Group common room, curled up on one of the armchairs with Kylie's journal on her folded knees. Her goggles were lying on the table and the rims of her eyes were red. Tears stained her cheeks. Finn wondered if she was still angry with him.

"I'm sorry," he said, sitting beside her. "In your

shoes, I'd want to keep the journal too."

"It's okay," she replied.

"Have you found anything?" He was glad they were still talking.

Zoe wiped her eyes. "I don't know. Nothing she's written adds up. I knew she was having a hard time, but nothing like this."

"Do you mind if I look?"

She paused for a moment, and he thought he might have over-stepped the mark. Then she handed him the journal. "Go ahead. Maybe you can make sense of it."

Scanning the page she'd been looking at, Finn read:

Heard them again after lights out. Same voices, different words. Still can't understand what they're saying. Ten minutes of babble then nothing. Took me ages to get to sleep. Then the same nightmare.

Finn turned to another page.

I'm definitely being followed. Only, when I look there's nobody there. Blink and you miss it. But I know it's after me. I know it wants me. I just wish I knew why. No. That's not true. I don't wish that at all. Here's what I wish - that it would GO AWAY AND LEAVE ME ALONE.

He read on, but it was more of the same. She was hearing voices and struggling to sleep. Getting told off in lessons for her lack of concentration. After a while the entries weren't even dated.

"She was losing it," said Zoe softly.

Finn skipped back a little, and saw that the first half of the journal was neatly written, the pages filled. He saw the name Callum a few times, but didn't look too closely – it felt private.

"She thinks someone was spying on her," said Zoe.

"And she was right," said Finn, recalling the report in Kylie's file. "The Dean?"

"I don't know," said Zoe. "Someone working for him, at least. But why? What was Kylie to him? Until Callum left, she was a model student. Never even as much as a detention."

He kept flipping through the pages. It was like looking at a mind unravelling as the handwriting became uneven and randomly spaced with certain words double-underlined, or scribbled out so violently that the pen had torn the paper. Towards the latter pages, drawings began to appear among the writing: strange symbols that looked like Druidic runes, or crude sketches that might have been fragments of maps.

And scattered throughout, sometimes in the corners, and sometimes occupying whole pages, were drawings of six-pointed stars.

One of these hexagrams headed a page on which Kylie had scrawled, in large letters:

What does he want from me?

Leafing further through the book, Finn saw the same thing repeated, only each time Kylie's handwriting got worse and the message more garbled:

Why won't he stop asking me?

Later:

Stop stop stop stop stop

He closed the book and ran his hand over the smooth plastic cover.

"It looks like the Dean was harassing her," said Zoe.

"I don't know," said Finn. "That doesn't explain the voices. And why would she call him 'it'? It's like it was something else."

They sat in silence. After a moment, Zoe retrieved her goggles from the table and wiped them with a tissue.

"Crying plays havoc with the lenses," she said, feebly attempting a laugh.

"I'll bet." Finn couldn't think of anything else to say.

"Look at the last entry," said Zoe.

Finn leafed to the spot, about three-quarters through. On the page he read, in perfect handwriting:

He's calling me to the sea.

The line was repeated. "Six times," he said.

"I should have been there for her," said Zoe.

"You would have been, if you'd known," said Finn. He closed the journal and handed it back to her. His stomach growled. "Have you eaten anything? It's been a long time since lunch."

Zoe shook her head.

"There's this buffet thing in the canteen," he said. "I could bring you something back."

"You go," said Zoe. "I'll be all right."

Finn went to his dorm and changed into a fresh jumpsuit. Closing the wardrobe door, he glanced at the mirror, remembering the secret symbol that Kylie had scratched there.

Why hexagrams? he thought. *Why was Kylie of all people, a model student, interested in the sixth sense? And why was the Dean interested in her?*

He stuck his head round the door, but Zoe was engrossed in her sister's journal again, poring for clues.

Looking for answers, when they didn't even know the question.

CHAPTER FOURTEEN

"That's a big monkey," said Finn, staring at the gigantic sculpture poised above their heads.

They were standing at the main door to the Touch Clann wing. The walls of the entrance hall were a jumble of rough timber, smooth steel and coarse stone. Muffled dance music sent ripples through a drape of crinkled silk.

Clinging to the ceiling was a crystal chandelier. Clinging to the chandelier was a carved wooden monkey that looked exactly like Pogo, only twenty times as big.

"His name's Felan," said Lucy. "But I call him King Kong."

"Do all the Clann mascots have names?" said Finn.

"Of course. Now, are you going to paste a smile on your face or what? This is a party."

Finn did his best, but he was still thinking about Zoe.

"Don't feel guilty," said Lucy. "Zoe will be fine on her own."

"I thought your powers were kind of zonked."

Lucy blinked. "They are, but I don't need Taste powers to see what you're thinking. Are we going in or what?"

The Touch Clann common room was like a huge woodland lodge, with thick log walls and an uneven wooden floor. Colourful flags hung from overhead beams. At the far end, an open fire blazed beneath an enormous copper chimney breast. The whole place was warm and welcoming.

A dozen or so people were dancing in the middle of the room. The rest of the space was filled with happy, chattering students. Best of all, the music wasn't deafening. His brother would be fine here.

"This is cool," Finn said to Lucy.

"Makes a change from those plain grey walls, don't you think?"

"Are the other Clann common rooms like this?" Finn said.

"They're all different," said Lucy. "I used to hang out

in Taste Clann. That looks less like a cabin in the woods and more like an American diner. Lots of chrome."

"Every time you turn a corner at Alyxa you see something different," said Finn.

"Tell me about it."

Adriana strolled up. She'd swapped her leather jacket and jeans for a leather dress. Her hair was unexpectedly pink.

"Hey there, you two," she said. "There are drinks on that table. Finn – want to say hello to your brother?"

Her smile was warm, but she didn't hold his gaze. Finn and Lucy followed her past the dance floor to the fire, where John was holding up a glass of what looked like lemonade.

"Presto!" he said, and the liquid froze instantly. Firelight flashed off the tiny bubbles trapped inside. Laughter broke out among the watching students.

"Do mine!" said a girl wearing purple-rimmed glasses.

John tapped her glass with an outstretched finger.

"Hasta la vista!" he said, and the girl's cola turned to a solid brown block.

"Do it again," she laughed.

Grinning, John wrapped his hand around a bottle standing on a nearby table.

"Incoming!" he cried. The condensation on the

outside of the glass froze, and the bottle cracked from top to bottom. John snatched his hand away.

"Oops," he said, prompting yet more laughter.

"You're such a show-off," said Adriana.

Across the dance floor, people started moving aside and began to clap as a girl pulled off her shoes and socks and began to climb the wall on all fours.

"Touch powers seem a lot more, well, powerful than the others," he said to Lucy, staring at the liquid fizzing out of the cracked bottle and on to the table.

"Not really," said Lucy. "They're just a bit more in your face."

Finn had been hanging back, waiting for the right moment to get his brother's attention. But he saw there was no rush. John was relaxed and having fun. He said to Lucy, "Come on. Let's leave them to it."

They left the warmth of the hearth and went to the drinks table, where Finn poured them both glasses of fruit punch. The music shifted uptempo and they watched as the dance floor filled up. John was at the centre, throwing shapes that made everyone laugh.

Finn glanced across at Lucy, expecting her to be staring at John. He was surprised to see her looking at him. He blushed, but it was dark enough that she probably couldn't tell.

"You do belong here, you know."

"So everyone keeps saying," Finn replied, "but I think I'll be a Numbskull until graduation."

Lucy laughed. "Nah! Anyway, you heard this song, Zoe said?"

"I *think* I did," said Finn. "Nothing much makes sense at the moment, if you'll forgive the pun."

"Forgiven," said Lucy.

After a silence, he asked her, "Do you believe in ghosts?"

Lucy pursed her lips. "One of the things they teach you at Alyxa is to trust your senses. As in trust *only* your senses. If you don't see it, hear it, smell it, taste it or touch it, then it's nothing you need to know about. I think that's why the idea of a sixth sense freaks them out so much – it goes against the whole ethos."

Finn understood. But could he trust his own senses? Had the song been real? What about the strange figures by the standing stone in the woods? If they had been real, had they been of this world? Or was his mind just experiencing some kind of weird mental indigestion because of all the crazy stuff that had been poured into it over the past few days?

"So you don't believe in ghosts?" he said.

"I didn't say that," said Lucy. "I'm just a big fan of concrete proof. Comes of having a scientist for a dad, I suppose."

They fell into silence for a moment watching the dancers. At that moment, John was tottering around in a handstand. The mention of Dr Raj brought a thought worming into Finn's head. A wild thought, but one which might provide more answers.

"Lucy ..." he began.

"Uh-oh," she replied jokily. "This sounds ominous."

He smiled. "Your dad has a sense-enhancement tool."

"I prefer 'brain-scrambler'."

"Maybe we could ... I don't know ... borrow it?"

"*Borrow?*"

Finn nodded. "It might help me focus more."

"Or it might turn your brain to custard."

"Or that," he said cheerfully. "So could you get it?"

Lucy shrugged. "I guess so. He's off to a conference tomorrow and I've got a key. But for the record, I think it's a ridiculous idea."

"Objection noted," said Finn. "Or we could just ask him?"

Lucy shook her head. "No way. The Wardens keep a really close eye on Dad, and the Dean doesn't like him at all. I don't think any of them really trust him."

"Because he's not from Alyxa?" said Finn. Lucy nodded. Finn wondered why he'd stayed after Lucy's mum had walked out – if that was really what had happened. "If they don't want him around, why don't they just tell him to go?"

Lucy downed the rest of her fruit punch. "They're not allowed."

"Allowed by who?" said Finn. "They're in charge, aren't they?"

Lucy looked sideways at him. "They like to think so. They're responsible for the curriculum, and the welfare of the students, but they answer to the Trust." When Finn looked at her blankly, she continued. "The Alyxa Trust. I suppose they're a bit like the School Governors. Mostly ex-students, but super-secretive."

"I didn't realise," said Finn.

"How else do you think this place keeps going?" said Lucy. "It must cost a fortune."

Finn nodded, feeling a little dim. *Of course it would.*

"So this Trust keeps your dad here?"

"Sort of. He brings other benefits, too."

"Like the Overloaders?"

"*Especially* the Overloaders." She paused. "Anyway, I think he likes it on the island."

Out on the dance floor, a forest of arms was waving at the ceiling as the dance music echoed around the log-lined room. Lucy had started bobbing her head in time. Of all the students at Alyxa, she was definitely the most *normal*, Finn thought.

The information about the Trust was interesting though. If they were above the Wardens, perhaps *they* would be the ones to go to with any evidence.

Lucy nodded towards the fire. "Your brother's waving at you. I'm going to get something to eat. You hungry?"

Finn shook his head. As Lucy made her way towards another table piled with snacks, he spotted John briefly sharing a dance move with a girl at the edge of the dance floor, before finishing making his way over.

"Glad you could make it," John said. "Isn't it awesome here?"

"It's a cool party," Finn agreed, meaning it.

"Not the party, dumbo," said John. "Well, yeah, the party's excellent too. I meant Alyxa."

"Oh, that," said Finn. From John's point of view, he supposed it was. He'd just won the Hunt. Everybody loved him. Never mind what might be going on underneath the surface. "Yeah. Alyxa's great."

"Have you sussed out what your power is yet?"

"Hearing, maybe," Finn replied, not because he really believed it but because it was something to say.

"Well, this place is the best thing that ever happened to me. Are you getting another drink?"

Without waiting for a reply, John filled up Finn's glass with cola and poured one for himself.

"Here's to Alyxa!" John chinked Finn's glass hard enough to make a splash.

"To Alyxa," said Finn, giving John's glass a gentle tap.

Over by the fire, Adriana's eyes seemed to be following Finn's every move.

"I don't think your new girlfriend likes me much," he said.

John glanced over his shoulder, then shuffled his feet. "Ady's not my girlfriend. And of course she likes you! She'd just hard to get to know."

"Her hair's cool," said Finn.

John laughed. "Her mum doesn't think so!"

Adriana turned away from them and stared into the fire. Her newly-dyed spiky hair looked like a pink bomb blast above her head. Finn thought she looked a little strained and sad.

John too, looked serious suddenly. "You know, Finn – I heard about your history lesson this morning." He frowned. "You should watch what you talk about. Some things here are, you know, taboo."

"Like Kylie's death?"

John's frown deepened. "Not so much that. But all this sixth sense stuff. I couldn't believe it when I heard you were making trouble." His lips made a smile that didn't reach his eyes. "I mean, my little brother, Finlay

Williams!"

Finn hated the fake chumminess in his brother's voice. "I was just asking questions," he said. "It wasn't that bad."

"Whatever it was, it wasn't cool," said John. "I'm just looking out for you here."

Finn opened his mouth but no words came out. This was all backwards. He didn't need looking after; it was John's freak-out at Amelie's party that had caused all this.

I should just tell him, he thought. *If I can't talk to my brother about all this, who can I talk to?*

The music switched to a truly ancient track by Elvis Presley, remixed to a thumping dance beat. As the dancers thinned out, Finn saw Adriana beckoning across to John.

"You like this song," Finn said to his brother. "You should go and dance."

"Don't be like that," said John, looking hurt.

"Like what?" said Finn. "I just don't want to spoil your street cred."

John gave him a play punch on the arm. "All right, bro." His gaze had wandered and his shoulders were gyrating. "Take it easy."

Finn watched the dancers part to absorb his brother, then headed for the door. Lucy caught up with him.

"Bored already?" she said, dropping an empty paper plate into a nearby bin.

"I want to see how Zoe's doing," said Finn.

"I'll join you."

The dungeon-like corridor leading to Finn's dorm didn't feel nearly as grand as the Touch Clann entrance hall.

"Why doesn't Nurture Group have a mascot?" he said as he reached for the chrysalis touchpad on the wall.

Something banged behind the door.

"There's someone in your room!" said Lucy.

His hand froze and he stared at her, startled. Another bang came from inside the room. The door was definitely closed, so how could anyone get inside?

"It could be Zoe," said Finn. "Looking for clues again."

He saw from Lucy's expression that she believed it about as much as he did. Then he heard footsteps behind him. No sooner had he spun around than Zoe appeared from around the corner.

"Oh, you're back," she said.

Finn pointed at the door. "You're not in there."

"Ten out of ten for observation," Zoe replied. "I went for a walk."

Steeling his nerves, Finn pressed his hand against the touchpad. But when he turned the door handle and pushed, something pushed back.

He banged on the door. "Hey! Open up!"

Gathering his strength, he slammed his shoulder against the door. This time it gave way. Finn flew into the dorm and landed sprawling on the floor.

"Are you all right?" called Zoe.

As Finn stood up, a blast of cold wind sprayed water across his face. The window was swinging to and fro, banging against the wall. Outside, rain fell from a glowering sky stained orange and purple with the last remnants of sunset.

Finn's breath caught in his throat. The room was empty, but on the blank grey surface of the wall above his bed, someone had used what looked like red crayon to scrawl a large six-pointed star.

Finn jumped on the bed and peered through the open window. Rain lashed his face. A cloaked figure darted from behind a stone cabin, clearly visible against the orange sky.

"There!" cried Zoe, pointing.

Lucy squeezed past her through the doorway. "They're getting away!"

Without thinking, Finn leapt through the window. Just as he had before, he used the nearby ventilation duct to get safely down to the ground, then sprinted after the fleeing figure.

Beyond the cabin was some kind of electrical plant. Buzzing coils rose from a line of squat metal sheds, and the air was filled with the tang of ozone.

The fugitive scrambled up a chain link fence, threw his legs over the top and dropped to the ground on the other side. The figure then climbed a ladder on to the roof of the first shed. Finn followed, easily clearing the fence and using a large boulder to propel himself up without touching a single rung. Grabbing the metal gutter, he swung himself on to the flat expanse of the roof. Electrical coils rose on both sides, their hot curves sizzling in the rain. Finn's jumpsuit was already soaked through, but he wasn't going to stop.

The cloaked figure jumped on to the roof of the next hut. Finn cleared the gap between the two buildings with ease, and was pleased to see he was gaining on his quarry. By the time the figure leapt to the third shed, Finn was almost close enough to touch the cloak's flapping tails.

"Stop!" he shouted.

The fourth shed was much farther away, and Finn felt sure the running figure would be forced to stop. But the person just kept running, and cleared the enormous gap with a tremendous leap that reminded Finn of the way the boy had jumped into the tree in the forest.

No way can I make that! he thought. *No way!*

Pumping his legs harder, Finn accelerated to the edge of the roof and kicked off. A pair of coils sent a dazzling arc of electricity over his head. He flew through the air, flailing his arms.

His chest hit the parapet of the fourth shed, knocking all the wind out of him with a single, shattering impact. His fingers scrabbled on the rough felt of the roof. But there was nothing to grab hold of. Finn slithered down the wall and dropped to the ground, landing with a squelch in a patch of mud.

He lay there with the rain lashing his face, fighting to draw air back into his lungs. The last of the sunset fled, turning the sky to a thick tapestry of purple and black.

The cloaked figure appeared on the roof above, then leapt down, landing softly. It approached with slow, steady strides, and fear descended over Finn. He tried to lift himself up but the mud sucked him down. His chest hurt, and his lungs were still refusing to work. He opened his mouth, managing to croak, "Who are you?"

"You know me as Morvan!" boomed the figure in a gravelly voice. The man's face was completely hidden by the cloak's dripping hood. "On your knees, servant. Kneel before me!"

Finn clawed at the mud, terrified. He tried to stand,

but his legs wouldn't work. When he opened his mouth again, the rain filled it up.

"Obey me!" the figure intoned. "Obey your master! Morvan will not be denied!"

"Get away from him!" shouted Lucy, appearing from nowhere and battering at the looming figure's chest. Finn looked on in astonishment as the hood fell away, revealing the grinning face of Xander.

Laughter burst from behind the shed. Three students emerged wearing rain capes. They were the same kids that Xander had been sitting with when Finn had first met him in the canteen.

Finn tried to wipe the rain from his face, but only succeeded in smearing himself with mud.

"It's not funny!" said Lucy. "He could have got hurt."

"I'm all right," panted Finn, wishing his voice sounded stronger. He lapsed into a fit of coughing.

Laughing uproariously, Xander joined his friends. Together they vanished into the twilight.

Lucy extended her hand to Finn. He pushed it away.

"I'm all right," he said, clambering awkwardly to his feet.

"No thanks to that pea-brain," said Lucy. "Speaking of thanks, do I get any?"

"Thanks," Finn muttered. He kicked at the mud,

wishing it had swallowed him all the way up.

"You could say it like you mean it."

Finn's shame grew when he saw the hurt in her face. "Sorry," he said. "Thanks for sticking up for me."

"That's more like it." She stared into the darkness. "Glad you started digging into the sixth sense?"

Finn thought about how John had tried to warn him off. Was this what he got for not listening to his brother's advice?

"Not really," he said. "But I can't stop now."

They trudged back through the mud in silence, while all around them the rain poured down.

CHAPTER
FIFTEEN

"*Help me,*" *said the girl.*

Finn couldn't see her. His body was floating.
Or falling? The girl called again.

"*Help me, please.*"

Finn opened his eyes. Cold water squeezed into his
nose and ears. When he moved his lips, it squirmed into his
mouth. Drowning.

He reached out, and right away his hand hit something
hard. A wall of ... of glass. Starting to panic, he looked up
and around. Glass walls on every side. He was trapped
inside a coffin of glass, and the coffin was filled with water.

Finn slammed his hands against the glass wall.

But the glass held.

Finn's lungs were on fire. He clamped his lips together but the water pushed relentlessly against them.

"Help me," said the girl, and still he couldn't see her.

The water tightened around him like a vice.

Finn couldn't hold his breath any longer. Eyes bulging, heart exploding inside his chest, he opened his mouth. The water flooded in, a devastating tsunami, liquid death ...

***

At assembly next morning, Finn took his place with Lucy on the Nurture Group bench. He looked around for Zoe – she'd retired to her room by the time he'd got back after chasing Xander and he hadn't seen her since. She arrived a few moments later. Finn gave her a weak smile as she sat down beside him. After the events of the previous evening, and a night spent tossing and turning, he felt exhausted.

Even though Zoe's goggles masked her eyes, Finn could see the dark circles lurking beneath them.

He wondered if she was having nightmares too.

"You two look like death warmed up," said Lucy.

"Just tired after the Hunt," said Finn.

He looked for John in the Touch Clann seats. To his annoyance, the first face he spotted belonged to Xander. When he realised Finn was watching him, Xander whispered something to his friends, prompting a bout of snickering. Finn wondered how he'd managed to get past his door security.

As usual, Professor Panjaran led the assembly. He began by recapping the result of the Hunt, and congratulating everyone on a safe and successful event. Finn was only half-listening, but the next thing Panjaran said made him sit bolt upright.

"It is my pleasurable duty to invite one of our newest students, John Williams, on to the stage," said the professor.

Finn watched in astonishment as John – who had been sitting several rows behind Xander – made his way up to the platform. He looked a little tentative, and also somewhat confused. Murmured conversation followed him. Pogo was back on his shoulder, preening his hair with nimble fingers.

"As you all know, John was a member of the winning team in yesterday's Hunt," Panjaran went on. "A vital member, some would say." The murmuring continued. "In light of his remarkable performance as Quarry, and in recognition of his equally remarkable progress in baseline power control, it gives me great pleasure to recognise his achievements publicly. I therefore award John with Touch Clann Level Three status."

There were gasps from the audience as the Sight

Warden presented John with a new silver badge with three lines beneath the monkey symbol. As John turned on the spot, waving and grinning, the gasps melted into a ripple of applause. When Pogo started chattering, the audience rose to their feet and cheered. The only unhappy face that Finn could see belonged to Xander.

"This is crazy," said Lucy. "Nobody goes from zero to Level Three. Nobody."

Finn was glad to see his brother looking so happy. But did John really understand what was going on here at Alyxa?

Do I?

After assembly, Finn joined Lucy and Zoe at the nearest timetable screen. He ran his finger down the multicoloured graph, looking for the little chrysalis icons that would indicate where they were due to go next. He'd just spotted his name in the scrolling display when Ben trotted up.

"Forget lessons," he said. "Dr Forrester wants us."

"All of us?" said Finn.

"Yes," said Ben. "It's sort of a Nurture Group catch-up. She just wants to monitor our progress, see how we're coping with the rehabilitation process."

Before Finn could go after them down the corridor, Kildair stepped into his path.

Finn's heart sank as his friends disappeared

into the distance. He squirmed, all too aware that the students still filtering out of the hall were giving him and Kildair a wide berth. Even in the crowded corridor he felt exposed and alone.

"I was just getting ready to go and see Dr Forrester," he said.

"Not any more," said the Dean.

Finn followed the Dean away from the hall. One of the corridors took them past a row of display cabinets containing stone tablets covered in some kind of engraved writing. On another day, he would have stopped to examine them - perhaps they were relics from the days of the Druids. Right now he felt no curiosity at all, just a sense of unease.

Approaching the Dean's office along the familiar passage, the dread made his legs heavy. How had he ever thought they'd get away with it? Kildair probably had a camera in there, and had spent the previous evening reviewing footage of Finn and his accomplices breaking in and searching the place.

But then why aren't Lucy and Zoe here with me now?

Inside, the office was hot and stuffy and he wondered if the Dean had switched off the air conditioning. A bead of sweat rolled down the small of Finn's back.

The Dean, standing silently on the other side of the desk, pressed a fingertip to a seemingly random spot on the surface. Having held his finger up for scrutiny, he wiped it against his jacket. Could he see fingerprints as well as Zoe?

Finn's gaze wandered to the filing cabinet where they'd found Kylie's journal. Not wanting to draw attention to it, he jerked his head around and found himself staring instead at the wall directly behind Kildair.

The empty wall.

He's removed the photo ...

"Your brother has an impressive set of skills," said the Dean.

"He's doing really well," said Finn. He didn't know where this was going, but the more he could agree with whatever the Dean said, the quicker he might get out of here.

"Yet you have shown no abilities at all," said Kildair. He spoke as if Finn was being stubborn in not demonstrating any sense capacity.

"I suppose I'm a bit different."

Kildair smiled wolfishly. "Oh, the two of you are more alike than you know."

As the Dean eyed him, Finn shifted his hands behind his back. But that felt odd, so he clasped them in front again. *Could I look more guilty?*

"How are you finding things in Nurture Group?" said the Dean.

"Uh, everything's fine," said Finn. He didn't know which version of the Dean scared him more: the intimidating one or the friendly one.

The Dean nodded. "I understand you've made friends with Zoe Redmayne."

Finn tightened his fingers against each other. Discussing Zoe would undoubtedly lead to discussing Kylie. He wasn't sure he wanted to go there again in the Dean's presence. "Not really," he said.

"But I assume she talked to you about her sister?"

"Everyone knows what happened to Kylie," said Finn carefully.

"Just as everyone appears to know about your remarks during Warden Blake's lesson," said the Dean.

"Do you mean the history class?" said Finn, wondering how far the Dean would take this. "It was good. We talked about all sorts of things."

"And you were the one who displayed a particular interest in the sixth sense." Kildair placed his palms down on the leather of the desk. The tendons on the backs of his hands stood out like steel cords. His eyes fixed on Finn. "In Morvan."

How detailed a report had Beaky given to the Dean?

Finn decided she'd probably told him everything. Which meant that lying now would only get him into more trouble. Easier to say nothing.

"Tell me, Finn, where did you first hear about the sixth sense?"

Finn made a show of frowning. "I'm not sure."

"But you're convinced you want to find out more about it?"

"Not really," said Finn. "It sounded funny, that's all. I know it's not real."

"Is that right?"

"Sure. Just a legend. A fairy story."

The Dean leant forward over the desk, and Finn felt like Kildair's gaze was a laser, trying to cut through his skull and see inside his brain. "Of course it is. But fairy stories have a way of spreading. Like disease."

The silence dragged out, then the Dean seemed to relax, lifting his hands from the desk and breaking eye contact. He sat in his desk chair, which creaked as he reclined.

"I'm sorry," said the Dean. The ice was gone from his voice. "I've been far too hard on you. I thought that if I pushed, it might release your hidden powers. I was mistaken."

Finn shuffled his weight from one foot to the other. It was the first time he'd heard the Dean own up to having any kind of weakness.

"It's not a problem," said Finn.

The Dean smiled. Almost human. "Would you like to talk to your mother?" he asked casually.

The words took Finn's breath away.

"M-my mum?" he said.

The Dean nodded.

"Of course. When can I ...?"

He watched in a daze as the Dean opened a drawer and withdrew a mobile phone that looked older than Finn. He put it down on the desk and slid it across. Finn couldn't take his eyes off it.

"You must promise not to tell anyone I allowed this," Kildair said, standing again.

"Yes, sir," said Finn. He picked up the phone and turned it over in wonder. "Thank you."

"You have five minutes."

With that, the Dean left the office.

Finn continued to stare at the phone in disbelief. Coming to his senses, he stabbed his mum's number into the keypad. She picked up on the second ring.

"Mum? Is that you?" he said.

"Finn!" she replied. "Where are you calling from?"

He could hardly speak. "Alyxa – the Dean said it was okay."

"Oh, it's wonderful to hear your voice."

"Yours too." *You have no idea.*

"How are you doing?"

Finn swallowed. He could hear the concern beneath her eager tone. "Okay, I guess. Better." He didn't want her to worry, so he let out a small laugh. "This place takes some getting used to."

She started to say something, then stopped herself. At last she said, "Are you ... have your powers come through yet?"

The last thing Finn wanted to do was disappoint her, much less worry her. "I might be in line for Hearing Clann," he said. Before she could respond, he added, "John's doing well. Incredibly well. He just got Level Three today."

"That's amazing," his mother said. "I always knew there was something behind his ... condition." She hesitated. Finn looked at the clock on the wall. He imagined that when the Dean said *five minutes*, he meant exactly that. "I wish I'd told you more about all this," his mum said. "But I couldn't. I just ... couldn't."

I wish you had too.

It suddenly occurred to Finn that the Dean might be listening in on the conversation. Even if he was, this might be the last chance he got to speak with his mother for a long time. Just to be sure, he crept to the door and opened it a crack. To his relief, the lobby beyond was empty.

"How well do you know Geraint Kildair?" he said, easing the door closed again.

"What's that?" said his mother. "Speak up."

"The Dean. Did you used to spend a lot of time together?"

"What makes you ask that?"

Finn glanced at the empty patch on the wall where the photo of Kildair and his mother had been hanging. "No reason."

"Well, we did study together. After we graduated, Geraint wanted to go travelling around Europe and I went with him. We had some good times, saw some sights. And it was good for me. It gave me time to work out what I really wanted."

"What was that?" said Finn.

She hesitated. "A fresh start. On the day Geraint told me he'd decided to go back to Alyxa, I told him I wanted out. When he turned up at the hospital the other day it was the first time I'd seen him since ... oh, since before you were born, I think."

Finn held the phone away from his ear and listened. *Was that footsteps outside the door? Or just his imagination?*

"Kildair's very strict," he said.

"He can be," his mother said. "But he's fair. He's a

223

good man, Finn, he really is."

"But did you trust him?"

The door opened and the Dean walked in carrying a brown folder. Stopping in the open doorway, he pulled out a sheet of paper and started scanning what was written on it.

"I've got to go," said Finn. "I'll try and call again when ..."

As the Dean glared at him over the paper, he let his voice trail away.

"Thanks for calling," said his mother. "Hang in there, and give my love to John. I love you."

"Love you too," said Finn.

He ended the call and held out the phone. "Thank you," he said. "Really, I appreciate it."

"Put it on the desk," said the Dean, eyeing him over the folder. "You should probably go and keep your appointment with Dr Forrester."

So that's it?

Finn placed the phone down, then made for the door. But the Dean hadn't moved. He blocked the way out, and clearly wasn't going anywhere.

"Excuse me," said Finn.

The Dean looked at him again for a long moment. "Since you're so interested in the sixth sense, perhaps you can do something for me?" he said.

"Sure thing," said Finn, feeling like he'd just swallowed a mouthful of curdled milk.

"If you should hear anyone talking about it – perhaps even stumble over something yourself – do come and tell me."

"Er ... yeah. No problem."

The Dean moved aside, and all the way out of the office and down the corridor, Finn could feel Kildair's eyes – no, all his senses – following him.

***

Finn climbed the spiral staircase to find Zoe seated in the infirmary waiting area gazing out through one of the big angular windows. Her legs were curled beneath her, and her chin was resting on her hand.

She was looking straight at the South Cliff.

"Where are the others?" said Finn.

"Lucy's in with Dr Forrester," said Zoe, not moving her head. "Ben's been and gone."

Finn sat beside her. After the rain of the previous night, the sky was a clear vivid blue, slashed with sharp white lines of high cloud. The sea was a vast, moving blanket.

"What did the Dean want?" said Zoe. Still she wouldn't look at him. *Was she still fretting over the*

contents of Kylie's journal, or had he done something new
to upset her?

"I'm not sure," said Finn. "It was ... odd."

"Did he mention the diary?" Zoe asked, confirming Finn's first suspicion.

"No. He might not even know it's gone."

"He knows," said Zoe, with a careless tone. "He can think what he likes. I'm not going to stop. Not until I know for sure what happened to Kylie."

The dead sound of her voice scared him.

"We've got to take this one step at a time," he said. "We can't afford to take risks."

Lucy emerged from the clinic, looking glum.

"Behold the perpetual Numbskull," she said, spreading her arms.

"What did she say?" said Finn.

"My power's only just above baseline – still," said Lucy. "It'll come back eventually, supposedly. I just have to be patient." She beamed. "Not my strongest suit."

Finn smiled back. He wondered if her dad had been tempted to use his apparatus on his own daughter. Perhaps not, if it was really as dangerous as she said.

Dr Forrester put her head around the door.

"Patience is indeed the key," she said to Lucy. "You can't rush these things. Finn – good to see you again. Come in, please."

226

With Zoe staring doggedly at the cliffs, Finn was reluctant to leave her, but there'd be time later. He followed the doctor into the same little room as before.

"How have you been?" Dr Forrester said once he'd seated himself.

"Er, okay," Finn replied.

"That was a brave move, getting involved with the Hunt the way you did."

News travels ...

"Some might say stupid," said Finn.

"Not me. Your brother did well."

"He always does."

She gave him a long appraising look. "Did you experience anything unusual when you were out alone on the island?"

You mean like standing stones that shouldn't have been there and a group of wild-eyed Druids eating raw dead rabbits?

"Nope," said Finn, smiling. "I got shot pretty quick."

Dr Forrester's face didn't seem to share the joke. "Shall we begin?"

After running through the same basic sensory tests he'd had before, the doctor tapped the results into her tablet and pronounced Finn as being normal.

"There's nothing out of the ordinary," she said with a frown, scanning the figures. "Which is ...

227

extraordinary."

"So being normal is weird now?"

Again, Dr Forrester didn't seem to understand he was joking. "Everyone's normal, just in different ways. Have you experienced any fugues?"

"What's a fugue?"

"An absence." The doctor leaned forward in her chair. "Like a waking dream."

Finn thought again about Druids and standing stones. Also glass coffins filled with water. If he said yes, she'd think he was crazy.

"Nothing out of the ordinary," he said.

"No feeling that you're tapping into something new? Some new sensory experience that you've never had before?"

"If you're asking whether I can feel my powers coming on, the answer's no," said Finn.

Dr Forrester sat back. She stared at Finn, rubbed her eyes, then stared again.

"Honestly, I would expect an older candidate like you – at your age – to respond quickly to the Alyxa environment. Just being around other students is usually enough to trigger dormant abilities."

Finn stretched the muscles in his shoulders, suddenly aware of how tense he'd been while in the Dean's office. "Maybe I just don't have any powers," he said.

Dr Forrester shook her head. "Given your mother's history, and your brother's remarkable abilities, that's quite impossible."

"Maybe they got it all and it just skipped over me."

"It doesn't work that way. Finn – when I asked you whether you had dreams, your eyes flicked away for a moment. Are you ready to tell me the truth now?"

Finn felt his cheeks flush. "Yes," he said softly.

"Yes, you're ready to tell me the truth? Or yes, you've been having dreams?"

"I didn't mean to lie," said Finn. "It was just a couple of bad dreams, that's all."

Dr Forrester tapped the screen of her tablet. She kept it angled so that Finn couldn't see the display.

"Tell me more," she said.

Finn squirmed in his chair. "It's no big deal. You know what dreams are like. As soon as you're awake they sort of fade away."

"Please try to remember something," Dr Forrester said. "Even the smallest detail might be relevant." Her eyes were boring into his.

"I thought I heard some music," he said. "When I was down in one of the meditation chambers. I thought maybe there was some kind of Hearing thing going on."

She peered at the tablet display. "There's nothing in

the tests to indicate that would be the case. Is that all?"

"It's all I can think of." Finn looked away, suddenly desperate to get out.

"You're perspiring," said Dr Forrester. "Are you all right?"

"I'm fine," he replied. "Just homesick."

As soon as he said the word, homesick was exactly how he did feel. He closed his eyes against the tears he felt brimming there, and in the darkness found himself imagining the immensity of the surrounding ocean, and the insignificance of the tiny speck of land on which he was trapped.

"What happens if my power doesn't come through?" he said, opening his eyes again. "Will they kick me off the island?"

"Kick you off?" said Dr Forrester in surprise.

"Yeah. Send me home."

She put down the tablet and regarded him thoughtfully.

"No," she said. "I don't think that's very likely. It may just be that your powers are buried deeper than most. For now, you can go."

Finn rose from the chair. "So what happens next?" he said.

Dr Forrester dropped the tablet in a drawer and opened the door for him. "I'll recommend you remain in Nurture Group until the end of term, which is only a few days away now. But we'll keep monitoring you." She cocked her head, and the look she gave him wasn't altogether friendly. "We'll figure you out, Mr Williams."

CHAPTER SIXTEEN

After their sessions with Dr Forrester, Finn and Lucy hurried along the south-east arm of the Alyxa building, the main corridor of which was covered in green carpet – floor, wall and ceiling. Their footfalls were muffled and the air felt oddly still. All Finn knew was that their next lesson was due to be held in something called the Interaction Suite, and that if they didn't get a move on they were going to be late.

They arrived at a set of low double doors, just in time to meet Pietr Turminski on his way inside.

"Fresh from your assessment, Lucy?" said Turminski, ushering them both through the doors. "You will be returning to us in Taste Clann?"

"Not any time soon," Lucy replied.

"Yes, well, better to take it slowly," said Turminski. "Rebuild yourself one piece at a time."

The Interaction Suite was long and narrow, with strange walls that looked like egg boxes standing end to end. A metal panel hung from the ceiling. Its entire surface was covered in buttons and knobs. Cables dangled from little round sockets.

Beneath the panel, two rows of chairs ran the length of the room, facing each other, very close together. On the arm of each chair was a small monitor.

"Is this some kind of sound studio?" Finn asked Lucy as they joined a knot of students at the far end of the room. To his dismay, Xander was among them.

"What makes you say that?" said Lucy.

Finn nodded at the ceiling panel. "That looks a bit like a mixing desk."

"Sound plays its part in here," said Pietr Turminski, as he squeezed past them carrying a fistful of multicoloured cables. "As do all sensory triggers. The Interaction Suite is holistic, you see?"

"That means this is where it's all happening," Xander said with a smirk.

"I know what it means," said Finn.

Turminski went down the line of chairs, using the cables to connect the monitors to the overhead panel.

When he was done, he clapped his hands together.

"Truth," he said. "That is the subject for today. Truth, and the ability to detect it. Or conceal it. These are useful life skills – among the most important, some might say."

"Are you going to teach us how to lie?" said Xander.

"Today, I teach you nothing," replied Turminski. "Today, you learn for yourselves."

"Including the Numbskulls?" said Xander.

Turminski showed his teeth, but he wasn't smiling. "Everyone has five senses, whatever Clann they are in. Even if they have no Clann. In the Interaction Suite, everyone gets the chance to use them all. Holistic, you see?" He clapped again. "Now, choose a partner, please. Each pair will take two chairs facing each other."

"May I have this dance?" said Lucy, offering Finn her hand and performing a mock curtsey. He wiped a palm that felt suddenly clammy on his jumpsuit before taking her hand, managing to laugh a little in the process.

They chose two seats in the middle of the row. The chair backs were upright and the cushions were hard. Finn examined the monitor on the arm of his chair, and was disappointed to see that the screen was blank. He and Lucy were so close together that their knees bashed.

"This exercise has two parts," said Turminski.

"First, lie detection. Each student will make two statements. Their partner must decide if the statements are true or false. The polygraph will then display the correct result."

A meek-looking boy with spots on his cheeks put up his hand.

"What's a polygraph, sir?" he said.

"It's a lie detector, stupid," said Xander.

"For the second part of the task," continued Turminski, ignoring both boys, "each student will ask two questions, to which their partner can answer yes or no. The interrogator must decide if the answer is truthful or not. Again, the polygraph will verify the outcome."

Turminski walked along the row of seated students, passing behind Finn, nudging chairs into line as he went. When he reached the end, he stretched up his arm and flicked a switch on the ceiling panel. Blue lights flickered along its length, reflecting off his bald head. All the chair monitors flashed blue as well.

"Take the square pad off your monitor and attach it to the inside of your left wrist," Turminski said.

Finn fumbled around the back of the monitor until he located a flexible pad about the size of a postage stamp. A thin wire attached it to the monitor. He pressed it against the skin of his wrist, where it stuck fast.

"With your free hand, hold the wrist of your partner," said Turminski. "Again, over the pulse, please."

Lucy's fingers closed immediately on the inside of Finn's right wrist. They felt very warm. He hesitated, then pressed his fingers against her wrist. He felt her pulse fluttering like a trapped moth.

Down the row, giggles broke out as the rest of the students did the same.

"This feels weird," Finn whispered.

"Says the boy whose big ambition is to stick his head inside an experimental brain-scrambler," Lucy whispered back.

"No laughing, please," said Turminski seriously. "Concentration is essential. Now – begin the exercise."

Finn stared at Lucy. She stared back, barely suppressing a grin.

"Who goes first?" said Finn.

"Flip a coin?" said Lucy.

"I don't have a coin."

Lucy rolled her eyes. "Oh, for goodness sake. I'll go first. Ready?"

"Yes," said Finn.

"Okay, here it comes. When I was six, I fell off a swing and broke my collarbone."

"Really?" said Finn.

"That's my statement, you pretzel," said Lucy.

236

"You've got to decide if I'm telling you the truth or not."

"Oh, right, yeah."

Finn tried to read her expression, but he couldn't tell if her smile was evidence of a lie, or just Lucy feeling mischievous. A broken collarbone? It could be true, but how could he know for sure?

"True," he said, because he had to say something.

A large green tick flashed on to his monitor.

Beneath his fingers, Lucy's wrist pulsed with a slow, steady beat. He wondered if his was racing. He certainly felt like it was.

"Your turn," said Lucy.

"Um, I'm allergic to cats," said Finn, wondering if she would taste the lie in his words.

"False," Lucy answered immediately.

This time the green tick appeared on her screen – she'd read him.

"That's one all," said Finn. "Now you go again."

Lucy gazed up at the overhead panel, then down again at Finn.

"My dad's favourite food is gumdrops," she said with a straight face.

Finn imagined Dr Raj doing experiments with a face full of sweets and burst out laughing.

"No way!" he said. "But ... I'm going to say true!"

This time, a red cross on his monitor told him he'd

guessed wrong.

"What is it then?" said Finn. "I knew gumdrops was wrong."

"Totally ridiculous, more like. Dad's favourite food is jelly beans, obviously. Now I'm one up. Your turn."

Finn thought for a moment.

"One day last year I took all the slats out of my brother's bed," he said. "When he jumped on it, his mattress collapsed right through to the floor."

Lucy snorted. "Absolutely, definitely, one hundred per cent true!"

"Wrong!" said Finn, and a second later the polygraph monitor confirmed her mistake. "It was the other way round – it was me who ended up on the floor. One all!"

"Well, we're done with the first part," said Lucy. She removed her fingers from Finn's wrist, stretched her arms, then took hold of his arm again. Finn did the same. He peeked down the row, where the rest of the students were exchanging their statements and responses. There was quite a bit of laughter going on, not to mention plenty of groaning. This was a lot more fun than history.

"I saw the Dean call you away," said Lucy, leaning closer. "Think he's on to us?"

Finn shook his head. "I think he's on to *something*."

He's a good man, Finn, he really is.

"Well, we're on to him," said Lucy. "He must have stolen that journal."

"It looks that way. And the journal was filled with stuff about how the Dean kept bugging her with questions."

"Bugging her enough to jump off a cliff?"

"Who knows?" he said. "I suppose Kylie had just split up with her boyfriend. Maybe that was the final straw. Or maybe she didn't mean to do it. The fall really could have been an accident."

Lucy treated him to a sceptical arch of her eyebrow. "The Dean's up to something."

Finn admired her certainty, and wished he could share it.

A phone-like device hanging from Turminski's belt beeped. He swiped it awake and stared at the screen. His lips tightened.

"Remain in your seats," he said, hurrying towards the door. "Continue the exercise until I return."

"What was that all about?" said Finn after the Warden had gone.

"Search me," said Lucy. "But he's worried about something." She planted her fingers back on Finn's wrist. "Want to go first with the questions?"

"If you like."

"Okay. Ask me your worst!"

Finn looked into her brown eyes, studied the turned-up corners of her mouth, and thought hard.

"Have you ever had a boyfriend at Alyxa?" he said.

Lucy's olive-skinned cheeks went two shades darker. "No, I have not," she answered.

"I think you're lying," said Finn.

A green tick on the monitor. He was right.

Now the corners of Lucy's mouth turned down. Finn could feel her pulse racing.

"Are you jealous of your *awesome* brother?" she snapped.

Finn blinked, startled. It wasn't something that had ever occurred to him. Was it true or not?

"No," he said.

Lucy half-closed her eyelids. "Oh, you're *definitely* lying."

Finn only had to see the flash of green to know that her monitor was displaying a big fat tick.

"I was right," said Lucy. "How interesting."

"In your opinion," he replied.

"The lie detector doesn't lie," said Lucy. "One more question each. What have you got?"

For a moment, Finn's mind was empty. Then a thought rose up like a balloon.

"Are you just pretending that you've lost your sense

powers?" he said.

Lucy flinched. "No," she said.

"That's a lie," said Finn immediately.

Another green tick. Given her strange intuitions about other people, Finn wasn't surprised. But he hadn't expected Lucy to look so horrified.

"I won't tell anyone," he said gently. "Why are you faking it?"

"You've had your last question," said Lucy with a sniff. "Now it's my turn."

Finn steeled himself.

"You *do* have powers, don't you?" she said, staring at him intently. "But you're keeping them a secret."

Finn blinked, bemused. He hadn't expected Lucy's final question to be so easy to answer.

"Afraid not," he said. "Dr Forrester just did a bunch of tests on me and I failed them all."

"You're lying," said Lucy.

"I wish I was," said Finn.

He stopped in shock as the polygraph delivered its verdict on Lucy's answer: yet another green tick.

"Eh?" Finn thumped his monitor. "This is nuts," he said. "I wasn't lying, really."

Lucy shrugged. "You can't argue with science. That's what my dad always says, anyway."

She pulled her fingers away from Finn's wrist. He

did the same. They leaned back in their chairs and stared at each other. Finn coughed, wondering which one of them would break the silence first.

"The questions got kind of personal, didn't they?" said Lucy at last. She was smiling a lopsided smile.

Finn managed to smile back. "I really won't tell anyone," he said.

Lucy held his gaze. "I just like being in the Numbskulls right now. How about you? Do you really think you don't have powers?"

Finn shrugged. "I just know that I wasn't lying. Not on that last question."

A scrunched-up ball of paper hit Finn's ear.

"Hey, new boy," called Xander. "Seen any more ghosts lately?"

"Ignore him," said Lucy.

"With pleasure," said Finn, fighting to control his breathing.

Xander's partner – one of the boys who'd been hiding behind the power shed in the rain – tossed another wad of paper in Finn's direction. This time Finn ducked.

"You wet your pants, didn't you?" said the boy. "I could smell the pee. Thought the Sixth Warden was going to eat you, I bet."

"Shut up, Chen," said Lucy.

"Chen's a Level Three," said Xander gravely. "Smell Clann. He'd know."

"Oh, get lost, both of you!" said Lucy.

"It's all right," Finn said to her. "They're idiots. Just ignore them."

"Finn and Lucy sitting in the pee," Xander chanted. "K-I-S-S-I-N-G!"

A girl further down the row said, "Xander, you're such a loser."

"Lucy loves Finn!" Xander laughed. Laughter rippled down the row of chairs. "Or maybe she loves the older brother, but Adriana got there first."

"What's your problem?" Finn said to Xander.

"I'm looking at it," said Xander.

Shooting a quick glance at the door, Xander rose to his feet and kicked back his chair. The cable jerked out of the monitor and writhed snake-like around him. Xander advanced towards Finn. All down the line, students shuffled their chairs back.

"You've had it in for me since day one," said Finn, standing up to face Xander. "What's wrong with you?"

"What's wrong with *you*, more like?" said Xander. "You think you're better than the rest of us."

"No, I don't," Finn replied.

Another red cross filled his monitor.

Finn ripped the sticky pad from his wrist and

hurled it aside, clenching his fists as Xander drew near.

Xander laughed and pointed to the two stripes on his badge. "Think you're ready to fight me?"

"You're not worth it," said Finn. He could feel his fingernails digging into his palms.

"That's what all the cowards say."

"Leave him alone!" said Lucy.

"At least your girlfriend's got some fight in her," Xander said.

"She's not my girlfriend!" shouted Finn.

He threw himself at Xander, who instantly sidestepped. Finn flew past him, tripped on a chair leg and fell to his knees. Xander's hands locked around Finn's arm and twisted it behind his back. A spike of pain drove through his shoulder. It was worse than the Overloader, worse than anything Finn had ever felt before. He clamped his teeth shut to stop himself screaming, biting his tongue in the process.

"Big mistake," said Xander.

"Get off him!" Lucy made a grab for Xander's shoulders, but Chen bulldozed her aside. Out of the corner of his eye, Finn saw her hit the floor.

Xander tightened his grip. The spike of pain grew teeth, and Finn groaned.

"Are you crying?" Xander said, breathing into Finn's face.

Finn writhed, trying to ignore the agony in his arm. Lucy was attempting to get up, but Chen was holding her down. Something flared inside Finn. It wasn't pain.

"If you hurt her ..." he gasped.

Keeping a tight grip on Finn's arm, Xander flipped his captive around and planted one foot on his chest. Now Finn was lying on his back, staring straight up into Xander's face. The pain in his arm had lessened, but he still couldn't get up.

"Teach him a lesson," said Chen.

Xander drew back his foot. Finn tensed, trying to prepare himself for the blow ...

... but the blow never came. Xander froze, then lowered his foot to the floor. A look of puzzlement creased his brow. His top lip curled back.

Slowly, Xander lifted his right hand. His eyes followed the tips of his fingers as his arm extended out to the side. Then – *WHACK!* – Xander slapped himself on the side of the face. The onlookers gasped.

Finn heaved himself on to his elbows and watched in disbelief as Xander slapped himself a second time, then a third. A red mark bloomed like a flower on his cheek.

Balling his left hand into a fist, Xander punched himself in the stomach.

A girl called Sandy let out a burst of laughter, only

to cut it short. Her face creased with confusion.

"Hey, mate," said Chen to Xander. "What are you doing?"

Xander started thumping himself on the chest, again and again.

"Make it stop!" he gasped. He looked shocked. Scared. As he spoke his feet tangled in one of the cables dangling from the overhead panel. He fell backwards, knocking over three of the chairs and yanking the cable sideways. The plug stayed in its socket, but the socket ripped free from the console and whipped across the room, trailing a nest of coloured wires. Sparks flew. A bank of lights flashed red and a hidden alarm managed one mournful beep before the entire control panel went dark.

Xander glared at Finn from the floor. The red mark glowed on his face, the outlines of his fingers clearly visible. Nobody spoke.

Xander raised a trembling finger and pointed it directly at Finn.

"What did you do?" he said, his voice cracking on the last word.

Everyone was looking at Finn.

The door flew open and Pietr Turminski rushed in. His thin face was pale. Finn held his breath, waiting for the Warden to remark on the scattered chairs, the broken control panel, Xander looking as if someone had just beaten him up.

Instead, Turminski started waving them all towards the door.

"Everybody to the main hall," he said.

Sandy raised a cautious hand. "Can I collect my PE kit from the laundry block on the way? I forgot to ..."

"No delays!" said Turminski. "As of this moment, the school is in lockdown."

CHAPTER SEVENTEEN

"**I**s it some kind of drill?" Finn asked Lucy, as they made their way to the hall with the other students.

"It won't be anything," she replied. The way she was bouncing along told Finn that she wasn't nearly as calm as she wanted him to think.

The hall was filled and buzzing with chatter. Hardly anybody was sitting down. The hawk was turning rapid circles above the platform, and for the first time Finn saw the bat that was the mascot of Hearing Clann. A tiny black arrow, it was darting back and forth between the banners hanging from the high ceiling.

While Finn and Lucy headed for the Nurture Group bench, Pietr Turminski hurried up on to the stage, where he joined the other four Wardens in a whispering huddle. Moments later, Zoe scurried up looking anxiously from side to side.

"Ben came and got me from the common room," she said. "What's going on?"

"Search me," Finn replied.

The Dean marched into the hall. The conversation died away. As Kildair climbed on to the platform, the Wardens took their seats.

"Silence!" said the Dean, although by then not a single person was talking. "I am ashamed to say that we have a thief among us."

A breeze wafted the banners and the bat retreated into the shadows. Holding himself rigid, the Dean scanned the audience.

"A book has been stolen," he continued. "A precious book."

Finn's stomach contracted into a painful knot. Beside him, he heard Zoe's breath catch in her throat.

The Dean began pacing around the perimeter of the platform, looking out across every section of the pentagonal hall. "I want the person responsible to step forward now."

Nobody spoke. A shadow flickered near the skylights and Finn watched as the Sight Clann hawk alighted on one of the banner poles.

The silence dragged out, then the Dean nodded to the Wardens.

One by one, the five Wardens took up positions facing out into the hall. When Professor Panjaran turned his penetrating gaze on the Nurture Group bench, Finn took in a long, slow breath. His breath was a wave and he was floating on it. In and out went his breath. The meditation calmed him, allowed him to focus. Carried him away.

Finn kept his breathing slow as the five Wardens moved steadily around the platform. After Panjaran came Pietr Turminski, who had picked up the Taste Clann snake from somewhere and now carried it wrapped around his neck. His lips were slightly parted, and the snake's tongue flickered. When Turminski moved on, Susan Arnott took his place. Her blind stare swept over Finn unnervingly. Next came Beaky, head tipped back, then finally the hulking figure of Magnus Gustavsson. Every so often, he would reach out, fingers splayed as if they were organic aerials, picking up some hidden signal.

Throughout, it took all of Finn's self-control to keep his breathing slow and steady.

When the Wardens had completed a second circuit, they fell in together with bent heads as they conferred.

They know, thought Finn. At any moment he

expected them to turn in unison towards him, or Zoe. But they didn't. The Dean faced the assembly once more.

"All students will return to their dorms. All prefects will keep their senses attuned to monitor behaviour and report any suspicious activities directly to me. Any student who does not obey these instructions will be considered guilty."

Ben, Adriana and the rest of the prefects started directing crowds of students out through the doors. Finn joined Zoe and Lucy as they shuffled along to the end of the bench.

"Where is it?" Finn hissed in Zoe's ear.

Zoe turned away from him, her eyes lost behind her goggles.

When they reached Nurture Group, Finn palmed his door control as usual. Nothing happened. He wiped his hand on the sleeve of his jumpsuit and tried again. Still nothing.

"Finn?" called Lucy from around a bend in the corridor. "Is your door working?"

Once they'd established that all the doors were locked, Finn, Lucy and Zoe slumped down in the passage with their backs against the wall.

"We're in such deep trouble," said Lucy.

"Don't panic," Zoe said. "Kylie's journal is safe."

"If it's in your room, they'll find it," said Finn.

"It isn't," Zoe replied.

"I told you we shouldn't have stolen it," said Lucy.

"I didn't steal it," said Zoe. "If there's a thief here, it's the Dean."

Finn nodded. "Exactly. How can he accuse us without incriminating himself?"

Ben arrived with Adriana and Jermaine. The three prefects stood in a line, blocking the corridor, each wearing the same grim expression. Finn was about to ask what was going on when Kildair appeared behind them.

Ben addressed Finn and his friends. He looked almost apologetic. "Is there anything you want to tell us before we go in?"

Finn held Ben's gaze and shrugged. He knew the others wouldn't spill the beans, and he had no intention of blabbing.

None of them spoke.

"You'd better hope we don't find that book in your room," Jermaine said to Finn. His nostrils twitched as he spoke.

"I don't even know what this book is," Finn said.

"Plus this is total invasion of privacy," said Lucy. "We've got rights."

The Dean nodded to Jermaine, who plucked the prefect's badge from his lapel and touched it against

Finn's door panel. The end of the pin blinked green and the lock clicked.

Replacing his badge, Jermaine pushed open Finn's door and disappeared inside. Adriana opened Zoe's door in the same way, leaving Ben to let himself into Lucy's dorm. Finn was glad he'd managed to scrub away the hexagram that Xander had drawn on his wall. But what would happen when Jermaine spotted the cracked mirror? Would he find the six-pointed star scrawled behind it?

The seconds ticked by painfully slowly, and Finn watched the Dean's inscrutable face. *What are you hiding?* he thought.

Finn's door reopened and Jermaine emerged. Finn's leg muscles tightened.

"Anything to report?" asked the Dean.

Jermaine shook his head.

Finn exhaled silently. Beside him, Lucy was kneading her hands together. Zoe sat utterly motionless.

Ben emerged next.

"Lucy, you've got one of the messiest rooms I've ever seen," he said.

"Every girl needs a floordrobe," Lucy replied brightly. But Finn could hear the tension in her voice.

"Nothing," said Ben to the Dean.

All eyes turned to Zoe's door. The Dean tapped his

foot, sending little echoes clicking down the corridor. Finn licked his lips.

When Adriana reappeared she said nothing, just stood in the doorway with a white face and a shocked expression. Finn half-rose, but Lucy pulled him down. Zoe didn't move a muscle.

"What have you found?" said the Dean.

Adriana flicked her pink fringe out of her eyes. "I think you should come and see this, sir." She glanced at Zoe and added, "Sorry, kid."

The Dean followed Adriana inside. The door closed behind them.

The next wait was even worse. Ben and Jermaine huddled near the bend in the corridor, exchanging whispered words. Finn sat and stewed. They'd found it! So much for being "safe".

The door opened and out came the Dean, with Adriana close behind. He was carrying a book, but Finn saw immediately that it was smaller than Kylie's journal, and bound in ancient brown leather instead of slick green plastic.

"Zoe Redmayne - do you have anything to say?" The Dean raised the book.

Zoe's mouth was hanging open. "I ... uh, I don't know. I've never seen that before."

"And yet the missing book was under your pillow,"

said the Dean.

Confused, Finn finally realised that the Dean hadn't been searching for Kylie's journal at all. The book that had been stolen was something else altogether. *But what?*

"It wasn't there before, honest," said Zoe. She clambered to her feet, her gaze darting from the Dean to Adriana and back again. "Someone planted it."

"You are lying," said the Dean.

"I'm not!" Zoe sounded close to tears.

"I see it in every spasm of your face," said the Dean. "I smell it through every lying pore." His voice rose in pitch. "I hear it. I taste it. I can feel your lies on my skin."

"No ..." said Zoe, trembling.

Adriana crouched and put an arm around the younger girl's shoulder.

"Maybe there's an explanation, sir," she said, looking up at the Dean. "Zoe's been under so much pressure lately, what with Kylie and ..."

"This is not about pressure," said the Dean. "This is about integrity. Clearly this girl has none. The rules of Alyxa are clear. The punishment for your crime will be swift and severe."

Zoe pulled her goggles down so that they hung around her neck. Tears were streaming from her eyes. She wiped them away with the palms of her hands.

"Do what you like to me," she said. "I don't care."

"Your cares don't concern me," said Kildair. "Your crimes do. Jermaine – take Zoe to Meditation Chamber One for interrogation. No one else is to talk to her."

When Jermaine started steering Zoe away down the corridor, Finn sprang to his feet. This time Lucy didn't try to hold him down.

"You can't do this," he said. "She's done nothing wrong."

"I can," said the Dean. "And she has."

"We know what you're up to!" said Finn. "If you take her away ..."

"Finn!" hissed Lucy, grabbing the arm of his jumpsuit. "Shut up!"

"When you're on thin ice, you should avoid jumping up and down," said the Dean through pursed lips. "Listen to your friend, Mr Williams."

Finn was so close to saying something, but with Ben and Adriana looking on nervously, he found the words wouldn't come.

"Very wise," said the Dean, who turned and left.

"Just take it easy," said Ben. "Zoe will be okay."

Then he and Adriana followed Kildair.

As soon as they were alone they headed into the Nurture Group common room. Finn sank into the nearest armchair. He felt totally lost.

"What was that book they found, anyway?" said Lucy.

"No idea. Oh God – you don't think the Dean put it there? If he really did do something to Kylie, what's to stop him setting this whole thing up to get rid of Zoe, too?"

"That's some serious paranoia. Anyway, Adriana found it. She's Kylie's friend. Move over."

"Huh?" Finn didn't see how there was room for two of them on the chair, but he moved.

Lucy pried up the cushion and plunged her hand down into the springs.

"What are you doing?" said Finn.

"Hang on," said Lucy. She rummaged around. "Here we go!"

She extracted a familiar green book from the depths of the chair.

"How did it get there?" said Finn.

"It was my idea," said Lucy. "Zoe wanted to keep it in her room, but I knew that was a recipe for disaster. Good job one of us was thinking."

Finn took the book. It felt strangely heavy, as if Kylie's secret thoughts had somehow gained weight.

"Hide it again," he said, handing it back to Lucy. "We don't need it for what we're going to do next."

"We don't?" said Lucy.

"No. Now the Dean's got Zoe, the game's changed. We can't go it alone any more."

**

Finn lifted his hand towards the Hearing Warden's door.

"Come in," said Susan Arnott before he had a chance to knock.

Finn entered cautiously, holding the door open for Lucy to follow him through. He was immediately struck by the scent of fresh flowers. Thick white carpet stroked his feet, a stark contrast to the black leather sofas and sleek steel desk. Jazz music played from speakers somewhere – a double bass, drums and a trumpet tumbling over one another.

The Warden was standing beside a large globe on a polished wooden stand. Her long dress was striped black and white, matching the stark decor of the room. As Finn and Lucy loitered near the desk, she opened up the patterned sphere to reveal its contents: a clinking array of bottles and glasses.

"Uh, it's Finn ..." Finn began.

"Yes," Arnott replied, without moving her head in their direction. "And Lucille Raj also."

She poured herself a drink and closed the globe.

When she turned to face them, Finn saw that her eyelids were open. Her eyes were pale, like pools of milk.

"You have no need to stare," Arnott replied. "Just as I have no need to see. Please, make yourselves comfortable."

Finn perched on the edge of one of the sofas. Lucy sat awkwardly beside him. When he shuffled his legs, the smooth leather squeaked.

"How can I help you?" the Hearing Warden asked. Her skin was as smooth as marble. Resting her elbow in her upturned palm, she sipped her drink.

Finn swallowed. "It's ... it's about Kylie Redmayne." Arnott nodded encouragingly. "There's something not right about the way she died," he went on. "Before it happened, she was writing about the Dean in her journal." He hesitated. "We think that maybe the Dean had something to do with what went on."

He half-expected Arnott to order them both out of her study. Instead she just took another sip from her glass.

"That is quite a statement," she said. "Do you have evidence to back it up?"

Finn sat forward. "A few things," he said. "It started when I saw the Dean down at the South Cliff. He was acting really suspiciously. I found a prefect's badge when I was there. I think it might have been Kylie's."

"Quite possibly," said Susan Arnott, "given how she met her death." She was still smiling, but Finn was finding those blind eyes impossible to read. "You said that Kylie wrote something about Mr Kildair. What was it, specifically?"

Finn stood again and began pacing back and forth, his feet dragging on the carpet's deep pile. "She said: 'Why does the Dean keep asking me questions?' And she thought she was being followed."

"Followed by whom?" said Arnott.

"I don't know." Finn considered telling her about the song, perhaps even about his peculiar dreams. There was so much inside him that wanted to come out. But would the Warden see the connections between those things and the Dean? Were there connections?

"And now he's taken Zoe away," Lucy said with a sideways look at Finn. "He thinks she's a thief."

"And is she?" said Arnott.

"We don't think so," Finn said miserably.

Arnott lowered her glass on to the desk, depositing it right in the centre of a small round coaster. She clicked her fingers three times and the music stopped. Her face was impassive. Finn held his breath, suddenly aware that the allegations they were making against the Dean were really very grave. And that the evidence they actually had against him was paper-thin.

"Your concern for Zoe is commendable," she said. "But I assure you that she is in no danger from Mr Kildair."

Finn sighed inwardly, relieved that she hadn't blown up at them. But she hadn't said she believed them, either. "What about all the stuff to do with Kylie?" he said.

Arnott glided from the desk to the sofa, her dress swishing as she moved. She turned and seated herself with a single, fluid motion. Her frown was almost imperceptible, just a line of silky creases in the smooth skin of her brow.

"You've heard of the sixth sense?" she said.

"You mean that sixth sense we're not supposed to talk about?" said Lucy.

One of the folds of silk deepened. "Yes. Many people here regard the sixth sense as a myth. Not the Dean. He's spent years trying to warn the Wardens – myself included – that the sixth sense is a real threat to the safety of Alyxa."

"And this has something to do with Kylie?" said Finn, thinking instantly of the hexagrams she'd drawn in her journal. Not to mention the one he'd found behind the mirror. Until now he'd mostly found the six-pointed stars mysterious, perhaps unsettling. It had never really occurred to him that they might be dangerous.

"I will tell you what I know," Arnott said. She

steepled her hands before her face. "The Dean believed that Kylie Redmayne had fallen under the influence of the sixth sense. Therefore he took steps to keep an eye on her. He regarded it as -" she waggled her fingers "- as a student welfare issue. I believe he even took the drastic step of acquiring her journal, in case it contained clues about her state of mind. He was devastated when Kylie took her own life. As we all were."

Finn sat down. Student welfare. He hadn't thought of that.

Lucy gave Finn a silent nudge and arched her eyebrows at Arnott.

"I know you do not believe me, Lucy," said the Hearing Warden. "Nevertheless, I am telling you the truth. More truth than I should, perhaps, but then you are Zoe's friends, after all. Now tell me, why are you afraid for her?"

"Because she had the missing book in her room, and we don't know how it got there," said Finn.

"Did she now?" said Arnott, and for the first time in the meeting she looked genuinely surprised. "That's rather curious, I must say. But perhaps not completely inexplicable, in light of her sister's diversions."

"What's so special about that book, anyway?" said Lucy.

"Probably nothing," said Arnott. "But the problem

is that it was stolen from the Wardens' private library."

"But you can't think Zoe stole it?" said Finn. "I mean, why would she?"

"The title in question is called *Liber Morvani*," she said.

"*The Book of Morvan*," whispered Finn, translating. Just the name made him shudder.

"You are right to flinch," Arnott said. "The *Book of Morvan* contains an ancient text purportedly discovered after the death of the Sixth Warden, over a thousand years ago."

"So is this guy real or not?" said Lucy. "Beaky ... I mean, Ms Blake, said it was a legend."

"Oh, Morvan was real," said Arnott. "By all accounts, he was a powerful Druid, capable of *unusual* feats. He was ostracised for his radical ideas, but encouraged renegade followers to join him. After a time, he became a threat and was ... dealt with."

"You mean killed," said Lucy.

"The records aren't clear," said Arnott. "But you must remember, this was long ago. Things were different."

Finn was wondering if he was ever going to get a straight answer on *anything*.

"Your breathing betrays your frustrations, Finlay," continued the Hearing Warden. "But I am not being deliberately opaque. It is almost impossible to say the exact events that occurred a millennium ago. History, remember, is written by the victors. But in its margins countless other stories can linger."

"But the Dean believes in the sixth sense?" said Lucy.

"By her own account, so did Kylie Redmayne," said Arnott.

So maybe Zoe did take the book, thought Finn. *She broke into my room to look for clues. Why not the Wardens' library too?*

Yet she'd seemed genuinely shocked when the Dean had accused her of the theft. Was that a lie too? And if she had taken the book, had she actually found anything in it?

"What's in this book?" he asked.

The Warden faced him. For an instant he seemed to see clouds building inside her featureless eyes, cold white plumes of vapour boiling in the places where her pupils should have been.

"Prophecies, spells, incantations, rituals," said Susan Arnott, with a dismissive wave of her hand. "It is said the contents were gathered by the six acolytes of Morvan after his death. They feared, with their master gone, that their Clann would be disbanded, its members exiled or worse, and so made several copies of the teachings."

"Have you read it?" asked Lucy.

"Parts of it," said the Hearing Warden. "It bears some relation to what the faithful would call a *grimoire*, inviting the reader to commune with the spirits of darkness." She closed her eyes. "All nonsense, of course, but there are always those ready to believe it is real. Ideas are powerful things, regardless of how true they may be."

"I don't get it," said Finn. "You seem to be saying the sixth sense is just a load of rubbish."

Arnott was silent for what felt like a very long time. Finn couldn't tell if she was considering his question, or simply lost in her thoughts.

"True or false, the sixth sense caused Zoe's poor sister to take her life. It cannot be allowed to prevail. That is why the Wardens work tirelessly to keep even the idea of it at bay. I thank you for bringing all this to my attention. I promise that I will speak to my colleagues about everything that has happened."

Arnott rose to her feet, the black and white stripes of her dress cascading around her like an optical illusion.

Lucy started pulling Finn towards the door.

"I suppose we'll be going then," she said.

"What about Zoe?" said Finn. He hung back, frustrated by her eagerness to leave. Surely there was more to say here?

Susan Arnott smiled. "Don't worry. I can assure you that Zoe Redmayne is perfectly safe."

CHAPTER EIGHTEEN

As soon as they left Susan Arnott's study, Lucy made for the nearest timetable monitor.

"According to this we've got a free period," she said, tapping the screen. "That lockdown thing really messed up the timetable. Race you to the canteen!"

She hurried away down the corridor. Finn followed, finally catching her up at a four-way interchange. A hanging mobile made of driftwood turned lazily above the crossroads.

"Why were you were in such a hurry to leave?" he said, tugging her arm. "There's still a thousand questions that need answering."

Lucy glanced first up at the mobile, then down the

diverging corridors. Finally she smiled. "Arnott cleared everything up, don't you think?"

With that, she started walking again. Finn stomped after her. "How do you know she's not in on it?"

"Now you're really being paranoid."

"Am I?" By now he'd caught her up again. He tried to stop her but she showed no sign of slowing. "When the Dean had me in his office, he wasn't just asking me questions. He was trying to find out what I know. He's hiding something."

"Arnott said she'd look into it," said Lucy, turning the next corner. "I think we should let it go."

When they reached the canteen entrance, Finn leapt in front of Lucy and barred her way. "What's wrong with you?" he said. "I thought we were in this together."

Lucy placed a finger to her lips and glared at him intently.

Bemused, Finn followed her through the doors. At the counter, he poured himself a hot chocolate from the machine while Lucy picked up a tall glass filled with pale grey liquid that he guessed was some sort of protein shake. They carried their drinks to a quiet corner of the canteen and sat down. Lunch wasn't for another hour so the room was almost empty. The conveyor belts hung motionless. Faint clattering sounds came from the kitchens above.

"Right," said Lucy in a low voice. "I think we're far enough away now."

"Far enough from what?" Finn had to resist the urge to shout.

"Susan Arnott. You know how good her ears are. She could probably hear you jabbering halfway across the school."

Finn felt himself deflate like a balloon. How could he have been so dumb? "Do you think she heard everything I said on the way here?"

Lucy nudged him. "Don't beat yourself up. I was just being careful. Hopefully she thinks she's thrown one of us off the scent."

"There's a scent?" said Finn, surprised that it was possible to feel stupid and relieved at the same time.

"Not a literal one. Look, I don't know if she was actually lying to us," said Lucy slowly. "But I don't think she was telling us the whole truth."

They sipped their drinks and Lucy pulled a face.

"Now who isn't telling the whole truth? Seriously – is it really worth keeping up the pretence? I mean, if you owned up that you've still got your powers you could get off the prison rations." Finn was exasperated.

"I prefer to do it this way," was Lucy's reply. "My point is, the best liars mix lies in with the truth. For the most part, Arnott *was* telling the truth, but there were a couple of moments when she felt … funny."

"*Funny?*"

Lucy nodded. "It was when she said that Kylie took her own life."

Finn swallowed. He'd suspected it all along, but hearing it from Lucy made his skin prickle. He looked around at the empty canteen. This was just a school. Kids didn't get murdered at school, did they? He felt very small, and completely powerless, just like in his nightmare, submerged under water. They'd taken their suspicions to the top, but they'd got nowhere. There were no other avenues to follow.

Except one …

"Your dad's away now, right? Do you still think you can get hold of that gizmo?"

"The one that'll liquify your brains?" Lucy stirred the straw around her glass.

"This all started when I heard that song. It's the one piece of the puzzle that makes no sense at all."

"The *only* one?" said Lucy.

Finn thought about his dreams, or visions, or whatever they were. The girl's voice calling him to help. He couldn't just ignore it - not when Zoe was under the Dean's control. He drained his hot chocolate and thumped his mug down on the table. "You said before that I should I trust my senses, and I know what I heard. Let's go to your dad's now."

"Your funeral," said Lucy.

A nearby monitor blinked yellow and a message began scrolling across the screen:

ALL STUDENTS WILL REPORT TO SECTOR G IMMEDIATELY.

Finn frowned. "I thought it was a free period," he said.

Around them, the handful of students scattered throughout the canteen were looking at the screens in obvious puzzlement.

"They're always updating the timetable," said Lucy, getting to her feet. "I didn't realise Sector G was ready for operation, though."

Finn shoved his empty mug across the table and wished he'd thought of going to Dr Raj's laboratory straight from Arnott's study. "And Sector G is ...?"

"Something new," Lucy said. "That's all I know. The Wardens have been working on it for months. They'd have finished it sooner, only Dr Forrester held things up."

"Why?"

Lucy shrugged. "She thought it was unethical or something."

Three girls bustled past on their way to the exit.

"Everyone knows it's Beaky who's behind Sector G," the tallest girl said.

"Yeah," said one of her companions. "Blake's a real sadist!"

Sector G felt like one mystery too many to Finn. "Is that all you're going to tell me?" he said.

"It's all I know," Lucy replied.

"Well, let's get it over with," said Finn. "The sooner we get into Sector G and out again, the sooner we can get back to business."

"Copy that, Commander," said Lucy, standing with a brisk salute. "Come on. We don't want to be the last ones there."

"Aren't you going to finish your drink?"

Lucy picked up her glass, poured the thick grey liquid into a nearby spiky pot plant and said, "You've got to be kidding."

***

Sector G was a black, bubble-like structure standing beside one of the arms of the Alyxa building, and connected to it by a glass tunnel. Instead of a roof, it had a transparent dome looking up into the sky. As he followed Lucy into the hangar-sized space, Finn tilted back his head to watch a flock of cormorants soar past.

In the middle of the room stood a squat black cylinder, maybe twenty metres across. It could have been an alien spacecraft from a sci-fi movie set.

Finn and Lucy circled the cylinder along with a growing crowd of curious students, all of whom were chattering excitedly. Finn counted five silver doors punctuating the cylinder's curved wall. Beside each door was a silver keypad and an illuminated panel. All five panels were glowing red.

John was loitering with his Touch Clann friends, but there must have been well over a hundred students.

"I think everyone's here," said Lucy.

Everyone except Zoe, thought Finn. He wondered what was behind those five silver doors.

A whistle blew and everyone fell silent. Beaky made her way through the crowd and climbed a short flight of stairs to a narrow platform jutting from the side of the cylinder. The bag she carried matched the tweed of her trouser suit. A single giant geranium clung to her jacket's lapel. A microphone awaited her on a spindly metal stand.

"The human mind!" said Beaky. The microphone amplified her shrill voice so that it filled the cavernous hangar of Sector G. She pulled a grey plastic brain from the bag and held it up into a shaft of sunlight. "It's a remarkable thing. No living creature on Earth has a brain this big, compared to the size of its body."

"You should ask to borrow that," Lucy whispered in Finn's ear. "You might need it after you've worn my dad's helmet."

"Very funny," said Finn. He looked again at the circular hall's central cylinder. This whole place looked pretty high tech – was Sector G one of Dr Raj's inventions too?

"The human brain has allowed *Homo sapiens* to achieve many things," Beaky went on. "We create great art. We develop extraordinary medical care to look after our bodies. Thanks to our brains, we have colonised the planet. The human brain is a gift." She paused. "But it is also a curse, because we are all of us slaves to our brains."

Finn craned his neck, looking for Zoe. What was the Dean doing to her?

"We are slaves to our brains because everything we know about the universe comes to us through our senses," Beaky went on. "Here at Alyxa, you are all learning to take your sensory abilities to the next level. But sometimes it's important to do the opposite. Sometimes you need to abandon your senses completely. That is why you are here: to learn silence. To learn blindness and numbness. How not to taste, how not to smell. In short, you are here to learn how to throw off the shackles of your senses."

"I thought we were supposed to use our senses," said a boy's voice. It was the young kid called Rufus.

"Switching off your senses is only the first step," said Beaky. "When you have learnt that, you will learn to switch your senses on again one at a time. Sector G is about focus. The lessons you learn here will teach you to cut through the confusion and concentrate only on the one sense that matters to you at the time."

"This is cool!" said Lucy.

"I don't get it," said Finn. "Senses aren't like light bulbs. You can't just turn them on and off."

Beaky tapped the curved black wall of the cylinder. "This is the Gauntlet," she said. "It's designed to disturb the senses of anyone who enters."

"I changed my mind," said Lucy. "It doesn't sound cool at all."

"The nature of the disturbance varies," Beaky continued. "The Gauntlet may project visual or audio interference. It may emit toxins to overwhelm the olfactory system. The air regulators can change the temperature from Arctic cold to the burning heat of Death Valley. Only by switching off your senses will you be able to complete the task I'm going to set you."

A few nervous giggles bounced off the bubble-like dome. "First I need you to gather into groups of five – the same teams you were in for the Hunt."

Now it was Finn's turn to put up his hand.

"We've only got four in our team," he said. "Zoe Redmayne has been ... uh, she isn't here."

Beaky folded a large tissue around her nose and blew hard. "Then you'll have to participate as a foursome," she said. She clapped her hands. "Hurry up, now. Assemble your groups."

As the students started to move, Xander pushed towards the platform. Finn watched him with sinking spirits.

"I don't want to go with the Numbskulls again," Xander said to Warden Blake.

"That's fine," Lucy called. "We don't want to go with you."

"Anyway, there's no point in them going in there," Xander went on. "They haven't got any powers."

Beaky looked down her nose at him. "The Gauntlet algorithm is designed to compensate for all abilities," she said. "Now join your team."

"But they'll get shredded and we'll lose," said Xander.

"This is not a competition," Beaky replied. Raising her voice to address the whole assembly, she added, "And nobody will get 'shredded', whatever that means. The Gauntlet is designed to disturb but not to harm."

Xander opened his mouth to argue but Ben swept

in and ushered him over to where Finn and Lucy were waiting.

"All together again," Ben said cheerfully. "Are we ready for this, team?"

Beaky clapped her hands again.

"In a moment, the first team will enter the Gauntlet," she said. "Once they are inside, a panel above each door will flash a sequence of five numbers, one every five seconds. Each student will memorise his or her numbers. After twenty-five seconds, the doors will open again."

"Is that it?" said Chen. "Just a memory test?"

Beaky gave him a baleful glare. "It may sound simple, but the Gauntlet's sense-disruptors will be functional the whole time you're in there."

Sandy put her hand up. "Does everybody feel the same ... stuff?" she asked nervously.

Beaky shook her head. "The Gauntlet's ID scanners will detect each student's dominant sense, calibrated to their skill level according to the details on Dr Forrester's database. For example, if you're Level Four in Sight Clann, you might see a kaleidoscope of brilliantly flashing lights. If you're Level One Touch, you might feel a gentle electric current." A ripple of unease passed through the crowd. "Now, first team, take your positions, please. One student outside each door. Touch your hands to the panels so that the Gauntlet will recognise you."

Jermaine moved first, directing his squad to fan out around the cylindrical chamber. Finn lifted himself on tiptoe to get a better view.

One by one, the students touched the red panels. After a second the panels turned green and the doors swished open. A tall boy moved in front of Finn, blocking his view. Finn craned his neck, trying to see what was inside the cylinder, but already the doors were closing again. All he got was a glimpse of bright white walls dotted with tiny points of black.

Utter silence followed. The students surrounding the cylinder shuffled their feet. What was going on in there? Up on her platform, Beaky's face creased into a cold smile.

Less than half a minute later the doors slid open again. The five students emerged and made their way round to the front, where Beaky was waiting on her balcony. One girl had her hands clamped to her ears; another was pale and drenched with sweat.

Jermaine looked surprisingly cheerful. "That was awesome!" he said. A puzzled look crossed his face, his eyes rolled back and he slumped to the ground. One of his teammates wobbled past, tripped over Jermaine's legs and went sprawling.

"I think I'm going to be sick," the boy said. Then

he was.

"Gross!" cried someone from the crowd.

The fifth student was Sandy. She just stood by her door batting her hands weakly in front of her face. "Make them go away," she said quietly. "I don't like them."

Beaky opened a hatch in the wall to reveal a bank of buttons and flashing lights. She fiddled with them for a moment then closed the hatch again.

"It's possible the calibration is a little high," she said.

The boy who'd thrown up looked up at her in disbelief. He opened his mouth as if to say something, then vomited again. Beside him, Jermaine was clambering groggily to his feet, his nose wrinkled in disgust.

"Everyone, tap your number sequence into the keypad beside your door," said Beaky. "Then tap the *Enter* key to submit your answer."

Three of the students obeyed. After each of them had entered their string of numbers, their panel flashed up the words: *INCORRECT SEQUENCE*. Jermaine and the girl with her hands over her ears just stood in front of their keypads and looked bemused.

"I definitely saw some numbers," said Jermaine. "Just don't ask me what they were."

Finn couldn't decide whether to laugh or be afraid.

It had been sort of funny seeing the first batch of students rolling around, but he knew that sooner or later he'd be the one going through the door.

The second group came out even worse than the first. Oddest of all was Chen, who left the Gauntlet at a dead sprint and didn't stop until he slammed straight into the far wall of the Sector G hangar. Rubbing his head, looking as if he had no idea where he was, he staggered slowly back to enter his numbers along with the rest of his team. Once again, nobody got it right.

Beaky looked as if she was loving the whole spectacle. "Meditation will help," the Smell Warden said. "Use what you've learnt. Prepare yourself in advance."

Ben slapped Finn on the back. "Come on," he said. "We're next."

"Here we go - like lambs to the slaughter," said Lucy as she set off. Xander trudged after her.

Finn chose the door immediately below Beaky's platform. Pressing his hand against the glowing red panel, he tried to slow his breathing. But the more he got a grip on his lungs, the more his heart thumped out of control.

The panel turned green, the door opened and Finn entered the Gauntlet.

Everything was brilliant white inside. Black dots covered curved walls and a flat floor and ceiling. It was like standing inside a map of the galaxy, only with all the colours in reverse.

The door closed with a hiss.

Finn wondered what happened next. Then he remembered what he was supposed to do. He turned just in time to see the number *5* disappear from a panel above the closed door.

As he waited for the next number to appear he imagined the vast power of the Gauntlet building around him. He almost expected the whole place to start spinning like some giant food mixer.

The number *3* appeared on the panel.

Finn waited. Any second now, something would hit him.

The panel flashed up the number *1* ...

Any second now!

... *8 ... 6 ... 5 ...*

The door slid open.

Finn stepped out of the Gauntlet feeling exactly as he had when he'd gone in. *That wasn't so bad*, he thought in surprise.

Ben appeared from around the cylinder's curve and tottered towards him with his arms clasped to his chest. His dark skin had acquired a distinctly greenish tinge. Lucy arrived looking even worse. Her hair stood up in a wild tangle and her face was a mask of horror. She stuck out her tongue and spat, then spat again.

"It was like eating rotten eggs!" she moaned. "Someone get me a plate of mush, please."

Xander couldn't walk. Much as it amused Finn to see his arch-enemy crawling on his hands and knees, he couldn't help wondering what nightmare Xander had endured in there.

"Don't tell me," said Lucy. She draped her arms over Finn's shoulders. "You feel totally fine."

"Actually, I do," said Finn, supporting her and hoping she wasn't going to throw up on him. "No powers, no disturbances."

"Enter your numbers," said Beaky.

Lucy returned to her door and Finn started punching the sequence into his keypad.

5 ... 3 ... 1 ... 8 ... 6 ...

He frowned.

... 5.

The light in the panel went out completely. After a pause, a message flashed red:

INCORRECT SEQUENCE.

Several of the onlooking students started mumbling things to each other. Beaky tinkered again with the controls, then called down to Finn.

"You entered too many numbers," she said. "Try again."

"I just put in what I saw," Finn answered. "There were definitely six numbers. The Gauntlet's new, isn't it? Maybe it's not set up properly."

"You must have been mistaken," said Beaky, glaring at him. "Of all the faults I despise in a student, over-confidence is the worst."

"But I ..."

"Thank you, Mr Williams," the Smell Warden said. "Next group, step up!"

Finn wanted to tell Beaky that she should try going in there herself. He couldn't stop running through the numbers in his head. He hadn't made a mistake. He was sure of it.

He stepped away from the panel, aware of the suspicious glances he was getting from some people in the crowd. But there was no time to dwell on it. It was John's turn to go inside.

"Are you going to be all right with this?" Finn asked his brother. "Maybe you don't have to go in."

"I'll be fine," John replied.

Finn wanted to remind his brother that they'd only been at Alyxa a few days, but he bit his tongue.

"Just be careful in there," said Finn, touching his brother's sleeve as John sauntered towards his door.

"No sweat, Finn," John replied with a sunny smile.

The next twenty-five seconds felt like the longest

of Finn's life. Sweat prickled in his armpits. He could almost hear the time ticking by.

What's going on in there? he wondered. *What's happening to my brother?*

Maybe it was best not to imagine.

The doors swished open. Adriana limped out with her eyes pinched shut. Seconds later, three more members of the team emerged, all looking equally distressed.

Finn waited. And waited. Still no sign of John.

Unable to restrain himself any longer, Finn barged forward through the crowd. He was halfway to the Gauntlet when John staggered out. Finn stopped dead, his heart thumping, as his brother put out his hand to support himself on the door.

Then John straightened up and flicked back his long hair to reveal the enormous grin on his face. He flexed his biceps first to the left, then to the right, before ending his little routine with a spin and a bow.

"The Gauntlet is *wild!*" he announced, and most of the watching crowd broke into laughter.

Finn waved to his brother, relieved. When John spotted his younger brother, he winked and jabbed a number sequence into his keypad. The panel lit up green with the words:

CORRECT RESPONSE.

The laughter turned to applause.

"Congratulations, Williams Senior," said Beaky. "I wonder if anyone else will match your performance."

Finn joined in with the cheering. What else was there to do? Maybe John was right. Maybe his sessions with the Touch Warden really had helped him turn the corner.

Maybe there were good things going on at Alyxa after all.

***

Finn kept John in his sight while the rest of the students went through the Gauntlet. Some of the later entrants tried meditating before entering, which seemed to help. In total, seven students including John succeeded in passing the test. It wasn't only those with highly-rated senses though – a couple of one-stripers managed to enter the correct numbers.

After the session was over, Finn led his brother to a quiet spot behind the curved wall of the Gauntlet's central cylinder. After his uncomfortable encounter with Susan Arnott, he needed to talk to someone he could trust.

"What was it like in there?" he said.

John's eyes seemed to blur a little. "It was like ...

like all my bones were aching," he said. "It felt like they were about to break. Then I remembered what Gustavsson taught me."

"Which was what?"

"That you don't feel pain in your body – you feel it in your head." John's eyes focused on Finn's again. "It's all just neurons firing. The trick is to turn them off. So that's what I did – well, I did it enough so that I could remember the numbers." He grinned. "First time I ever beat you at maths, right?"

Finn could have argued that the Gauntlet was more about memory than maths, but that was hardly the point. Anyway, happy though he was about his brother's success, this wasn't really what he wanted to talk about.

"It's amazing," he said, meaning it. "Really, you've just done so well. I mean, Beaky was pleased with you today and she doesn't seem to like anyone. And Gustavsson's obviously on your side."

John swept his hand through his hair. "They're okay, as teachers go," he said.

Here goes. "So if you said something to them, they'd listen to you?" said Finn.

"I guess." John's brow furrowed. "What's up? Are you okay?"

Finn pulled his brother closer to the wall. "Not really," he said. "There's something weird going on here.

The Dean's taken Zoe away. I think it's got something to do with Kylie's disappearance."

"Wait a second," said John, frowning. "I know Zoe's your friend, and she seems like a nice girl, but she's kind of a mess, don't you think? It's not surprising, after what her sister did."

"But you don't know what the Dean's like."

"He's strict, I know, but he's just doing his job," said John. "If he's got Zoe he'll just be, you know, making sure she doesn't do anything stupid."

"Who's stupid?" Adriana appeared with her leather jacket slung over her shoulder.

"No one," snapped Finn. "Me. For putting in the wrong numbers."

John frowned but didn't contradict him.

"Yeah, about that," said Adriana. "You should probably stop doing weird stuff. First all that talk about the sixth sense, then picking a fight with Xander. You know what they're calling you, don't you?"

Finn could imagine only too well. "What are they calling me?"

"Ady – don't go there," said John.

"A freak," said Adriana, ignoring him. "I'm sorry, but trust me, when someone calls you that at Alyxa, it's not good."

"Like I need advice from you," said Finn.

"Chill. She's only trying to help," said John.

"Is she?" said Finn. "Because I just want to talk to my brother for a minute without her listening in."

John's face tightened. "That's uncalled for," he said coldly. "You need to apologise, Finn."

Finn scoffed. "Whose side are you on?"

John looked hurt. "No one's," he said. "I'm looking out for you."

"Oh, please! It's your fault I'm stuck here."

John took a step backwards. Adriana's mouth was a silent O.

"Whoa," John said. "Where's all this coming from?"

"From me!" said Finn. "Little old me, who would like his life back."

He pushed past them both, knocking the jacket from Adriana's shoulder. Finn's feet caught in it and he nearly fell.

"Nice trick," he said. "Try to trip up the freak."

He snatched up the jacket, only to feel the sharp point of Adriana's prefect's badge jab into his finger. As he pulled it free, he noticed a line of clumsy stitches running through the leather lapel, right beneath the badge.

He jammed his bleeding finger into his mouth and thrust the jacket back at Adriana.

"Leave her alone," said John, putting his arm round Adriana and marching her away. "Come back when you've stopped behaving like a six-year-old."

Finn was still fuming when he got back to Nurture Group. But his anger dissipated as soon as he entered the common room, because there was Zoe sitting in one of the chairs. Her freckled face was pale and her hands were limply holding her goggles in her lap. Lucy sat beside her.

"What happened?" he said, kneeling beside the chair. "Are you okay?"

"I have to go," Zoe replied in a monotone.

"Go where?"

"Away from Alyxa," said Zoe. "He said it's for the safety of the other students."

"The Dean expelled her," said Lucy.

"He can't do that!" said Finn.

"He can," said Zoe, wiping away her tears. "I'm glad he has. My dad never wanted me to come to Alyxa in the first place. Last time I saw him he said he'd kept my room just the same as it was before I left. Now I know I'm going back, I can't wait to get in my own bed again."

That made Finn think about his own bed, and his own room, and for a moment all he wanted to do was go home himself. Then he remembered the reason Zoe had been expelled.

"Zoe – *did* you steal the *Book of Morvan*?"

Her wide pupils locked on to his eyes. "Of course I

didn't," she said.

"That's what I thought. Which means you don't have to go."

Zoe groaned. "But I told you, I'm ready to go. I just want to ..."

"I know what you want. Your old life, your real home. I get it. I really do. But don't you see what's happened here?"

Slowly, Zoe shook her head. Lucy hugged her tighter and stared at Finn, waiting for him to speak.

"Someone planted the book in your room," Finn said.

"The Dean?" said Lucy.

"Probably. The fact he set you up means he's scared. Scared that you'll find out something about Kylie. That *we'll* find something out. It might even mean we've got him on the run."

"But nothing is going to bring Kylie back," said Zoe. She stood up. "You've both been amazing, but it's time to stop."

Finn watched helplessly as she took herself off into her room.

CHAPTER NINETEEN

He couldn't sleep – the shaft of moonlight beaming in through the window was too bright. He turned on to his side, his mind jangling. His room was filled with unanswered questions, like the puzzle of what had really happened to Zoe's sister.

The more he thought about it, the more certain he was that the Dean was hiding something about the night Kylie died. Had the Dean actually killed her? Finn didn't want to believe that. If it was true, then he'd spent far too much time in the past few days alone in the presence of a murderer. But how to be sure?

The song. It was the only real evidence Finn had, from his own senses, that something strange was going on at Alyxa.

Finn tossed back his covers and sat up. The night air was cold on the back of his neck. He grabbed the dressing gown, crept out into the dark common room and knocked gently on Lucy's door.

The door opened immediately to reveal Lucy standing wide awake and fully dressed.

"I was just coming to get you," she said. She opened the door wider to reveal her bed. On the duvet rested Dr Raj's sense-enhancement helmet. Coloured wires crisscrossed its gold-foiled surface. At the front, a cluster of tiny mirrors caught the light like an insect's eye. Finn drew in a sharp breath.

"You're sure about this?" she said.

"No," said Finn. He entered, and picked up the helmet, which was lighter than it looked. Gingerly, he placed it over his head while looking in her mirror. It was cushioned and surprisingly comfortable.

Lucy fiddled with the wires, adjusted the neck strap, then peered at a small button on the side.

"Do you know what you're doing?" said Finn.

"Most of the time," said Lucy. "Now, not so much."

"Wow, way to be comforting."

She pushed the button. The cluster of mirrors on the front of the helmet trembled and tinkling sounds filled the room. Some of the tangled wires began to glow, creating a spider's web of reflections in the helmet's shiny gold surface.

"Does it run on batteries?" said Finn, eyeing his reflection apprehensively.

"I have no idea what it runs on," said Lucy. "I'm not even sure I know how to turn it off. There's a remote control, here."

She made Finn sit on the bed and pressed a small square box into his hand. A couple of seconds later, the tinkling noise stopped.

"What next?" he said. He turned his neck experimentally. He looked ridiculous.

"Turn the dial," said Lucy, "and see what happens."

Finn looked at the remote control. The little box had two buttons and a dial marked with numbers from one to a hundred.

"I'm going to try it at ten to start with," he said, not liking the way his voice was trembling.

He turned the dial.

The room grew immediately bright. Rainbows of vivid colour chased through the grey-painted walls. The smell of soap from Lucy's sink grew suddenly overwhelming. The night wind battered her window, ridiculously strong. He could hear the breath scraping in and out of Lucy's lungs. He could also hear someone breathing in the next room: Zoe, fast asleep.

He could taste his own fear, a sharp metallic tang.

Dizziness crashed over him. He dropped the remote and raised his hands. His arm muscles snapped like electricity. He could feel every single hair standing proud of his skin. He yanked off the helmet and let it fall on the bed. His breath flew in and out of his lungs in short, sharp gusts. His exhilaration was matched only by his exhaustion. When he tried to stand, he nearly fell. Lucy grabbed him and eased him down on to the bed again.

"Are you okay?" she said. "What did you feel?"

"Everything," said Finn. The dizziness was passing. "I wonder what it's like when you turn it up to a hundred."

"Well, you're not going to find out," said Lucy. She snatched the helmet away from him, her eyes wide with alarm. "Look at you. You're shaking! I'm taking this thing right back to ..."

"No," said Finn. "I don't think it's dangerous. I just think this is the wrong place to use it."

Lucy looked around her room. "Where do you want to use it?" Then sarcasm crept into her voice: "I know, let's wake up the Dean. Maybe he'd lend us his office."

"Don't be dense." Finn thought for a moment. "The whole point of this is to cut out distractions, right?"

"I suppose so."

"It's just that it's hard to do that when I'm sitting on a lumpy bed knowing you're watching me."

"Who says my bed's lumpy?"

Finn took back the helmet and turned it over and over.

"I need to be somewhere, I don't know ... neutral," he said.

"You mean like a sensory deprivation tank?" said Lucy.

"I guess," said Finn. "Do we have one of those here?"

"No," said Lucy. "But we've got the next best thing."

***

While Lucy ran the bath, Finn found a plastic bag and wrapped it around the helmet. When the bath was full she turned off the taps, dipped her hand in the water and swished it around.

"Not too hot, not too cold," she said. "You're good to go."

"I need *you* to go first," said Finn. When she didn't move, he added, "I need to get undressed."

"I'm not leaving you alone with that thing on your head," said Lucy. "Keep your boxers on."

Blushing furiously, Finn stripped down to his boxer

shorts and lifted up the helmet. Then he stopped. Did he really want to go through it all again?

"You don't have to do this," said Lucy.

"Yes," he replied. "I do."

Finn put on the helmet and stepped carefully into the bath. As they'd agreed, Lucy rolled up a flannel and pressed it over his eyes. The warm water seemed to cling to Finn's skin. The faint sloshing sounds it made sounded like somebody chuckling, far away.

"Are you ready?" said Lucy.

"Give me a minute," said Finn.

He waited for his body to relax. He breathed in, he breathed out. For a while nothing changed, then gradually his heartbeat slowed, and his mind began to float. Soon he was hardly aware of his arms and legs bobbing in the water. He was a wave, free to wash wherever the current chose to take him.

"Okay," he said. "I'm ready. Dial it up to twenty."

"*Twenty?*" Finn thought she was going to argue, but she said no more. There was a pause, then the faintest of clicks.

Immediately the pressure of the helmet on his head went away. But he could still feel the bathwater rippling against his limbs, the weight of the flannel over his eyes. He felt poised, like a parachutist ready to jump. But he hadn't jumped yet.

"Keep going," he said through dry lips. Lucy drew in her breath with a hiss.

Finn heard another soft click and then his whole body was suddenly weightless. Everything around him drained away. Now there was just him, Finn Williams, floating in emptiness. Even his breath was gone. There was just ... nothing.

Something chimed in the void. Music. No, someone singing. A girl. Her voice rose and fell, rose and fell, just a simple, lilting pattern of repeating notes. He knew it at once.

Kylie's song.

Finn swam along with the song until it reached an end, as softly as driftwood washing up against the sand. And as the music stopped, he heard words. Speech. The voice of the girl.

Help me, she said. Her words were clear but very faint. Distant. Deep. *Find me, please.*

Finn wanted to ask her where she was, but he had no mouth, no lungs, no breath. All the same, Kylie seemed to know that he'd spoken.

Please, hurry. I don't like it here. Come and find me. Please! I'm scared!

Where are you?

Underneath. Come, quickly. Please. Under the ...

The urge to respond to her was overwhelming, but

the instant Finn found a way to open his mouth water flooded his throat and he began to choke. He tried to sit up but his arms and legs wouldn't move. The weight of the helmet was dragging him down and the water was sucking him under. His head was full of needles.

A pair of hands grabbed him under the armpits. Another pair seized his ankles. Warm water turned to cool air and for an instant he was flying. Then cold tiles slammed against his back and he was flopping on the bathroom floor, coughing out water, flailing like a stranded fish. The helmet flew off his head and the blindfold unravelled.

Finn blinked and saw Zoe staring down at him. Her goggles were nowhere in sight and her eyes were wide and shocked. Behind her, Lucy looked ready to cry.

"What were you trying to do?" said Zoe. "It sounded like someone was strangling you."

"I thought you were going to drown," said Lucy, her voice distraught.

Another bout of coughing sent pain shooting through Finn's skull. He looked wildly around, convinced that the ghost of the girl had followed him in here. But there was just him, and Lucy, and Zoe. He managed to lever himself into a sitting position. He was relieved to see he was still wearing his boxer shorts.

"Take your time," said Lucy.

"I'm okay," he said, wiping his mouth with the back of his hand.

He let Zoe pull him to his feet. "You're so stupid!" she said. When she tried to yank her hand away, he kept hold of it. His teeth were chattering.

"I heard her."

Zoe's mouth closed with a snap. Her lip began to tremble. "Kylie? Singing?"

Finn nodded. "More than that. She spoke to me."

"W-what did she say?"

Finn grabbed a towel and hugged it around his dripping body. Zoe had already been on a rollercoaster ride of belief and doubt about her sister's fate. Did he really want to send her on another plunge into who knew what?

But he knew what he'd heard.

"She needs our help," he said firmly. "And I think I know where she is."

***

The long stone corridor leading to the assembly hall was deserted. The main lights were off, leaving just a dotted line of blue emergency LEDs running along the bottom of each wall.

They'd all changed into their regular grey jumpsuits.

Finn did his best to keep up with the girls, but his legs felt as if they might buckle any minute. At least the headache had mostly gone.

Zoe was first to reach the door to the hall. There she stopped and furiously beckoned to the others.

"Hurry up!" she said. The goggles were back on her face. The reflections of the LEDs made the lenses look like pools filled with stars.

"We're coming," said Lucy. "Finn - are you okay?"

Summoning his energy, Finn trotted the last few metres to the doorway.

"Feeling more human with every step," he said.

Together they peered into the darkened hall. The Clann banners hung limp. The rows of seats were empty in the grey light.

"You're sure this is it?" said Zoe.

"*Under the main hall*," said Finn. "That was the last thing Kylie said. I almost missed it because that's when I started choking."

"I've been in the main hall hundreds of times," said Lucy. "I never knew there was a basement."

Finn stepped over the threshold on to the hall's solid stone floor. "Follow me," he said.

Once inside the hall they spread out. While Zoe and Lucy explored the seating areas, Finn circled the central stage.

"Anything?" called Lucy in a loud whisper.

"Nothing," said Zoe. "Keep looking."

Finn ran his hand over the stage's curved edge. The stone was smooth and cold.

He hopped up on to the stage and made his way past the chairs to the raised platform that Professor Panjaran always used when addressing the students. The platform was wooden, and looked very old. When Finn touched the wooden planks he felt them vibrating.

He knelt and ran his fingers around the base of the platform. The wood was slightly discoloured.

"Up here," he called.

When the girls had joined him, they split up and worked their way methodically around the platform.

"This whole thing is damp," said Zoe. "Why do you think that is?"

"Here," said Lucy. "I've found something."

Finn and Zoe circled back to find Lucy crouched in front of a square hatch no bigger than a paperback book.

"You'd have to be a leprechaun to fit through there," she said. "Any ideas, anyone?"

Finn ran his fingers round the edge of the hatch, but the crack was too narrow to get a grip. He tried pushing the wooden panel down. There was a click and the hatch popped open on silent hinges, revealing a magnetic catch and a shallow interior space. In the middle of the backboard was a brass lever pointing up at the ceiling.

"Here goes," said Finn.

He gripped the lever and pulled it.

Something squealed and the entire platform began to rotate. The low surrounding wall retracted out of sight and Finn watched in amazement as the decking on top started collapsing in on itself. One by one, the individual planks sank down into the stone stage, each one dropping lower than the next, until a spiral staircase had appeared miraculously before their eyes.

Finn cautiously approached the edge of the circular shaft that had opened up in the stage. The newly-formed staircase curled downward into dark shadows.

"Ben told me there were caves under Alyxa," said Finn. He stared down into the abyss. The blackness looked thick and impenetrable. "Are you sure you want to do this?"

"Duh," said Zoe. "Kylie's down there."

Please let that be true, thought Finn. If he'd got Zoe's hopes up for nothing, he'd never forgive himself.

"Like I'd let you two have all the fun," said Lucy.

Finn went first. The staircase had no handrails, but the curved wall of the shaft was cluttered with a complex system of ropes and cogs, which gave them plenty to hang on to. When the wooden stairs ran out, a set of rough stone steps took over. At the junction between the two stood a wooden podium. On top of it was a lever identical to the one at the top.

Finn gazed up into the silvery moonlight filtering down from the hall.

"We don't want anybody following us down," he said, and pulled the lever.

The ropes jerked and the cogs turned. One by one the wooden steps spiralled back up to their starting points. Little by little the moonlight disappeared. When the final plank thudded into place, the shaft turned as black as pitch.

"Let me go first," said Zoe. "I can see a little."

She took Finn's hand and put it on her shoulder. He put Lucy's on his. Together they made their way cautiously down the stone steps and headed deeper into the darkness that lay beneath Alyxa. *Who knows about this place? The Wardens? The Dean?*

Finn counted twenty-six steps before Zoe said, "It levels out here."

Sure enough, the steps gave way to a hard, sloping floor. The walls of the corridor seemed to close in on Finn and he lost count of the times he banged his shoulders on them.

"The passage splits," said Zoe. "There's the middle way, then there are two passages to the left and two to the right."

"Shush a minute," said Finn. "Let me listen."

Even though the darkness was total, he closed his eyes. Being underground felt a bit like being in a meditation chamber, after all. The dripping sound filled his ears, but sure enough there was something else too. A girl's voice.

Here. I'm here. This way.

"Far left," he said, stepping in front of Zoe. "Trust me."

"Wait," said Zoe. "Let me go first. You can't see."

"No," he replied. "But I can hear."

"Without the helmet?" said Lucy.

"Yes," said Finn.

As he walked, he let his hands trail along the walls of the narrow corridor. The stone was cracked and crumbling.

The corridor split into five again. Finn couldn't see it, but he knew it all the same. He took the middle way without hesitation.

"Wait!" Zoe called. "This place is a maze. If I can't see you we're going to lose you!"

But Finn couldn't slow down. His muscles felt strong again and his feet were eager to carry him on. His fingers blurred against the walls. The damp air of the underground labyrinth filled his lungs. The darkness sucked him forward.

Another junction ... *far right.*

Another ... *centre left.*

On and on, with Zoe and Lucy yelling after him and the sound of Kylie's voice growing louder and louder and louder in his ears.

I'm here! Kylie cried. *Help me!*

Another split. Finn chose the tunnel that was second from the right. Not only were Kylie's calls louder down there, but the stone walls were brighter.

"Can I see light?" came Lucy's voice from somewhere behind.

Finn was running now. Water glistened on the walls, shining green as they caught the light that lay ahead. He raced left around one corner, right around another, and slid to a halt just before he tumbled down a descending set of steep stone steps.

No sooner had he recovered his balance than Zoe and Lucy crashed into him.

"Leaving us behind?" said Lucy.

"Careful," said Finn, lowering his foot on to the first step. "It's slippery."

Water dripped from a vaulted ceiling on to the steps. They held on to each other all the way down to the bottom, where a low archway framed a dazzling green glow.

Finn stepped through the arch and into a chamber

that looked as if it had been clawed out of the rock by a troll. Huge gouges disfigured the walls. The floor was pitted and uneven. Great cracks ran across the ceiling.

You found me.

In the middle of the chamber stood an upright glass cylinder filled with glowing green liquid. Floating in the liquid was a girl with pale skin. An Alyxa jumpsuit clung to her body and her red hair billowed around her like a flame. Her eyes were closed.

Finn took a hesitant step forward, waiting for the girl's eyes to flick open, and for her fists to start hammering on the glass. But she didn't move. In fact, she looked as if she was fast asleep.

Or dead.

Zoe ripped off her goggles and fell to her knees.

CHAPTER TWENTY

"Is it her?" said Finn. Lucy nodded, but seemed unable to speak.

"Kylie!" said Zoe, hammering on the glass. Her goggles swung from her neck. "Kylie!"

Finn approached the vat slowly. He couldn't take his eyes off her. Here was the girl whose song he'd heard in his dreams. But who had kept her trapped down here? And why? The closer he got, the more he could see the likeness between the sisters – the same red hair, the same freckled cheeks. But where Zoe was filled with frantic energy, Kylie's body looked utterly lifeless.

"Can you still hear her voice?" said Lucy.

Finn tried to listen the way he'd listened in the

tunnel. He couldn't focus as well as he had before, but he was sure of one thing.

"No," he said. "She's gone."

Peering into the cylindrical container, he saw that Kylie was hanging from a kind of harness. Tubes and wires curled from the back of it and disappeared into an array of sockets near the top.

"What is this place?" said Lucy, looking around the cave. The faintly glowing liquid cast an eerie green glow across her upturned face. "And who did this to her?"

"We know who did it!" said Zoe. "What matters right now is getting her out."

Finn glanced back at the archway through which they'd entered. "Then let's get to it," he said. "We don't want the Dean to catch us down here."

"Take a look at this," called Lucy from behind the vat of liquid.

They circled the cylinder to find her bent over a rack of metal shelving. One shelf carried a line of metal boxes studded with blinking lights. The boxes were emitting a faint beeping sound.

The top shelf held a glowing screen. Zigzag lines danced across it at regular intervals. Along the bottom, a row of numbers flickered with constantly changing values.

"Is that a heartbeat?" said Zoe. She raised a

trembling finger to point at a bright green line bouncing its way across the screen. She pressed her other hand to her mouth.

"I think it's a touchscreen," said Lucy.

"I don't think we should touch anything," said Finn. "This thing might be keeping her alive. If we mess with it ..."

But Zoe was already reaching for an icon at the top of the screen. When she pressed it, an image of a number keypad appeared, just like the door locks scattered throughout Alyxa. Below it, a text label read: *ENTER SECURITY CODE*.

"Uh, I think we should back off," said Lucy.

"Lucy's right," said Finn. "If we do the wrong thing we could hurt her."

"Dr Forrester might know what to do," said Lucy. "Or maybe one of the Wardens."

Zoe's finger hovered over the keypad.

"I'm not leaving until we get her out!" she said.

Finn ran his fingers down the side of the vat. The glass was seamless, its smooth surface interrupted only by a round metal valve near the bottom.

"Look at the screen," Finn said suddenly. "Do what you did outside the Dean's office."

"What?" said Zoe.

"The screen should be cleaner over the keys that get

touched the most. You'll be able to see that."

Zoe's enormous pupils seemed to grow even wider for a moment.

After a moment she said, "One, three, five, six, eight."

"Five digits," said Lucy. "That figures. Go on, Finn, you're the mathematical genius. How many combinations are we going to have to try? Oh, and let's not forget that we probably only get three chances before the whole place blows up."

Finn calculated. "A five-digit code has a hundred and twenty possible combinations," he said.

Zoe's shoulders slumped. "We've got no chance."

Finn ran through the five numbers that Zoe had given them. There was something familiar about them. What was it?

Then it came to him.

"Different order," he said.

"What?" said Zoe.

"You said the numbers in ascending order," he said. "Lowest to highest. But that's not how it goes."

"Of course it isn't," said Lucy. "That would be too simple."

"That's not what I mean," said Finn. "I know those numbers."

He tapped out the sequence he'd seen inside the

Gauntlet.

5 ... 3 ... 1 ... 8 ... 6 ...

He paused, then said, "But it isn't a five-number sequence. It's six."

... 5.

The keypad vanished. A bewildering grid of icons popped up in its place. Finn counted at least fifty of the little pictures. Beneath each was a tiny strip of text.

"You did it!" said Zoe, grabbing Finn's arm. "What next?"

Finn scanned the icons. Some of the labels might as well have been in a foreign language:

INTERNAL RETICULATION

PLANCK DEFIBRILLATOR

METASYNAPSE

Others made at least partial sense:

DIAGNOSTICS

SYSTEM UPDATE

BUFFER SPEED

"I don't know." He ran his hand through his hair. "Where do we start?"

"What about this one?" said Zoe, pointing to an icon in the middle of the screen. Its label read:

EMERGENCY LIQUID DRAIN

"Do you really think that's a good idea?" said Lucy.

"We've come this far," said Zoe. "I'm not stopping

now!"

She stabbed her finger against the icon.

A red circle flashed up. Inside it were the words:

DRAIN IN PROGRESS

Something clunked inside the vat. They all spun around to look. Bubbles started streaming up through the liquid inside the vat. One of the pipes on the floor twitched, then the valve at the bottom of the vat sprang open and gloopy green fluid started flowing out.

"Look out!" Finn cried.

Together they clambered up a heap of fallen rocks until their backs were pressed against the wall of the chamber. Below them, the liquid continued to exit the vat. It oozed like syrup and smelt like honeysuckle. By the time it hit the floor it was no longer glowing.

Thick and glutinous as it was, the liquid flowed quickly along a rough-hewn channel in the floor. When it reached a crack in the opposite wall it vanished.

Inside the fast-emptying vat, Kylie's body sagged in its harness. Meanwhile the screen reverted to its original display. As Finn watched, the zigzag lines began flattening out. The heart rate, if it was that, began to drop. Green panels turned red. Warning lights began to flash.

"We've got to get her out of there!" he said, realising they'd just made a colossal mistake.

They scrambled back down the rocks and reached the vat as the last of the green liquid drained away. As Finn bent to the valve, the harness ripped and Kylie slumped down against the glass like a puppet whose strings had been cut.

"Smash it!" Zoe cried, battering uselessly against the side of the vat. "Help me!"

Finn stuffed his hand into the open valve, grabbed the inside edge and tugged. Nothing happened. He pulled again, throwing all his weight into it. The valve creaked and a tiny crack appeared in the glass above it.

"Stand back!" he said.

He grabbed one of the black control boxes. The wires jerked free, showering the floor with sparks. He didn't care. His muscles protested about the weight of the box, but he managed to raise it above his head and bring it crashing down on the valve.

The crack in the glass widened. The metal valve popped free and rolled away across the floor. Finn brought the box down again and felt a jolt through his shoulders as the wall of the vat shattered completely. Finn turned his face away from a shower of tiny transparent pebbles. Lucy screamed as they landed in her hair, but Finn brushed them off.

"It's okay," he said. "It's like the safety glass you get in cars. It breaks but the bits aren't sharp."

Zoe dragged her sister out of the broken vat. Kylie's eyes were closed and her lips were blue, but her jumpsuit was barely damp, which made Finn wonder exactly what the peculiar liquid was.

"Kylie!" Zoe cried. She sprawled on the floor with her sister half-draped over her lap. "I don't think she's breathing!" She threw a desperate glance at Finn.

"Does anyone know how to do CPR?" said Lucy. Her eyes were red.

"Turn her on her side," said Finn.

Zoe did so, and in a few seconds Kylie's chest heaved. Her mouth opened and her whole body convulsed. Then she coughed and out gushed a flood of green liquid.

Kylie coughed again, spat out more liquid, then started banging her arms and legs against the rocky floor. Zoe tried to hold her down but she broke free. Staggering to her feet Kylie took two stumbling steps before dropping to her hands and knees. Her bedraggled hair hung around her face.

Slowly, Kylie looked up at Finn. He took a step towards her, thinking she was going to speak to him, but she only frowned, and then her gaze moved on. When her eyes found her sister she gasped.

"Zoe!" she said in a kind of croaking gargle. "You've got to hide me!"

Zoe embraced her sister. Slowly Kylie's breathing

returned to normal. "Don't worry," said Zoe, combing her fingers gently through Kylie's hair. "We'll look after you."

"Just get me somewhere safe," Kylie whispered. "Hurry."

"Who are you hiding from?" said Finn. "Is it the Dean?"

When Kylie didn't answer, he turned to Lucy. "Where can we take her? It's got to be somewhere Kildair won't think to look."

"How about Susan Arnott's quarters?" said Lucy. "She listened to us before. Maybe she'd listen again."

Finn shook his head. "I still don't trust the Wardens." He thought for a moment. "What about your dad's?"

Lucy's eyes brightened. "That's not a bad idea. It's the last place the Dean would think of looking."

Zoe was helping her sister to her feet. "I like Dr Raj," said Kylie weakly as she tottered in Zoe's embrace.

"How do we get there?" said Finn.

"Back the way we came, obviously," said Zoe. "Kylie can hardly walk and it's the most direct route."

Finn shook his head. "Too risky. It means going back through the hall and down all the main corridors – we're bound to get caught. There's got to be another way out."

Zoe made a show of looking around the cavernous chamber. "I don't see one."

"Neither do I," said Lucy. She cocked her head and ran the tip of her tongue over her lips. "But there's fresh air coming from somewhere."

She crunched her way across the heaps of broken glass and headed for the crack in the wall through which the green liquid had vanished. "This way!"

They squeezed through, back into darkness, with Lucy leading the way. The tunnel soon widened out enough for Finn and Zoe to walk on either side of Kylie, holding her up and helping her along. Kylie winced every time her bare feet jarred down on the rough floor. Lucy went ahead, picking her way along the passage as it sloped down towards a dim and distant glow. A channel ran down the middle of the floor, stained green with the last of the liquid that had drained out of the vat. After a few dozen metres, the channel stopped at a circular metal grate, beyond which the floor was dry.

As they crossed the grate, Kylie stumbled and nearly fell.

"Kylie," said Zoe. "Are you still with us?"

"I'm okay," Kylie mumbled. "Keep going."

They came around a corner and a tiny circle of silver light appeared ahead. It grew as they approached, finally revealing itself as the tunnel exit. The light was the reflection of the moon on the waters of a broad lake. Finn had seen that lake before, on the day of the Hunt.

The exit was sealed by a battered metal grille. The bars were caked in rust but the padlock securing it looked brand new.

Whoever put Kylie down there didn't want her found ...

Handing Kylie over to Zoe, Finn grabbed the bars and rattled the grille. It shifted a little on its hinges and flakes of rust showered down. But the lock held. He slammed the heel of his hand into the metal.

"We should have brought John," he said. "He'd rip this thing out with his bare hands."

"Maybe we could rip it out anyway," said Lucy, jiggling the gate experimentally. "Look – the hinges are kind of loose."

The ground beyond the gate was strewn with fallen rocks. Finn reached through the bars and grabbed one that was twice the size of his fist. Raising it high, he smashed it against the topmost hinge. Shards of rock flew in all directions, stinging his hands and face.

"Stand back," he said. "Cover your eyes."

When the three girls had retreated to a safe distance, he hammered again at the hinge. After three blows the metal parted with an agonised screech and the gate tilted to the side. Dropping to his knees, Finn repeated the process with the bottom hinge. When that finally gave way, the gate tipped forward and crashed to the ground.

A narrow path took them from the tunnel exit to a steep gravelly slope. Finn's feet skidded on the loose stones, and several times Zoe nearly slipped over. The slope levelled out where it met the sandy shore of the lake. The night sky was a patchwork of moonlit clouds and the air was cool. Kylie began to shiver.

"We need to get her inside," said Finn.

"This way," said Lucy. "It's not far."

The path circled the lake then climbed towards a little stone building that Finn recognised from his earlier excursions. Only now did he realise that it was the home of Dr Raj. Beyond the cottage, the towering silver wall of the school loomed over a line of outhouses. But the cottage itself wasn't overlooked.

At the door, Kylie bent double and started coughing. Finn did his best to help Zoe hold her up. Lucy lifted the corner of the small brown doormat and picked up an ordinary key. There was just enough moonlight coming through the windows to illuminate a small, square hallway with rough plastered walls. Finn glimpsed a cluttered kitchen through a half-open door. The door opposite was closed. Directly ahead, a steep stone staircase led up into darkness.

Between them, Finn and Zoe managed to get Kylie

up the stairs to the main bedroom. While Zoe settled her sister on the bed, Finn rummaged in a cupboard for extra blankets. Even before they'd finished arranging them across Kylie's inert form, she was fast asleep.

"Well," said Finn, perching on the wide window sill. "It's a start. Now we've got to work out what to do next."

"You still don't want to go to the Wardens?" said Lucy.

"I don't think it's a good idea," said Finn. "If the Dean really is behind this, he probably had help. I don't think we can afford to trust any of the Wardens right now. We've got to think bigger."

"What do you mean?" said Zoe.

Finn glanced through the window. "We've got to get a message off the island," he said. "Tell someone what's going on here."

Lucy's eyes opened wide. "You mean like the police?"

"That's probably the best place to start," said Finn.

"You can't do that!" said Zoe. She glanced at the sleeping Kylie and lowered her voice. "This is Alyxa!"

"I don't care," said Finn. "And neither should you. Kylie's your sister."

"You think I don't know that?"

"Then why won't you ...?"

"Alyxa is the only place I ever felt safe," said Zoe. "The only place I've ever belonged. I can't betray that. I won't. Whatever's wrong with Alyxa has to stay at Alyxa."

Finn raised his hands helplessly. "Then what are we supposed to do?"

"Fix it," said Lucy. "Zoe's right. Contacting the outside world is a no-no. There'd be an investigation. They'd be swarming all over the island in protective suits. Can you imagine?"

"They might even shut us down," said Zoe.

"Shut us down and take us away," said Lucy. "They'd probably want to do experiments."

Finn knew they were right – he could see it all. He imagined swarms of helicopters descending from the sky. Would he and John escape the scrutiny because they were new here?

Who was he trying to kid?

He let out a long sigh. "All right," he said. "I suppose there is someone else we could try."

"Who?" said Lucy.

"Dr Forrester," Finn replied. Leaving Zoe with her sister in the bedroom, he and Lucy hurried back down to the hall. A phone clung to the wall beside the kitchen door. A scruffy notebook dangled from beneath it on a short length of string.

"It's my dad's phone book," said Lucy. As she leafed through the creased pages, Finn saw names and numbers scrawled in tiny, spidery handwriting.

"Doesn't your dad have all that computerised?" he said.

"Did that helmet look computerised?" said Lucy, running her finger down the list. "Here we go."

Lucy read out the number and Finn tapped it out. It took ten rings before Dr Forrester came to the phone.

"Who is it?" she said blearily.

"It's Finn Williams," said Finn. "I'm sorry to wake you up but it's kind of an emergency."

"Emergency?" Dr Forrester sounded more alert.

"Sort of. We've found Kylie."

"Kylie? Kylie *Redmayne?*" Fully awake now. "You've found her body?"

"No," said Finn. "We've found *her.*"

"She's alive?" Dr Forrester's confusion came through in the sound of her voice. "But ... how is she? What happened to her?"

"It's complicated," said Finn. "But she's basically okay. Can you come to Dr Raj's cottage?"

"Yes, of course. But why are you there? Have you ...?"

"Just come, please," said Finn.

No sooner had Finn replaced the phone on the little

321

table in the hall than a groan came from the bedroom. They rushed up the stairs to find Kylie sitting up in bed with Zoe holding her hand. Her face was scarlet and beaded with perspiration.

"You were in the cave," she said, staring at Finn. "Who are you?"

"My name's Finn," he said. Then to Zoe he added, "Dr Forrester's coming."

Zoe pressed her hand against her sister's forehead.

"You're burning up," she said. "Lie down."

"I've got to ..." said Kylie, flopping back on the pillow.

"It's all right," said Zoe, stroking her hand. "I'm just so glad I've got you back again. Do you remember anything about what happened?"

Kylie shook her head. "Not really. I think ..." Her brow creased as she rubbed her temples. "I remember the cliffs. I went there because ..." Her voice trailed away.

"Did you meet someone there?" said Finn. He could feel his pulse beginning to race. "The Dean?"

Again Kylie shook her head. "The Dean?"

"We found your diary," said Zoe. "You said he was following you. Giving you a hard time?"

"Did I?"

"And you drew things," said Lucy. "Weird things,

like hexagrams."

Kylie turned on to her side. "My head's on fire," she said. "I just want to sleep."

Zoe leaned over and kissed Kylie's sweat-soaked brow.

"Hang in there," she said. "We're not going anywhere."

Leaving Zoe to nurse her sister, Finn and Lucy went down to the kitchen where Lucy lit two candles. She was glancing nervously at the stairs.

"What's up?" said Finn.

"There's something not right about Kylie," Lucy said in a low voice. "She tastes different."

"What do you mean?" said Finn.

"Everyone gives off pheromones, right?" said Lucy. "Kind of a subliminal smell. And everyone's pheromones are unique – yours are different to mine, get it?"

"Like a smell signature?" said Finn.

"Exactly! But Kylie's is all wrong."

"Maybe it's all that green goo," said Finn. "Maybe that sort of messed with the signal."

Lucy shook her head. "I don't think so. I think Kylie's lying."

That brought Finn up short. "Why would she do that?"

"I have no idea. And there's something else that's odd about this whole thing."

Finn finished his drink and waited for her to continue.

"That keypad code we used to empty the tank," said Lucy. "You said that a five-digit code has, what was it, a hundred and twenty combinations? So what are the odds against you guessing a *six-digit* code?"

The numbers jumbled up in Finn's head. "I don't know," he said. "They're high. All I know is that I used the numbers I saw when I was inside the Gauntlet. And it worked."

"Yes. But why? Is the vat connected to the Gauntlet somehow? Or is it something else?"

A sharp knock broke the silence, making them both jump.

"Dr Forrester's here," said Finn, relieved.

They went out into the hall, but when Finn opened the door it wasn't the doctor standing outside on the mat.

It was Ben.

CHAPTER TWENTY-ONE

"Hey there, Finn," said Ben, leaning in through the half-open door. "What's happening?"

"Er, nothing much," said Finn. He tried to swing the door shut a little more, but Ben had jammed his foot against the threshold, preventing him from moving it.

"Hi, Ben," said Lucy. "How did you know we were here?"

"Smelt it, of course," said Ben, resting his hand against the door frame. "So are you having a party or what? Can anyone come?"

"Nothing like that," said Lucy. "My dad just asked me to look in on the cottage while he was away."

Ben stood on his tiptoes and tried to peer past them.

Finn moved to block his view.

"I don't think Dr Raj would want his house full of students," he said. "Anyway, Lucy and I were about to lock up and go back."

"I'm not students," said Ben with a grin. "I'm me. You're sure I can't help?"

"Positive," said Finn. "Why don't you go - we'll be following soon anyway."

"Do you think I'm an idiot?" said Ben. He kicked open the door and shoved his way into the hall.

"Wait a second," said Finn, pulling Lucy with him to the foot of the stairs. "You can't just come barging in here."

"This is trespassing," said Lucy. "My dad's going to be so cross."

Ben raised his arm and spoke into a metal band on his wrist. "They're in here," he said.

The bottom dropped out of Finn's stomach. "Who are you talking to?" he said.

Suddenly there was an Overloader in Ben's hand. He aimed it straight at Finn's chest. "Get out of my way." His thumb hovered over the activation switch.

Finn spread his arms. "Hey, no need for that."

"He's right, put it down, Ben," said an all too familiar voice. "We don't need to resort to violence. Yet."

Ben lowered his arm and stepped aside. Standing

immediately behind him was the Dean.

"Where is she?" said Geraint Kildair.

"Where's who?" said Finn.

"Don't get smart with me. I'm sick of your lies. Tell me where Kylie Redmayne is or I'll change my mind about using the Overloader."

Aiming the weapon at Finn again, Ben moved further into the hall, allowing the Dean to enter the cottage. The night breeze came with him, chilling Finn's skin.

"I don't know what you mean," said Finn. "Kylie's dead."

"I know there are more of you in the house," said the Dean.

"Yes, I'm here too," said Zoe, appearing at the top of the stairs. "We were just leaving."

"Ben – check the bedrooms," said the Dean.

Before Ben could move, Kylie walked calmly across the landing to join her sister. Her green eyes sparkled, bright and alert. Finn could hardly believe it was the same girl they'd left semi-conscious in the bed just moments before.

The Dean took a small step backwards. "Get back, Zoe," he said. "Don't let her near you."

"She's my sister," Zoe snapped.

"Just walk slowly down the stairs," said the Dean.

"Stay where you are," Finn called up the staircase. Then to Kildair he said, "I won't let you take her."

"You stupid fools," said the Dean.

Lucy shrieked as Kylie leapt down the stairs in a single, impossible bound. Dodging past Finn, she turned her shoulder sideways and slammed straight into Ben, who crashed back against the wall, grunting in pain and surprise. The Overloader flew through the air and landed at Finn's feet.

"Kylie, wait!" said Zoe, racing down after her sister.

Finn reached for the Overloader, but Kylie, moving with unnatural speed, snatched it up first. Spinning on her heels she hurled herself at the Dean. Though he was a head taller and must have outweighed her by twenty kilos, she forced him back and rammed the Overloader hard against his collarbone.

"Sweet dreams," she said. Her lips curled back from her teeth.

A shower of sparks filled the little hallway. The Dean's eyes rolled up white and he collapsed on to the floor.

Zoe had reached the bottom of the stairs. "Kylie?" she said uncertainly.

Finn threw a glance at the Dean's prone body, wondering if the Overloaders could be set to kill.

Kylie advanced on Ben, jabbing the still-sizzling

Overloader at his face.

"Back up," she said.

Ben scrabbled backwards until he was wedged into the corner of the hall. Sweat slicked his anxious face.

"Tie him up," said Kylie.

Nobody moved. Finn glanced at Lucy. She was clutching Zoe's arm, preventing her from running to her sister. Zoe was struggling, but only half-heartedly. Her face was creased with confusion.

"Get some rope," Kylie said, firing the words at Lucy. "Make it quick."

Lucy released Zoe. Instead of going to Kylie, Zoe sank down to sit on the bottom step with her legs shaking. Her naked eyes were wide, and her astonished gaze never left her sister.

From the corner of his eye, Finn saw Ben edging towards the front door. He ran to close it at the same instant that Kylie jabbed the Overloader forward with a hiss.

"Don't even think about it," she said.

Lucy returned with a roll of black duct tape. "It's what kidnappers use in the movies," she said. She might have been attempting a smile, but all Finn saw was a grimace of fear.

He helped her tie Ben's hands behind his back.

"You don't know what you're doing," Ben said as

they wrapped more tape around his lower legs.

"Sorry," said Finn. "But you're the one who brought the weapon to the party."

"She's not safe," said Ben.

With a loud groan, Kylie staggered sideways and collapsed on the stone floor in the middle of the hall.

"Kylie!" said Zoe, rushing to her sister's side. Finn knelt down with her and pressed his fingers against Kylie's wrist. A strong pulse.

"I think she's just fainted," he said.

Between the three of them they managed to get Kylie on to the couch in the living room. Zoe draped a sheepskin rug over her body and checked her sister's pulse for herself.

"Why don't you stay with her?" Finn said.

"She's out cold," said Zoe, marching back towards the hall door. "I'm going to get to the bottom of this."

By the time Finn and Lucy caught up with her, Zoe was crouching beside the tied-up Ben.

"Start talking," she said.

On the floor nearby, the Dean began to stir. Relieved that Kildair was still alive, Finn grabbed the tape and quickly used it to bind his arms and legs – and tried not to dwell on the knowledge that he was tying up the head of the school.

Meanwhile, Lucy had picked up the Overloader.

"Come on," she said, waggling the device in Ben's face. "How long have you been doing the Dean's dirty work?"

"You don't know what you're talking about," said Ben. "Without us, you'd all be finished."

"Us?" said Lucy.

Ben struggled in vain against the duct tape. "The Order," he said.

Finn saw Lucy flinch. "The Order doesn't exist any more."

"Ha!" said Ben. "The Order will always exist, as long as the sixth sense threatens our world." Ben looked towards Zoe. "That's the only reason we're after Kylie. She's in deep."

Zoe's eyes narrowed. "That's my sister you're talking about." She grabbed the Overloader from Lucy and held it just an inch from Ben's face. He shrank back.

"Was it you who planted that book in my room?" Zoe said.

"No," Ben replied at once. "I have no idea how it got there."

Finn looked at Lucy again. She licked her lips. "He's telling the truth," she said reluctantly. She glared at Ben. "Doesn't mean you're not a scumbag!"

The Dean gave out another groan. His eyes flickered open and he tried to sit up. Zoe swivelled a dial on the base of the Overloader and pointed it at his chest. Her hand shook, and for a moment Finn was convinced she was going to zap him.

"I have no idea what this will do to you," Zoe said, "but right now I don't really care." Like her hand, her voice was trembling. "Why did you put Kylie in that tank?"

"You have to let me go," said the Dean, firmly and calmly. In the faint light from the moon his face looked ghoulish.

"Answer the question!" said Zoe.

"I would if it made any sense," said the Dean. Unlike Ben, he seemed unconcerned by the tape binding him up. "Why would I go to all that trouble? If I'd got my hands on Kylie I would have simply killed her."

Finn's guts turned over.

"You'd what?" said Zoe. Her knuckles turned white on the Overloader.

"She's sixth sense," said the Dean. "Those stupid Wardens! The reality is that your sister has to be put down."

"You're lying!" shouted Zoe.

Finn glanced at Lucy, willing her to reassure them all that the Dean was lying. From the defeated look on her face, he guessed that simply wasn't the case.

"Your ignorance will kill us all," said the Dean.

"Then tell us what's happening!" said Finn. "What is it about this extra sense that's so bad?"

"The sixth sense is not an extra sense." The Dean's voice grew deeper and more guttural. "It is the culmination of senses. Those who have it can do extraordinary things."

"Such as?" Finn had already witnessed some pretty extraordinary things at Alyxa.

"Some believe that the sixth sense allows you to control minds. Others say it opens doors to parts of the world that nobody else can perceive." He glanced at the door leading into the back room. "Perhaps you should ask Kylic. Although I wouldn't recommend it." He glared at them. "Now let me out!"

"You said you didn't kidnap Kylie," said Finn, eyeing the door to the other room with unease. "So who did?"

The Dean grunted. "Some fool who thought they could help her. Someone who thinks Morvan can be toyed with."

"But Morvan is dead!" said Finn. "He was killed centuries ago."

"You don't understand anything," said the Dean.

Something smashed in the back room.

"Kylie!" Zoe leapt up and ran to the door. But when she grabbed the handle and pushed, nothing happened.

"Something's jamming it!" she cried, throwing

333

herself at the door.

"Let me try," said Finn. He tried rattling the handle but it barely moved. "Locked!"

He pressed his ear to the door. He heard muttered conversation, footsteps crunching on what sounded like broken glass, a sharp intake of breath.

"Kylie!" shouted Zoe, slamming her hand against the wooden panel.

Finn whirled and raced to the front door. Pulling it open, he sprinted around the side of the cottage, vaulting a low stone wall along the way. He rounded the corner of the building and into a blast of wind. There was Adriana standing in a pool of moonlight, peering in through a broken window. Strapped to her back with a leather harness was a quiver of blunted arrows. In her hand she held a short bow.

When she spotted Finn she raised the bow. "Stay back!" she said. The wind ruffled her spiky pink hair.

As she spoke, a figure appeared at the window. Kylie's limp body was draped across his shoulder. He knocked a loose triangle of glass out of the frame then started clambering out.

It was John.

"What?" said Finn.

Taken by surprise, John half-jumped, half-fell to the ground.

"Finn," he said, hoisting Kylie more securely on to his shoulder. "You shouldn't be here."

"What are you doing?" said Finn.

John backed away, his face a mask of distress. "We've got to do this," he said. "It's the only way to save her."

"Come on," said Adriana, pulling at the sleeve of John's jacket. "We've got to hurry."

"I'm sorry," John said to Finn, and then they both turned away.

"I can't let you take her," said Finn, moving forward.

Adriana spun round. In one smooth movement she plucked an arrow from her back and nocked it on to the string. Feet planted wide, she drew the arrow back. It was aimed straight at Finn's chest.

"I warned you," said Adriana. She let the arrow fly.

It struck Finn in the centre of his breastbone. The impact of the arrow knocked the breath from his body, stiffening every limb.

As he dropped helplessly to the ground, he heard John's voice calling as if from the other side of a canyon. "Stay away, Finn! Please!"

CHAPTER TWENTY-TWO

He wasn't sure if he passed out or not, but unseen hands hauled Finn to his feet. Wiping blurry eyes, he stared straight into Zoe's goggles.

"What happened?" she asked. "Where's Kylie?"

"They took her," he said, staggering as she let go of him.

"Who took her?"

"John and Adriana."

Zoe looked in through the broken window. "That makes no sense. Are you sure?"

Finn managed to nod.

Lifting the goggles from her face, Zoe scanned the bushes surrounding the cottage. Rough paths led in half a dozen different directions. Gusts of wind sucked the sand from the ground and whipped it skyward.

"I can't see their trail," she said, running first towards one path, then another. "They could be anywhere."

"Lucy!" said Finn. "Maybe she can track them."

Zoe helped him back to the cottage's entrance hall. Once there, Finn told Lucy what had happened, but the Dean interrupted before she could respond.

"You should have killed her when you had the chance," he said.

"Nobody's killing anyone!" said Zoe.

"This has gone far enough," said the Dean. "Untie me and let me do what needs to be done."

"In your dreams," said Lucy. She turned to Finn. "Why did they take her?"

Finn had no idea how John had got mixed up with all this. And he couldn't believe Adriana had actually shot him. How was she even involved?

His skin suddenly tingled as he remembered the tear on her jacket. *Of course!* He plunged his hand into his jumpsuit pocket and held up the prefect's badge. "What if this wasn't Kylie's? What if it was Adriana's? What if they were together that night?" He stopped, suddenly inspired. "And it was Adriana who found the *Book of Morvan* in your room?"

"Adriana Arnott?" said the Dean. He groaned. Somehow he twisted his body around so that now he was kneeling awkwardly with his legs still tied together and his hands bound behind his back. "I should have seen it! You see how the sixth sense infects everyone it touches?"

"But why would she do that?" said Lucy. "And how did she get hold of the book in the first place?"

"She's Susan Arnott's daughter," said Finn, frowning. His thoughts still felt muddy after the jolt of Adriana's arrow. "It can't have been that hard."

"Never mind why and how," said Zoe. "We need to know where they've taken her. And we need to get after them, now!"

Finn turned to Lucy. "Can you track them? Taste their trail or something?"

Lucy's face pinched up. Then she shook her head. "I'm better at tasting feelings."

"I can do it," said Ben. He tilted his head towards the open door and made a strange gulping sound. "The trail's there, but it's fading fast. The wind."

"Then what are we waiting for?" Finn glared at Ben. "How do we know you won't turn on us if we set you free?"

"I won't," said Ben at once.

"Is he telling the truth?" said Finn.

"Partly," said Lucy, frowning.

Zoe hefted the Overloader. "We can keep him in line."

***

By the time they reached the back of the cottage, the wind was gusting even more strongly. Airborne sand stung Finn's eyes and he found himself envying Zoe her goggles. The bushes thrashed from side to side and dust devils gyrated to and fro on the narrow paths.

Ben arched his head and made the same peculiar grunt in this throat.

"This way," he said, setting off at a trot. "Trust me."

"You've got a long way to go before we trust you again," said Lucy.

Finn followed with the others, trying to shake off the residual numbness from his legs. He didn't know who to trust any more. It was one thing knowing that Adriana was mixed up in such sinister goings-on. Knowing that his brother was somehow involved too ... that was another thing entirely. No wonder he'd been so eager to close down Finn's suspicions.

Ben led them down to the beach, where the trail became visible again. Two sets of footprints led across the damp sand.

"Even I can see they went this way," said Lucy.

"They were dragging her," said Zoe, pointing to a scuffed, straggling line between the trailing footprints.

They raced along the shore. The wind was even stronger down here by the sea. It blasted their faces as if trying to hold them back.

Finn wasn't surprised to find that the tracks were taking them straight towards the cave at the foot of the South Cliff. Splashing through the rock pools, they passed the giant boulders that had fallen on the night Finn had come here in search of Pogo. He glanced nervously up at the towering cliff face.

Waves crashed over a line of rocks sending white foam high into the air as they reached the sloping plain of shingle. Salt spray lashed their cheeks.

Finn stopped just outside the cave entrance.

"There was a big boulder there before," he said, staring into the cave's yawning black mouth. "It looked like it was blocking the entrance."

"I think I see it," said Lucy. She pointed to a pile of seaweed-covered rock fragments at the bottom of the slope. The broken faces were clean and dry.

"John!" said Finn. "He must have rolled it aside."

He stepped up to the edge of the shadows. Lucy and Zoe followed, but Ben hung back.

"I'm not going in there," he said. He retched, and

for a moment Finn thought Ben was going to be sick. "It tastes ... bad."

"Whatever," Finn replied. To the others he said, "Come on. We're close, I know it."

They scrunched their way up the shingle slope into the cave. As the darkness enveloped them, the wind howled around their ears. The floor was uneven and they had to drop to all fours a few times in order to clamber over an endless succession of slippery rocks. The whole cave smelt damp and rotten.

"I can see light ahead," said Zoe.

"I can't see anything," said Lucy.

"Careful," said Finn. "It gets really slippery here."

At last Finn began to see what Zoe was seeing: a fan of light reaching down like silver fingers from high above. Peering up into the haze, Finn saw circular polished stones set in the cave ceiling, which was peppered with holes.

"They're like mirrors," he said. "They're bringing in the moonlight somehow."

As they passed beneath the mirrors, he wondered who'd put them there. The Druids? How many moonrises had those reflective surfaces captured? How many centuries had they seen?

The captured moonlight illuminated a set of stone stairs. From the rough planes, Fin guessed they'd been hacked out by hand. He began to climb, trying his best to avoid the thick strands of seaweed that lay draped across the steps. Shadows lurked in distant crevices.

Halfway up the steps Finn was gasping for breath – the staircase was steeper than it looked.

"What's up there?" panted Lucy.

"We're about to find out," said Finn.

At the top of the steps, two archways led to a pair of narrow tunnels. The left tunnel led slightly down, the right slightly up. The keystones at the tops of the arches were engraved with cryptic runes. Blankets of lichen clung to the pitted surface of the stone. The lichen was glowing yellow.

Never mind centuries. This place looks thousands of years old.

"It's bioluminescent," said Finn, touching his finger to the strange shining stuff.

A deep thud echoed down the right-hand tunnel.

"This way," said Finn.

The tunnel opened on to a wide ledge overlooking a hexagonal chamber big enough to hold a tennis court. A vaulted ceiling held more of the polished stones. Silver light bounced in all directions, lacing the air with a criss-crossing maze of moonbeams. The ceiling was held up by six towering pillars of rock etched with twisting spiral patterns. All the pillars were cracked, and all looked very, very old.

Finn knew at once where he was. *The Large Ring. The house of the Sixth Clann*.

He ventured to the edge of the ledge. Many metres below – too far to jump – was a floor of rough stone slabs. He wasn't surprised to see that each slab had six sides. In the middle of the floor was a hexagonal altar. Kylie was lying on it motionless with her arms and legs spread out. Heavy manacles fixed her wrists and ankles to the altar's smooth stone surface. A metal collar enclosed her neck.

"No!" said Zoe, startling Finn by coming up behind him.

"Do you know what this place is?" said Lucy as she joined them.

"I think I do," Finn replied. "It's the Temple of Morvan."

Four slender standing stones surrounded the altar, each as high as a man. Like the pillars holding up the ceiling, they were covered in spiral patterns. Two identical stones lay on their sides. As Finn watched, one of the fallen stones began to rise up on end.

Finn gasped. *That's impossible!*

Then a familiar figure came into view: a tall boy crouched with his back against the stone, muscles straining, using all his strength to tilt it back into its proper place.

"John!" Finn cried.

The stone settled into position with a resounding thud – the same sound they'd heard moments before. John wiped his forehead and looked up, right into Finn's eyes.

"Finn!" John called. "I told you not to come!"

Finn scanned the chamber but Adriana was nowhere to be seen.

"Let my sister go!" Zoe shouted. Her voice echoed off the ceiling, sending shivers through the lattice of moonbeams.

"That's what we're trying to do," said John. "We're going to set Kylie free. Morvan's inside her and we're trying to draw him out."

Someone began to chant. As Finn searched the chamber to find its source, Adriana appeared from a low archway on the opposite side. Eyes closed, hands raised, she stepped out across the stone floor and headed straight for the altar.

Finn couldn't take his eyes off Adriana. But Lucy gripped his arm.

"Where's Zoe gone?" she said.

Finn looked too, but she was nowhere to be seen.

Down on the temple floor, Adriana began to speak. "*Beorht, galdor, tostinca, felan, nyss,*" she intoned.

"We want to help Kylie," John said again.

Finn didn't need superpowers to see the honesty in his brother's face.

Nor could he ignore the sly smile on Adriana's lips.

"She's using you," he called to his brother. He dropped to a crouch and gauged the distance to the altar. If he had a running start, could he leap on to it from here without breaking his ankle? Maybe, but he'd have to be desperate to try. "Adriana was with Kylie on the night she disappeared. She's behind all this. Whatever she's told you, don't trust her."

John threw a confused look at Adriana, who continued to advance on the altar. As she stepped through the alternating lines of shadow and moonbeam, her pink hair seemed to flash like neon.

"*Beorht, galdor, tostinca, felan, nyss ... yeldu!*" she said. He wondered briefly how she knew the words, but then it came to him. *Of course. The Book of Morvan.*

He had no idea what the words meant, or why they turned his whole body cold.

"You've got to stop her!" he shouted to John.

Adriana halted in a pool of light. "They're just a bunch of scared kids," she said to John. "Are you going to finish the job?"

John looked desperately up at Finn.

"I'm sorry," he said. "We've got to do this."

He ran to the sixth fallen stone and started heaving it back into place. As the grinding sound of the stone's movement filled the chamber, Adriana resumed her chanting. When she reached the altar she held out her hands and fluttered them over Kylie's expressionless face. John groaned, veins bulging on his temples, and with a hollow thump the sixth stone rocked finally into position. As it settled, a network of deep cracks opened up in the temple floor around it.

As echoes resounded around the chamber, Zoe appeared from the same archway Adriana had used.

"Leave my sister alone!" she shouted, and raced towards John. He put out his hands to stop her, but her arm flashed out and she slammed the Overloader against his chest. Dazzling blue lightning flared from the end of the Overloader and sank shining claws into John's body.

"No!" Finn shouted, rising from his crouch.

The energy from the Overloader held John rigid for an instant, then Zoe tilted her hand and he flew across the chamber floor. He landed hard against one of the standing stones and lay there immobile with his jaw hanging slack. From this distance Finn couldn't even tell if his chest was moving. He recalled how she'd rammed the dial to maximum in Dr Raj's house.

"Leave him alone!" cried Finn.

Backing up, he ran to the edge of the ledge and jumped out into space. For an instant he was convinced he'd misjudged the drop completely. Then his feet slammed down on to the corner of the altar, sending shock waves up his shins. He let his knees fold, angled his shoulders and kicked out sideways with his legs. His body made a complete rotation in the air and he came down on his feet again, this time flat on the floor.

Zoe was already raising the Overloader again. Finn sprinted to her and swung at her wrist to grab it. He misjudged, catching the Overloader and knocking it away. It spun through the air and vanished down one of the cracks in the floor.

"There's no reason to be scared," said Adriana. She seemed oblivious to what had just happened. "It's fear that's been causing all the problems. That's the only reason the sixth sense is taboo."

As she spoke, tiny flakes of stones rained past her face. Finn glanced up to see that the ceiling was shaking. As he watched, a crack appeared and a rock fell, smashing to pieces on the edge of the temple steps. A shower of pebbles came down near the standing stone beside which John was lying.

"Get out of there!" called Lucy from the ledge.

"We have to put fear aside," Adriana went on, oblivious, as stones continued to fall. The floor was

347

shaking, but she remained curiously balanced. "Forget ordinary life – it's time to explore our full potential. Imagine all the things we could do if we really started to use our powers."

Finn tottered across the unstable floor towards John. Adriana's eyes shone. Kylie's body started to vibrate on the altar. The chamber continued to shake. The standing stone near John began to totter. It looked ready to fall at any minute.

"*Beorht, galdor, tostinca, felan, nyss,*" Adriana chanted.

More cracks split the floor directly in front of Finn. He circled to the left, trying to pick out the best route to get to John. He heard Lucy scream and looked up just in time to see her foot slither off the ledge. To his relief, she scrabbled backwards to safety as the entire section of wall below her collapsed into a mound of rubble. Zoe was trying to get to the altar, but the falling rocks kept blocking her way. It was a matter of time before one struck someone's head.

"*Beorht, galdor, tostinca, felan, nyss ... yeldu!*" said Adriana. "*Yeldu! Yeldu!*"

Kylie's entire body jerked. The manacles kept her wrists, ankles and neck pinned to the altar but her back arched clear of the stone. Her eyes squeezed shut and her mouth flew open. An unearthly shriek rose from it.

Then her muscles relaxed and she slumped down again, only to undergo another spasm that lifted her into the air, then another. Finn had never seen a human body bent in two like that.

"Kylie!" screamed Zoe. Her foot had dropped into a crack and she was fighting to pull it free.

The shriek wasn't the only thing coming out of Kylie's mouth. With each lurch of her body, a pale shape rose further and further into view, like a billow of breath taking physical form. On the sixth spasm, it settled into the shape of a human figure.

The ghost – or spirit, or whatever it was – looked like a hunched man dressed in long rippling robes. His head was hairless and his face was tattooed with interlocking hexagrams. His eyes were dark, empty sockets. Kylie sagged back limply with an exhausted sigh.

"*Yeldu!*" cried Adriana, reaching up towards the floating entity. "Morvan! Rise into the light. Rise and ..."

A falling chunk of rock glanced off the back of Adriana's head and knocked her forward. She clutched helplessly at the altar, then crumpled to the floor.

The pale spirit drifted away from Kylie, who now lay unmoving on the trembling altar with her face tilted sideways and a line of drool running from her mouth. One by one, the manacles that secured her snapped open of their own accord. Freeing her foot at last, Zoe ran to her sister's side. The phantom circled the chamber, moving with a peculiar pulsing motion that reminded Finn of a jellyfish. The hanging robes hid its legs completely. Its arms probed the air.

Having completed its circuit, the spirit made straight towards John.

"No!" yelled Finn. He ran across the broken stones and threw himself in front of his brother.

The ghostly thing thrust out his arm. His fingers parted, expanded, and suddenly Finn's neck was inside them. The fingers closed and fire exploded in Finn's chest. His throat burned, his eyes seemed to expand with sudden pressure. He was dimly aware of Zoe climbing up on to the altar, of Lucy clambering down the rubble-strewn slope of the collapsed wall. But they were only fragments of dust in the light of the moon, and he was falling into the shadows.

"Come to me," a voice whispered, and the words poured over Finn, smothering him, blinding him, clogging his ears and his nose, filling his mouth and his mind and all the open pores of his skin. The world around him went away, leaving only darkness or nothing or both.

"Come," said the voice again, inside his head.

Robbed of its senses, Finn's consciousness collapsed.

CHAPTER
TWENTY-THREE

He floated through shadow, through silver, through shadow again.

The moonbeams pushed him through the air. He was a bird, or a ghost. Below him stretched the hexagonal floor of the Temple of Morvan. Patterned pillars climbed towards him. As he drifted, the cracks in the pillars sealed themselves up and the rubble on the floor melted away. Coarse stone became glossy and polished, shot through with streaks of colour: red and green, orange and purple, yellow and blue.

This is how the temple used to be, Finn thought. He floated down, until he was standing under an arch, looking in. No Lucy, no John, no Zoe, no Adriana or

Kylie.

Six figures surrounded the altar just as the six standing stones had done. Their faces were lost beneath enormous hoods, but Finn could hear the thick rasp of their voices, and he could smell the earthiness of their sweat. Standing at the head of the altar was Morvan, the ghost made flesh. His thick woollen robe was woven with intricate curling patterns, not just with spirals but an entire maze of tangled knots and swirls. It was a pattern you could get lost in, if you stared at it for too long. In one hand he held a gnarled wooden staff.

Finn had the same strange sensation – present, but not – as when he was in the Small Ring, seeing those crouched Druids skinning their rabbit.

Morvan raised his shaved head. Moonlight trickled down the six-sided tattoos on his face, making them glow. His nose was long and a little crooked, as if it had once been broken. His chin came to a sharp point. He looked at Finn and smiled.

"I escaped once," said Morvan, "only to be trapped again. They trapped me, but you heard my call. You set me free."

"You used me," Finn said.

"I have waited so long," Morvan replied. "Your body is what I need."

Finn shook his head. He wanted to get away.

The six Druids lifted their cowled heads as one towards him. They flowed out from the altar. Now the moonlight shone into those huge hoods. Instead of faces, Finn saw white bone, gaping eye sockets, grinning teeth. Human skulls.

One after the other, the Druids withdrew wooden staffs from beneath their robes. They seemed to lengthen before Finn's astonished gaze; soon each was as tall as the figure who wielded it. Finn turned a slow circle, but there were too many to keep in sight at once.

"Bring him to me," said Morvan.

A stick whacked into the small of Finn's back, driving him forward. A second blow struck the backs of his knees. Pain coursed through his legs and he crumpled to the ground. The six Druids circled him, sticks twirling, their skeletal faces grinning like Halloween masks.

Finn staggered to his feet. A stick jabbed towards his face. Finn dodged it – barely. But another stick cracked against his shin and he yelped with pain.

Calm yourself. Empty your mind and fill up your heart. Open your senses to the world. If you cannot see, then hear. If you cannot hear, then touch. Taste the threat. Smell your enemy. Take it all in.

Something hissed to his left. Finn ducked and knew that a staff had missed him by the width of his hand. Something rustled to his right – he threw himself backwards. A descending staff deflected the air against his face.

Tiny vibrations shook the floor.

Finn kicked off his trainers and planted his bare feet against the cold stone. Now the vibrations were tremors, six sets of heels springing this way and that as the Druid warriors made their rings around him. Letting the direction of the tremors guide the muscles of his legs, Finn danced to and fro, crouching and leaping, smelling the wafts of pinewood as the staffs slashed at his darting form, always just too late to make contact.

Wait ... wait ...

There! One of the Druids had over-reached. For an instant he was right in front of Finn's blind eyes, his staff held motionless before him.

Finn could taste the Druid's surprise.

Finn grabbed the staff and flung it around his head. The air sang as it spun. Whipping the wooden stick around, he smashed it straight down on to his frozen opponent and opened his eyes in time to see the Druid's flapping robe fill with an explosion of shattered bones. They dropped into an untidy pile of ribs and limbs and shredded cloth.

The five remaining Druids moved back, suddenly wary.

"Interesting," said Morvan, and Finn was pleased

to hear uncertainty, almost pride, in his voice.

The Druids closed in again. Fear sent quivers along Finn's arms, but he forced himself to hold the staff steady. He managed to parry the first blow but missed the second, which glanced off his left elbow and sent tingles all the way to the ends of his fingers.

One of the Druids darted sideways. Finn heard two more closing in from behind. He reversed his grip on the staff and, without looking, drove it straight back. He was rewarded by a satisfying thump and a series of hollow cracks. Splintered bones scattered over the floor around his feet, including a naked jawbone, flopping uselessly.

A staff hit Finn's left shoulder, then another smacked the side of his head. Tiny stars flashed in the corners of his vision and his ears rang. He closed his eyes again and sent all of his attention into the soles of his feet. As he did so, he began to see movement in the darkness behind his eyelids.

There's an altar, and hooded figures, and a boy.

The boy was him.

He was seeing through the eyes of one of the attackers. How was that possible?

The vision was murky, as if he was deep underwater. But it was enough. When the Druid raised his staff, Finn was able to move easily aside. He pinched his eyelids tighter and the view changed. Now he was inside another of the Druids. Skeletal limbs coiled ready for a strike and Finn dodged again. Another pinch, another viewpoint.

Wait ... wait ...

A Druid feinted left and Finn moved right, then swung his staff low. Leg bones splintered and the Druid went down. Finn smashed his staff into the twitching remains then immediately spun, lashing out and felling the enemy who had crept up behind him.

One left.

The final fighter took so long to come that in the end Finn went for him. The Druid made an attempt to parry, but dropped his staff. Finn side-stepped, driving a scything diagonal swipe, and felt his opponent's spine buckle.

He waited, listening for any further movement, tasting for signs of treachery in the air. All was still.

He opened his eyes in time to see Morvan stepping out from behind the altar. He placed both hands on the centre of his gnarled wooden staff and drew them apart. The two halves of the staff separated, revealing a shining blade that looked as if it was made of pure gold. Morvan tossed away the unwanted piece of staff and gripped the remainder, the hilt of a glittering sword.

"Your powers are coming along," Morvan said to

Finn, advancing with the golden sword held before him. "But they are rudimentary still." Finn backed away, dreadfully aware of the inadequacy of his wooden staff. "I will offer you a choice," continued Morvan. "Come willingly, or do not."

"Doesn't sound like much of a deal," said Finn as he continued to retreat. His bare feet scraped across a pile of scattered teeth. "What's in it for me?"

"Honour," said Morvan. "The knowledge that you alone were responsible for returning Morvan to the world."

Finn found himself up against the wall of the temple. There was nowhere left to go. Morvan loomed before him, the tip of his sword aimed right at Finn's throat. His chin jutted. His skin – under the shifting tattoos – was grey and lifeless like putty.

Finn ducked as the golden blade flashed towards him. It sank into the stone.

Striking the hilt of Morvan's sword with his staff, Finn leapt sideways and brought his weapon down on his opponent's head. Morvan dodged with uncanny speed, and the end of the staff whistled harmlessly through the air. Finn let his momentum carry him out across the floor of the temple. Planting one foot on a low plinth, he propelled himself up and on to the altar.

Morvan was two steps behind him. With a roar, he

slashed at Finn's legs. Finn jumped, allowing the blade to hiss past the soles of his bare feet, then sprinted along the altar's edge. When he reached the corner he hurled himself towards the nearest pillar.

Morvan grunted, his robe a blur as he followed. Suddenly he was there at the foot of the pillar with his sword swinging up towards Finn's flying body. Crying out, Finn twisted in mid-air. Morvan's sword sang. Finn's hands slapped against the pillar, but he knew he was falling back, right on to the blade ...

Except it wasn't a pillar any more. Now it was a horizontal stone pipe along which he was running at top speed. Ahead of him was a wall of moonbeams.

Not ahead - above, he thought. *Either the temple's tipped over or ...*

Morvan bellowed and launched himself in pursuit. Finn jumped across to the next pillar and ran down it just in time to avoid another swordstroke. He was heading for the altar again, only now the altar was tilted on its end.

Finn had no idea how he was climbing the wall. Nor did he have any time to think, because Morvan was closing in. The air whistled and Finn ducked. Morvan's sword carved a wedge of stone from the pillar, which groaned and trembled beneath Finn's feet.

He continued to run along the pillar, or down it,

until he reached the side of the altar. Morvan followed, proving that he was no more bound by physical laws than Finn was. Each slash of Morvan's sword took a slice out of the altar plinth, and sent chunks of stone skittering across the floor.

Finn jumped from the altar to the circular wall of the temple before springing on to the pillar that Morvan had hacked through barely a moment before.

The Sixth Warden was agile but slower, so when Finn reached the top of the pillar he had a few seconds to catch his breath. The ceiling of the temple was close enough to touch. The moonbeams held him like a shining spider's web.

"You should have taken my offer," said Morvan as he climbed effortlessly towards Finn. "It matters not to me whether your body is healthy or wounded. I will have it one way or the other."

Finn, with nowhere else to go, ran straight down the pillar towards his opponent.

Morvan's eyes shone with anticipation as he drew back his sword. As the distance between them closed, Finn accelerated. Morvan grinned. At the last moment, Finn planted his staff against the stone and pole-vaulted straight over Morvan's head. The golden sword came round, just missing him as it sang through the air.

As Finn landed, the pillar began to teeter first one

way, then the other. His feet slipped and he fell. His ribs cracked against the corner of the altar and suddenly the ground was back in its proper place.

It was also rushing up towards him.

Finn landed hard and all the breath exploded from his lungs. Black circles spun in the corners of his eyes and his ears rang.

Finn, get up!

But Morvan was already there, landing lightly on his feet, towering over him and cutting downwards. With arms that felt like wet clay, Finn held up the staff to block the attack. The sword sliced clean through the wood and Finn felt a cold shock to his shoulder. He looked down and saw that the blade was embedded in his flesh.

"And now you are mine," said Morvan.

Finn tried to sit up, but Morvan planted a foot on his chest and forced him down. His facial tattoos folded around his ferocious smile.

"Just let it happen," he whispered. "It won't hurt."

Finn saw no blood welling from the wound, and there was no pain.

Behind the altar, a huge crack opened up in the teetering pillar. It wouldn't hold for long. But something was happening to the golden blade. From Morvan's hands flowed the grey spirit-mist which travelled down the blade and into the wound. Into Finn's flesh. And as it entered him, a strength-sapping numbness eased through his bones. An evil. He imagined it like a snake's venom, slowly paralysing him.

What's happening to me?

He pushed back, while he still had strength, with every fibre of his being. And with the surge, the ghostly mist fell into confused currents.

Morvan's eyes narrowed and the foot on Finn's chest pressed harder. Once again the grey poison flowed into Finn's veins. Only now it felt almost good, rich and intoxicating and potent.

"No ..." said Finn desperately, gritting his teeth. With a cry, he fought the influx. This time, the mist reversed, creeping back up the blade, through the hilt, and into Morvan's hand. And as it did, Finn felt his mind untether, flowing with it, emptying himself. It pushed against the dark, vengeful, powerful thing that was Morvan.

"You cannot," said the Sixth Warden, and for the first time he sounded unsure.

The pillar above them crunched with a sudden jerk as the cracks widened. It began to fall.

Finn's mind tore free.

Now the thing that was *really* Finn – the very heart of him – was looking down at his own determined face.

Looking out through Morvan's eyes. He smelt the fear of the boy on the altar, the boy who was about to die. He heard the thick crackle of disintegrating stone as the pillar plunged groundwards.

He felt the weight of the golden sword in his own hands.

He stepped away.

What are you doing? It was Morvan's voice, only now Finn wasn't just hearing it. He was saying it. *Let me go!*

Finn considered this briefly, then delivered his response.

No, he said.

It hurts! Morvan cried.

The pillar was nearly upon him. Finn stepped sideways, stepped Morvan sideways, directly into its path.

Again, Finn replied.

Good.

Out in the world, gravity was back in charge and drawing everything down towards a single point. A target.

Morvan.

You cannot! Morvan screamed.

Yes, said Finn. *I can.*

A split second before the stone column smashed

down on top of Morvan, Finn tore himself from the Druid's mind and back into his own. Driving what little strength he had left into his aching muscles, he rolled out of the way just as the collapsing pillar crunched to the floor. Clouds of dust clogged his throat and stung his eyes.

For a moment, Finn lay there, wondering if he was dead or alive – the fact that he was wondering meant only one thing.

A strangled groan rose from beneath the pillar. Finn wiped his eyes, and blinking through the thick particles of dust, he rolled on to his knees and stood. Clambering over the debris, he spotted Morvan's head sticking clear of the rubble. Blood poured from a gash in his dust-covered scalp. The rest of his body was buried beneath tonnes of broken stonework. His eyes were open. One of them had turned completely red.

Morvan looked directly at Finn and opened his mouth.

"B-b ...?" he tried to say. His face contracted in agony. He spat out blood and spoke again. This time Finn heard a single word that might have been *bien* or *burn*. All he could really be sure of was that it sounded like a question.

A long gasp of air trickled out of Morvan's bloodied mouth. His lips closed and his eyes emptied, and Finn knew that he was dead.

A series of tremendous cracking sounds split the air and more stones began showering down. One struck the altar and exploded. A triangular section of ceiling broke loose and crashed to the floor of the temple. The next pillar split in half and fell, bringing yet more stones down from above. As the floor heaved, a third pillar started to fold.

The floor was rippling in great waves. Even as it was collapsing, the temple was going dark. Or was that light pouring in? He couldn't tell.

Water roared and a cold wave splashed across Finn's face. He spat out a mouthful of brine. He planted his hands on the edge of the altar and when he could see again, everything had changed. The pillars – what was left of them – were no longer smooth and new. Now they were pitted and ancient, just as they had been when Finn, Lucy and Zoe had first entered the temple. Morvan's body was gone.

Another wave sloshed against him, making him gag.

"Finn!" shouted a voice.

Finn looked up to see Lucy waving from the stone ledge. Zoe was beside her.

"You've got to get up here!" she said. "The tide's coming in! The whole cave system is flooding!"

John ...

Finn threw panicked glances through the ruins, and saw pale flesh. It was his brother, moving weakly as water splashed across his body. Finn crouched, took an arm, and dragged John half to his feet, before crumpling. His brother mumbled.

"Come on!" said Finn. "You've got to stand."

A wave crashed over the rocks, covering them both before flowing away.

"John, please, bro. I can't lift you."

John's eyes were half open, and he must have heard, because Finn felt him take some of his own weight. Another breaker covered the entire temple floor, up to their knees.

"Quickly!" cried Lucy from above. Finn heaved himself and John past the altar and into the water that now surrounded it. Clinging to each other, they waded towards the collapsed wall as the water washed around their waists. Halfway there, Finn stumbled on a submerged stone. John caught him as he fell, but his head went underwater and he came up spluttering. They forged on. With each step Finn took, the water sucked at his legs, threatening to pull him under.

Lucy turned and bent down towards something on the ledge that Finn couldn't quite see. Seconds later, she rose up with her arm wrapped around Kylie. On Kylie's other side was Zoe, her face pale and grim.

"What happened to you?" Zoe yelled over the roar of the water and the cracking of the temple walls. "We got Kylie but we couldn't see where you'd gone."

A massive boulder crashed down into the water just a few metres from Finn, drenching both him and John.

"I'll tell you later," Finn shouted back, though he wasn't sure he'd ever be able to find the words. "Go. We're right behind you."

They started scaling the pile of rubble that would take them up to the ledge. Halfway there, John froze, suddenly awake and aware.

"Adriana!" he said.

Shrugging off Finn's embrace, he plunged back into the raging water, which now reached up to his chest.

"Adriana!" he cried, looking helplessly around.

Finn scanned the disintegrating temple. Only three pillars remained standing. Falling stones turned the surface of the water to froth.

"She's gone," he said, reaching out his hand. "And we've got to go too."

With an animal cry, John floundered back to the rubble slope and climbed it to join Finn on the ledge.

The tunnel brought them back to the top of the wide stone staircase. Black water sluiced past them down the steps and splashed into the raging eddies below. Lucy,

Zoe and Kylie were clinging to each other on the topmost step, staring down into the maelstrom with desperation on their faces. Finn was glad to see that Kylie seemed able to stand for herself.

"We've got to jump," said Lucy. "It's the only way."

"It's too dangerous," said Zoe. "We'll drown."

We can't stay here ...

Finn grabbed Zoe's hand and she took Kylie's. Lucy took John's hand and together they all leapt into the water. At once Zoe's fingers slipped from Finn's grasp and his head went under. He came up choking, kicked out his legs and tried to scull with his arms, doing everything he could to stay afloat. It was colder than he ever thought possible, and in his chest he felt his heart punching in protest like a fist. Kylie's head bobbed up beside him, then Zoe's. He could just make out John and Lucy over the pounding waves. They looked a long way away.

The rip current swept them rapidly away from the steps and out towards the exit. The craggy walls of the tunnel raced past.

"Finn!" shouted John from somewhere far ahead. "Where are you?" Finn could just see Lucy floundering in the distance, but there was no sign of his brother.

Before Finn could answer, a giant wave reared up and blocked his view altogether.

"It's pushing us back!" said Zoe.

Kylie coughed out a mouthful of water and made a grab for her sister. The wave lifted them up and spun them around like riders on some crazy carousel. Finn waited for the moment his body would be smashed mercilessly into the rock. He just hoped it would be quick. Then the wave broke, and suddenly they were plummeting into a great trough. Finn went under again and came up spitting out more of the salty water. He saw black rock spinning, a spray of foam. The water pressed against his back and there at last was the mouth of the cave, and beyond it the bright eye of the moon hanging low above a line of distant trees.

The water carried them outside. They continued to spin around each other, but now Finn's feet were dragging through sand and stones. He kicked out his legs and half-ran, half-waded through a swirl of shallow water. A wave knocked him forward then retreated, leaving him sprawled with his drenched jumpsuit clinging to his body. Zoe and Kylie fell to their knees beside him, clutching each other and gasping for air.

Finn tried to get up, but couldn't. He felt more exhausted than he ever had in his life. He flopped back on the shingle, only to feel a hand grabbing his wrist. The hand pulled, and suddenly Finn was on his feet, staring into his brother's exhausted face.

"I thought I'd lost you," said John, embracing him.

"Same here," said Finn.

Feet crunched on the shingle and there was Lucy, bent double and hardly able to walk, but walking just the same. Finn extended an arm and hauled her in to form a little circle.

Meanwhile, Zoe was helping Kylie to stagger upright. The sisters leaned against each other for a moment, gasping for breath.

A woman shouted, and Finn looked up to see three people racing over the sand towards them. The silver moonlight threw their familiar faces into sharp relief: Ben, Dr Forrester and the Dean.

"What happens now?" said Lucy, straightening up.

Finn tugged a strand of seaweed out of his hair.

"I don't care," he said. "We've done everything we had to do."

"Not everything," murmured John, gazing back at the cave. Finn could only guess how hard it must have been for him to leave, knowing Adriana was still in there.

"Is it over?" said Kylie.

Finn gazed at the flooded cave. Somewhere deep inside it was a ruined temple, now lost forever.

"Yes," he said. "It's over."

But even as he spoke the words, he could tell they were not true.

CHAPTER TWENTY-FOUR

Finn sat looking out through the wide infirmary window. The morning light was crisp and bright. Tiny clouds sped past, sending brisk shadows racing along the rugged wall of the South Cliff. The sea, so tumultuous the night before, was calm as a millpond.

Dr Forrester had checked them all over on the beach already. Cuts and bruises, some torn clothes. Soaked through, and incipient hypothermia. She'd told the Dean in no uncertain terms that they needed to come to the infirmary before anything else. Finn had been too exhausted to worry about what Kildair might be thinking as he marched off.

The extraordinary events that had taken place in

the temple seemed almost like a dream. He'd tried to explain to the girls what had happened, but as he played the events back in his head they seemed jumbled, as if his memory had been shattered and put back together very clumsily. No one had seen Morvan or his skeletal acolytes apart from Finn. Whatever had happened – whatever parallel dimension they had entered – was hidden from the others.

But in all the confusion, he recalled one moment clearly. It stood out more than all the gravity defying acrobatics. Somehow, at the crisis point, he had left his own body and looked through Morvan's eyes.

And though that act had allowed him to live, it terrified him. Because there was only one word for what had happened.

Body-hopping.

His skin felt hot thinking what that might mean.

Finn stretched his legs and groaned at the twinge in his left knee. He couldn't remember injuring it, but then it felt as if his whole body was one big ache. His feet were bandaged inside his trainers, and there were bandages around his ribs.

John emerged from the treatment room grinning.

"Clean bill of health," he said. "Are we awesome or what?"

Dr Forrester followed John out. Her uniform

looked smart and hair was neatly tied, but there were dark circles under her eyes.

"You're all good to go," she said. "Except you, Kylie. I'd like to observe you for a little longer."

Zoe sat up straighter.

"No way," she said. "Kylie stays with me."

Dr Forrester's mouth opened, but it was Kylie who spoke first.

"It's okay," she said to Zoe. "I think it's a good idea. I still can't ... I'm still a little mixed up, you know?"

"That's understandable," said Dr Forrester. "With the proper care, I hope your memory will return."

Footsteps sounded on the spiral staircase and Ben climbed into view. His face was serious.

"Everyone is summoned to the Wardens' library," he said icily. "Now."

Finn glanced at his brother, who shrugged.

"I guess we've got nothing better to do," John said.

"You may take these four," said Dr Forrester. "But Kylie stays with me."

Ben moved between them and the doorway. "I said everyone has to come," he said.

"Like we actually care what you've got to say," said Lucy.

"I don't make the rules," Ben mumbled.

Dr Forrester glared at him. "And my rule is that

Kylie stays with me."

Ben held her gaze for a moment. Then his eyes dropped and he let them pass.

"Don't think the rest of you are getting out of it," he said.

They followed Ben down the stairs. On the way over, it looked as if the prefect was going to try to initiate a conversation on several occasions, but each time he silently gave up. Finn wanted to ask him questions, but a part of him enjoyed seeing the prefect suffer, too. By time they reached the library Ben's shoulders were slumped. His mood darkened further when Professor Panjaran refused to let him in.

"I brought them like you said," Ben grumbled.

"Yes," said Panjaran. "And now it is time for you to pursue your prefect's duties elsewhere."

While Ben remained in the corridor, Finn and his friends assembled in the library. The room had a high, ornate ceiling moulded with plaster animals, and the walls were lined with bookcases. Ladders hung from wheeled rails, offering access to books on the highest shelves. Glass cabinets contained enormous volumes that looked much older than the rest of the books on display. It wasn't hard to imagine Adriana sneaking in to steal the *Book of Morvan*. Finn wondered what else was contained in some of the volumes.

Professor Panjaran closed the door and joined the other three Wardens who were waiting in the middle of the room. The only Warden not there was Susan Arnott. Finn guessed why, but it was his brother who voiced the question that was actually in his head.

"Is there any news of Adriana?" John said.

Professor Panjaran shook his head sadly. "All evidence suggests that Adriana Arnott drowned," he said. "I am sorry."

John nodded, his face white. Finn said nothing. What was there to say?

"It is a tragedy," said Marissa Blake. "There will have to be an investigation, of course." All the Wardens looked grave.

"So many rules broken," said Pietr Turminski, holding out his palms in an oddly apologetic gesture. "Such rashness. This cannot be swept aside."

Finn felt Lucy's hand creep into his own. He squeezed it and stood as straight as his aching ribs allowed. Zoe and John were both looking down at the wooden floorboards, apparently unconcerned about whatever was coming.

"However," said Panjaran, "whatever wrongdoings have taken place, the Wardens are satisfied for now that the four of you are innocent in this whole affair."

Finn let out his breath silently. He sensed the others

relaxing too, all except John, who held his body stiff and continued to stare at the floor.

"So we're free to go?" said Lucy.

Blake eyed her. "The term is nearly over, so in a few days you will leave Alyxa along with the rest of the students. The school holiday will give everyone a chance to reflect on what has happened here. You should use the time wisely."

Finn could feel the pressure of Professor Panjaran's penetrating gaze, and so wasn't surprised when the Warden of Sight addressed him and his brother directly.

"John and Finlay Williams," Panjaran said. "You will be leaving a little earlier than everybody else. Today, in fact - immediately after this meeting is concluded."

"What are you talking about?" said John.

"Your mother has been notified and will be waiting for you on the mainland," Professor Panjaran said.

It took Finn a moment to process this. He'd been at Alyxa for less than a week and already the mainland seemed very far away. His mother even further. Professor Panjaran clapped his hands.

"Very well," he said. "You are dismissed. John and Finlay - there is a boat waiting for you at the East Jetty. As for you, Lucy and Zoe, I suggest that you -"

"Wait a minute," said Finn, taking a step forward. "That can't be it."

Panjaran's bright eyes settled on him again. "I'm sorry, young man?" he said.

"You can't just send us away without giving us some answers," said Finn. "For a start, who put Kylie's body in that weird tank contraption?"

Pietr Turminski shook his head with a small smile.

"The tunnels have been searched," he said. "We found no trace of the object you mentioned."

"That's because we smashed it getting Kylie out," said Finn. "But what about all the broken glass? And the computers?"

"No broken glass," said Turminski. "No computers."

"We've also received new testimony that confirms Adriana's involvement in all this," added Blake.

"What new testimony?" said Finn.

"Adriana met Kylie at the South Cliff on the night Kylie disappeared," said Turminski. "This we now know. Perhaps they argued." He gave a minute shrug, as if inviting them to fill in the rest.

"Why would they?" said Zoe. "They were friends."

"We cannot answer that," said Professor Panjaran, lacing his hands across his protruding stomach. "But it is possible that something unfortunate happened, and that Adriana covered it up."

Finn waited for John to say something. But his brother remained silent.

"The only way we'll ever know what really happened that night is if Kylie regains her memory," added Blake.

"Given the trauma she has been through," said Panjaran, "perhaps she will be happier if her mind remains a blank."

I didn't tell the Wardens about Adriana and Kylie meeting on the beach, Finn thought. *So who did? The Dean? Perhaps Susan Arnott.*

"Where's the Hearing Warden?" asked Finn.

"Given the situation with her daughter," said Panjaran, "she thought it advisable to take a leave of absence."

Zoe pointed her finger at each of the Wardens in turn. Her hand was shaking.

"You were in on it, all of you," she said. "You're the ones who kidnapped Kylie!"

Blake looked shocked. "That is quite an accusation, young lady. Where is your gratitude?"

"Gratitude?" Zoe stepped forward, her shoulders quaking.

"We are grateful," said Finn hurriedly, "... that you can see we're innocent, I mean. But Zoe's got a point. It feels like we've stumbled over something really big. We just want some proper answers."

"As do we," said Pietr Turminski. "When we find them, you will be informed, of course."

"As for your suggestion that we were involved ..." Blake began, taking a step towards Zoe.

"... we will consider that a side effect of your extreme physical and emotional fatigue," said Panjaran, smoothly completing her sentence.

Beside him, Magnus Gustavsson said nothing and gave a single nod.

Finn turned to Lucy and was pleased to see that all her attention was on the faces of the Wardens. He raised his eyebrows at her: *Are they telling the truth?*

She shrugged: *I don't know.*

Professor Panjaran spread his hands out wide.

"What is most important is that we thank you," he said. "You performed well in a difficult situation and in doing so prevented things from getting out of hand. There is only good news here. Zoe – I am pleased to tell you that we have already informed your parents that Kylie's death was misreported. They are overwhelmed but delighted, of course."

Finn tried to read Zoe's face, but behind the goggles her expression was inscrutable.

With that, Magnus Gustavsson ushered them to the door and opened it with one of his enormous hands. Professor Panjaran joined him while Blake and Turminski turned away, deep in whispered conversation.

Finn stood his ground. He was pleased to see his

friends were staying put, too.

"I believe we have discussed everything there is to discuss," said Panjaran. "I am certain you must all be tired."

"Tired of only getting half an answer to everything," said Finn.

At last John lifted his head. "Leave it, Finn," he said in a voice that was uncharacteristically soft. "He's right. It's time to let it go."

Finn didn't want to let anything go. But it was clear they weren't going to get anything more out of the Wardens today.

Some day soon, though.

"What do you think, Zoe?" he said.

She turned her goggles towards him. "Let's get out of here," she said. "I want to get back to Kylie."

And I'm going home, thought Finn, hardly able to believe it.

Lucy and John went to the door first, followed by Zoe. Finn brought up the rear.

"Enjoy the holidays," Panjaran said to them as they left the library. "And remember – we do not want to hear any more talk about hexagrams or the sixth sense."

"You must be discreet," said Gustavsson. "Remember the power of rumour. These fantasies about Morvan must not filter out into the rest of the school."

"So Morvan's a fantasy?" John muttered to Finn when they were all back in the corridor. "Tell that to Adriana."

Tell it to any of us, Finn thought, shuddering as he remembered what had happened in the temple.

"They're hiding something, aren't they?" he said to Lucy.

Lucy nodded. "A lot," she said. "The problem is that we have no idea where the truth ends and the lies begin. I don't know if you noticed, but they didn't actually say they weren't involved. The best way to cheat a lie detector is not to give a straight answer."

"They want to bury it all," said Zoe fiercely. "Just like they wanted to bury Kylie. Remember what the Dean said in Dr Raj's cottage? He said 'Those stupid Wardens ... thinking Morvan can be toyed with.' What if he meant they were the ones who locked Kylie up?"

Finn tried to wrap his head around it all. "He might just have been guessing."

"Or he might have been right," said Lucy.

"What you're saying is we don't know anything," said John.

"Like I said – they want to bury it all," said Zoe.

Finn summoned his strength and stood up straight.

"Well, we won't let them," he said.

Lucy showed them the quickest way to the eastern arm of the star-shaped Alyxa building.

"There's a track that goes down to the jetty," she said to Finn as she pushed open the exterior door. "Nice day for a walk."

"They don't need to walk," said a familiar voice. "I'll give them a lift."

"Dad!"

Dr Raj was standing in front of the old Land Rover he'd parked in the yard outside the door. His vivid orange jacket clashed horribly with the green paint of the vehicle. Lucy ran to him and gave him a hug. He ruffled his daughter's hair and kissed the top of her head.

"I know the Wardens went easy on you," he said. "But I say you're in big trouble for getting up to mischief while my back's turned."

"So what's new?" said Lucy, beaming. She turned back to Finn. "Well, I suppose this is goodbye for now."

"Nonsense!" said Dr Raj. "Farewells should be kept for railway platforms and airport terminals. Most of all seaside jetties. Everybody jump aboard!"

They piled into the Land Rover. With a crunch of gears, Dr Raj drove down the bumpy track. As the vehicle veered through a gap in a line of gorse bushes, Finn looked back at Alyxa through the rear window. Cloud shadows turned the smooth silver wall of the enormous school building into a mottled patchwork of light and dark.

The Land Rover slewed to the side, the gorse bushes rose up, and Alyxa vanished.

***

The ride was short but painful. Every jolt seemed to poke at a different injury on Finn's bruised body. He was glad when they reached the end of the track.

The East Jetty was a wooden pier thrusting out from a headland at one end of a semicircular rocky cove. The surrounding cliffs were steep and dotted with gorse bushes. Tied to the end of the pier was a small white boat with a short mast. Fishing nets hung from the stern. A man with a thick black beard stood waiting in the enclosed wheelhouse, fiddling with a large piece of radio equipment.

Leaving Dr Raj in the Land Rover, the four friends walked out to where the boat was moored. John leapt nimbly aboard, leaving Finn to say goodbye to Lucy and Zoe.

"I suppose I'll see you next term in Numbskulls,"

said Finn, "unless you recover your powers, Lucy."

"We'll have to wait and see," she said, smiling.

"Just try to find a way not to come last in the Hunt again," said Zoe.

She tilted her head and her dark goggles showed Finn the reflection of the sea, the sky and his own grinning face.

"I'm working on it," he said.

Finn clambered aboard the boat only to find the skipper leaning over the side and cursing.

"Always trouble coming out here," said the bearded man.

"What's the problem?" said Finn.

"The anchor is stuck," the skipper replied.

"Let me try," said John. "Hang on to my legs, Finn."

John leaned out over the gunwale and Finn grabbed his ankles. John plunged one hand below the lapping waves, yanked hard and lifted the dripping anchor up out of the water.

"Where d'you want it?" he asked the skipper.

"Wherever," the man replied, turning his back on them both and returning to the wheelhouse.

"Well, *I* thought it was impressive," called Lucy from the jetty.

The engine chugged into life and the boat pulled slowly away from the pier. As Finn waved to Lucy and Zoe, the topmost floor of the silver Alyxa building appeared again over a crag of rock. Someone was watching them from the roof: a tall, thin man in a grey suit.

"I knew the Dean would want to see us off, one way or another," Finn said to John. But his brother was too busy staring into the water to reply. Finn tapped his shoulder. "John – are you okay?"

"I'm sorry," John said quietly.

Finn sat beside him. "What for?"

"I should have listened to you," said John. "Like at the party. You knew something was going to go wrong and it did. Just like it did here."

"It's okay," said Finn. "I'm sorry too. I said some pretty mean things."

John looked up from the water. "Adriana really wasn't a bad person."

"I know."

"She spent her life in her mother's shadow," said John. "She told me that. I don't think she'd ever said that to anyone before."

Finn's heart broke a little when he saw the depth of sadness in his brother's eyes. "At least she got the chance to tell you," he said. He waited a few seconds before asking the question that had been brewing since the moment he saw John coming out of Dr Raj's window.

"How did you get involved in all this, John?"

His brother gripped the gunwale. "I knew something was up with Adriana," he said. "Most of the time she's ..." his knuckles whitened ... "she was so cool and chill, but a couple of times I realised she'd been crying. She said it was about Kylie Redmayne, but I could see she wasn't just upset – she was scared. Guilty. She swore me to secrecy, told me what had happened ..."

Finn let his brother talk.

"After the storm, Kylie started hearing voices. Adriana realised it was something to do with the sixth sense. She tried to help her. Then when Kylie went to the cliffs, she followed her and tried to stop her from going into that cave. But she said Kylie went crazy and attacked her. I think Morvan already had his hooks in her. Adriana panicked and ran. She was so scared ..."

"Or so she said," muttered Finn. "I saw her in the cave, John. She wanted that power for herself." He couldn't shake the memory of Adriana's gleeful chanting. "She planted the *Book of Morvan* in Zoe's room as well."

John flinched. "She'd told her mum about the cave. The Hearing Warden told her to keep it between them. I think she was worried what the Dean might do if he found out about Kylie meddling in the sixth sense. That guy's a fanatic, Finn."

"He *did* know," said Finn nodding. "He was spying

on Kylie already. Watching her every move. But what are you saying – Susan Arnott put Kylie in that chamber? Not on her own, she didn't."

John shrugged helplessly. "I don't know anything about that. Neither did Adriana. But she must have heard you guys talking about Kylie. Last night she asked me to come with her – told me it was the only way to save you guys from Morvan. I thought ... I thought I was doing the right thing."

Finn saw his brother was close to tears, and for a moment John looked a lot younger than fifteen. Finn put his arm over his broad shoulders.

"We all did," he said. "That place is so full of secrets and shadows, it's hard to see what's going on."

"Adriana thought the sixth sense would solve everything," John went on. "She thought she could control it. But she couldn't. I guess it sort of ... corrupted her."

The skipper pushed the throttle lever forward and the boat surged out over gently rolling waves. As they rounded the headland, more of the silver building came into view. From here it looked as if a spaceship had landed on the island from another world.

"We'd better get a move on," said the skipper. "There's a storm coming."

Finn scanned the blue sky. Most of the clouds had

disappeared.

"Are you sure?" he said.

The bearded man licked his lips. "Aye, I'm sure."

Back on the island, the air shimmered. The school seemed to blink, and flicker, and then Alyxa was gone. *The White Wall.*

"Secrets and shadows," John repeated.

As they struck out east across the ocean, Finn thought about what was waiting for him on the mainland: his own bed, next door's cat chasing birds in the garden, pizza delivered to the door, saving up movies to watch on TV. Familiar sights, familiar sounds, all the ordinary things that in his old life he'd taken so much for granted.

Mum.

He took a seat on the little bench tucked out of the wind behind the wheelhouse wall. As the fishing boat rocked beneath him, he tried to make sense of his thoughts. Since he'd gone to Alyxa, every discovery, every lesson, every hour practically, had brought confusion with it. Everything was new, everything was strange. At every turn, he'd had to change the way he looked at the world – it worked very differently from the way he'd always thought.

But in processing the differences, he'd lost sight of all the things that were the same. John, Lucy, even the Dean and the Wardens – they might have special powers that defied science and reason, but they were still just people. Normal people with normal thoughts, normal feelings. Flawed people who sometimes got things wrong, or kept things to themselves. Who sometimes lied. Remarkable though they were, in their hearts they were still just human beings.

Alyxa dwindled, shrinking into the distance. Eventually it was gone.

But I'm going back soon ...